DAY ZERO

Day Zero

A Novel
on Water Crisis

Muneef Ahmad

Publisher: Be-Civil
Editor: Wordplay Creative Services
Front cover design: Heather Morin

Issued in print and electronic formats.
ISBN 978-1-7387415-0-2 (paperback). -- 978-1-7387415-1-9 (EPUB).

This is an original print edition of *Day Zero*.

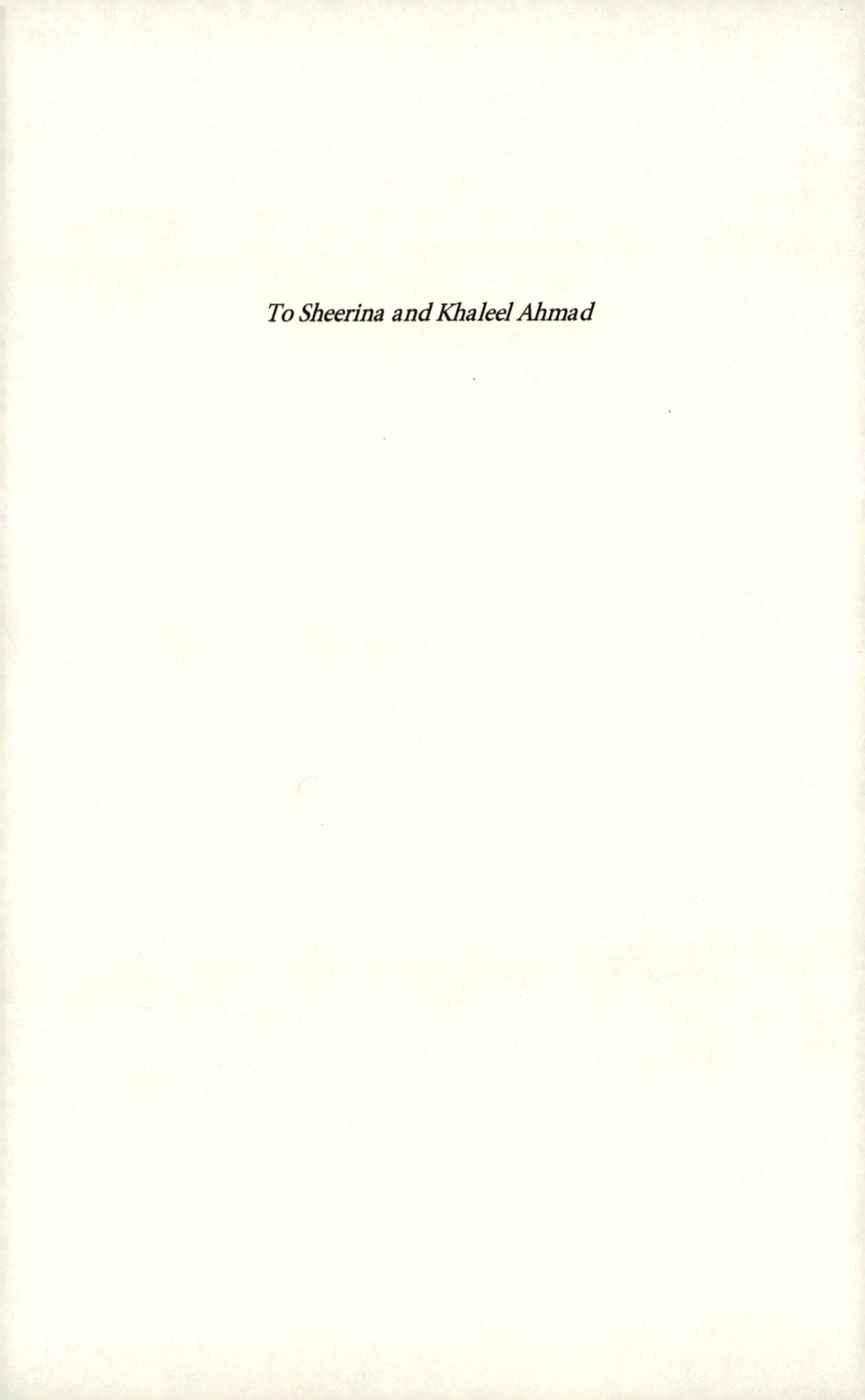

To Sheerina and Khaleel Ahmad

Prologue

Vegas has fallen.

It was the first city to succumb to the drought that plagued southwestern America. Crisis had loomed for years before today, but the critical point arrived when the 600,000 residents of Las Vegas were ordered to leave the city. Inside two months, they all became water migrants, or "wigrants."

For decades, cities have teetered dangerously on the brink of Day Zero. The day a city runs out of water. Around the world, the pursuit of water consumed the attention of cities. In Australia, the Middle East, South Africa, Brazil and others. Meanwhile, politicians ignored the warnings of future risks as cities hobbled along.

During the first five years of the American southwest drought, climate change was still in question as cities kept up their operations. After ten years, it was harder to challenge the implications as cities struggled to thrive with any effective water restrictions. After two decades, all skepticism had evaporated.

There was no end in sight. People decided they had to fend for themselves. Crimes related to water theft had risen. There were even those who were stealing and delivering whole shipments of water. Water and money being finite, cities chose to either outsource or enforce their water supply.

Carla Cole was in the fray, leading her global non-profit enterprise, Axiom Water, to find and supply water to many large cities in need around the world. Axiom Water would find money to provide clean water, or build pipes to carry water over even longer distances, or both when necessary. Cole's persistence streamlined ten-year projects down to two-years. And yet, this did not always solve the problem. The more water was made available to cities, the more it seemed to the politicians like the looming threats weren't real. People plodded forth using the same amount of water they always used.

Mira Senna was the counterpoint. She had established River Enforcement, now one of the largest private security firms in the world, to vigilantly enforce water restrictions using protocols for the imprisonment of water violators. When imprisonment wasn't enough for enforcement, there were questions around how far she would go.

As the residents of Vegas abandon their homes and seek refuge with family and friends, a haven has been identified for the 250,000 wigrants with nowhere to go. Toronto, on the north shore of one of Canada's freshwater lakes. It would be optimal, except for the fact that Toronto's water infrastructure cannot accommodate such a burst in population so quickly. A makeshift wigrant settlement is quickly cobbled together.

Senna's enforcement in Toronto has kept the city thriving. But now, the settlement and its water problems have fallen to her. How far will Senna go to rein in this unwelcome situation? Cole must intervene to wrest the reins from Senna's grasp, if there is to be any hope of survival.

The fate of the wigrants lay in the fallout between them.

Part One

The Flop

Chapter 1

Las Vegas

The ocean of people parted as he walked towards her against the current. Past the concierge, he could see her perched on the fountain in the middle of the cavernous casino foyer, issuing orders. The coolness of the massive marble walls and columns offered some relief from the heat of so many bodies crowded together, people looking for answers and seeking escape.

When he reached the fountain, he stepped into the empty basin where people once threw their coins and approached the elevated statue of the Three Graces in the center. There she stood, on a ledge, calling out instructions. To him, she seemed even larger than the Greek goddesses. Her curly hair was pulled back in a ponytail, with two cornrows on each side, and her ebony skin was aglow.

"You're late, Steele," she said. "I told them I didn't need protection. But they insisted, so make yourself useful." She glanced at his colorful shirt. "Take those acorns for a walk and help that family over there." She pointed towards an elderly couple.

Carla Cole was wearing dark trousers and a sleek gray crop necked top, and she was draped in a gunmetal-gray, full-length jacket that danced like a cape as she moved on the platform. A brightly colored bead necklace accentuated her strong jawline. Steele noted her athletic physique. He froze looking into her impossibly large, doe-like eyes, and saw the ferocity of a lion in them.

He cleared his throat and stretched his shoulders back as Cole answered a question from a sweaty man with a lit cigar and a southern accent. The cigar smell tracked ten feet away.

"Ma'am, it's ridiculous you herding us like cattle. You couldn't fix the problem here, and now you're shipping us off to be someone else's problem," he said, gesturing agitatedly with his cigar.

"Sir. Put that out and calm down. We had to gather everyone here. This was the last casino the owners agreed to keep open as Lake Mead dried up. We have enough buses and trains to get everyone out, but it's going to take time."

Steele cleared his throat.

"Why are you still here, Steele? Elderly family!" Cole said pointing again.

"Pineapples, Cole. These are pineapples on my shirt, not acorns. And I'm your bodyguard, not your errand boy. Finally—" Steele's protest was drowned out by a loud scream coming from one of the lobby's corridors.

Cole and Steele locked eyes, then she jumped down to where he stood.

"Behind me," ordered Steele.

As Steele dashed off, he felt a gentle bump on his left side as Cole breezed past him.

He followed her through the crowd in the direction of the scream until they arrived at a woman with strawberry-blond hair standing over a smaller version of herself. Her daughter lay on the ground, and she was having difficulty breathing.

"Cole. My daughter . . . she's asthmatic, and she hasn't had anything to drink in two days," pleaded the mother.

At Cole's direction, Steele picked up the young girl, and the mother followed behind them as they pushed through the crowd towards the casino's front entrance.

As they left the building and neared the lineup for the bus, the crowd muttered but begrudgingly gave way when they saw Cole. The mother spoke. "Cole? Will they have water on the bus for my daughter?"

"Very little," Cole shot back.

"And how long till we get to the settlement in Toronto? I hear it is very crowded where we're going."

"A couple of days, with all the stops," replied Cole, in a softer tone now. "Let's get you onboard and settled so you can be on your way."

"Thank you so much. I just . . . don't know what to do from here. My daughter and I brought everything we could in our suitcases, but it's nothing. It's like suddenly, *poof*, now you're poor. Did you hear they even have a name for us water migrants now? Wigrants. It's so demeaning."

Steele got the mother and daughter settled on the bus, and when he stepped out again he saw Cole heading back to the casino. He caught up with her. He needed to ask her a few things, and there wasn't going to be a better time.

"You know Las Vegas means 'the meadow' in Spanish, right?" he said. "I grew up in Spain, in Seville, before moving to the UK. My family is still there. Seville's water pipes had degraded beyond the city's ability to keep up. As disrepair mounted, we neared the verge of collapse. Axiom Water came in with critical repairs and took over the system. You brought life back to my home. Couldn't you do the same thing here? 'One People, One Water'—is that the Axiom slogan?"

"The Earth is vastly different from place to place, Steele. Getting water to people who need it can take years, and cost millions. Here in Vegas, the cost has already exceeded a billion dollars."

"Right. But when they built the Hoover Dam, they formed Lake Mead behind it to provide water. Isn't it the largest reservoir in America? I didn't think it was possible for Lake Mead to dry up," said Steele.

"It didn't have to dry up. It's just that the water level has dropped so low that it can no longer generate power or supply enough water to keep everything running. It's tough to explain all that from the top of a fountain in a tense situation, but . . . Vegas hit Day Zero before I arrived," said Cole.

"Day Zero?" asked Steele.

"The day a city effectively runs out of water," replied Cole.

Cole explained that the state of Nevada had failed to take action with water shortages looming. Finally, with Day Zero imminent, they'd called in River Enforcement to push strict conservation. "It might even have helped, if they'd done it years ago. But the casino owners weren't happy with what Senna from River Enforcement was about to do, so they lobbied the state to kick them out."

"What did Senna want to do?" asked Steele.

"Let's just say, Senna is not averse to unorthodox measures."

As the desert heat beat down on them, Cole stopped for a moment. They both looked around at the monstrous buildings of the Strip. And there was the once-cinematic water feature made of a thousand individual fountains, now dry and baking in the sun.

"This was the first thing River Enforcement shut down when they arrived, and the first thing back on after they were kicked out," said Cole.

When she spoke again, it seemed to Steele that she was speaking to herself.

"Vegas has fallen. But if it costs me everything I've built, I will save everyone here."

Chapter 2

Toronto

Tipping garbage cans wasn't helping anymore. He'd been running flat out for five minutes, ever since he was spotted, and he felt like he was being chased by a rabid dog. He turned and ran down an alleyway. Then came the gunshot.

"Two feet to the right, head height. Tell me where you want the next one, kid," a voice called out. It sounded as if it was coming from someone lounging in a beach chair by the ocean, not someone who'd been dodging garbage cans at top speed.

Another round of gunfire. This time he was hit!

The shooter approached down the alleyway and sidled over to him with a smile.

He was on the ground wincing, both hands nursing the pain. "You shot me in the ass, cop!"

Her shadow loomed over him now. As she walked around him, she pulled up the hood of her camouflage jacket, probably to get the sun out of her eyes. Then she just stood over him, motionless and kinetic all at once. Coiled, like a tightly wound spring. He studied her—wouldn't want to run into her again. The stillness of her hazel eyes finally met his gaze. He noted a tiny divot on her cheek, below her right eye, a small marring of her smooth, white complexion.

Then he dropped his gaze and saw the smoking gun hanging softly in her right hand.

"Trust me, I'm no cop," she said, and he froze in fear.

At that moment, a River Enforcement warden came running up to them, out of breath.

"Senna! Sorry it took me so long."

With a look of disappointment, the woman called Senna holstered her weapon.

"You didn't have to shoot me!" he grunted.

"You didn't have to run," Senna said as she stepped back and gave her warden room to handcuff him.

"You know, you can leave the field work to us," the warden offered shyly.

"And do what all day? Paperwork? I'll trade you the boardroom for this fun any day," replied Senna.

"Did they reach you yet about the termination?" the warden asked.

"Come again?" asked Senna.

An hour later, Senna was in the mayor's boardroom. She was unaccustomed to being out of the loop, and she was piecing the story together from snippets of his rant.

"You're responsible for what your wardens do. You got it? Especially in the settlement. *Those people* are not my problem! You got us into this mess, so you'd better figure out how to fix it, fast!"

Senna just listened, determined not to object to any of his nonsense, watching as his face turned deeper shades of red. His aides kept their eyes fixed on their notebooks.

"My residents are telling me those wigrants—"

"The polite term is 'settlers,'" Senna finally interjected, demonstrating the diplomacy that she knew would be expected of her.

"I don't care what they want to be called! They've squatted in my waterfront, packed in like sardines. I was forced to take them because *you* couldn't fix the problem in Vegas, and now, they want *my* water to look after all *those people!* My fine city is in the headlines for being a humanitarian refuge, and then one of your wardens goes and shoots one of the wigrants dead on *my streets!*"

Senna glanced at the aides, then looked the mayor in the eye.

"Mr. Mayor, you know that the city's well-being is my top concern. You gave River Enforcement responsibility for overseeing the settlement and the housing of water refugees, and I won't let that negatively affect the city's residents. I'll get to the bottom of this."

The mayor stopped, and took a deep breath. One of his aides finally looked up and nudged the other as the mayor walked over to the window to look out at his city. His face, Senna thought, was becoming noticeably less tomato-like. He combed his thinning white hair with his hands and sat in the chair beside her.

"What's that thing you say about luck, Senna?" he asked.

"Hard work makes its own luck," Senna replied firmly.

"Well, today is your lucky day. I'm not kicking you out of this city, yet. You get to work with Toronto's Finest to clean up this mess. Find out who killed the wigrant."

Senna bit her lip. She looked past the mayor, out the window, and waited to feel her breath steady. The aides shifted in their chairs uneasily as silence swept over them all.

The mayor looked over to his aides and they slid a folder to him. He opened it and then handed it to Senna, explaining that it was the few details they had compiled on the recent death. Another file was slid to him which he just handed her without opening.

"That is your police contact. I'm sure you'll be a deadly duo. Good luck."

◊ ◆ ◊

Senna arrived at the Toronto Police division noted in the file. No one on duty knew yet why she was there, but they definitely knew who she was. She took a seat to wait outside the office of the captain, and she saw a man inside, sitting with his back to her. The captain spotted her but made no effort to close his office door.

The man with his back to her leaned back in his chair. "Damn it! River Enforcement messed up big time." He tilted his head to glance up at the ceiling, and the fluorescent light cast a glow off the whiteness of his freshly shorn head. "I spend years criticizing their methods, calling them out on their limits and their tactics for inspecting and incarcerating people exceeding water quotas. We get clawed back to make room for them. And they finally mess up. Well, it's time to pay the piper."

"Gonna be tough to put that stuff aside, but you have to focus, Merchant," the captain replied. "This thing is going to go public, and with police involved, at least it'll be transparent. We need to have our best on it. And that's what River Enforcement wants, too. No one likes a rogue."

"But c'mon, Cap! We can do this without them. They don't have the data access that we do. I mean, our records, you know. They'd need to have all our stuff to find this guy!"

"Or girl," said the captain.

"Whatever. The person who murdered a wigrant. Who wrapped this gift up for them, Cap?"

"Right from the top, Merch, if it makes you feel any better."

Merchant sighed. "I'd have loved to get this guy myself."

"Or girl."

"Whatever. So, we're doin' this thing now?" asked Merchant.

"You'll be our liaison. She's just outside." The captain lifted his chin to acknowledge Senna.

Merchant turned around. All the blood from his body rushed to his feet. He turned back to the captain.

"Because you've decided that, rather than shoot me for insubordination, you're throwing me into Purgatory?"

"Because she's the top dog in her shop, not to mention the best. And we want this guy," said the captain.

"Or girl," said Merchant.

"Touché," the captain said as he waved Senna in.

She shook hands with the captain, then stood strong beside Merchant. Though they were the same height, the bulk he carried around his chest and waist somehow amplified the space around him.

"Let me be the first to introduce you to our acting captain. Mira Senna, meet Sergeant Tonio Merchant," said the captain.

Merchant lifted his shoulders and turned to greet Senna. She nodded, and they shook hands.

"Only till a proper replacement can be found," the captain added.

Merchant rolled his eyes.

"This captain stuff isn't all bad, you know. You might even like it," said the captain.

"Yeah, and I might volunteer for a prostate exam, too. I've got work to do, Cap. Even more now that I have to babysit the River Goddess, here," said Merchant.

"I won't stay up late, and I promise not to have friends over," said Senna.

The captain picked up a folder from his desk and handed it to her.

"Our resources, our files, whatever you need, Senna. But respect the rules. We all want justice. A murder investigation is clearly our territory, but the jurisdiction in the settlement area is blurry for us. River Enforcement is in charge of the settlement, so Toronto Police will partner with you on the investigation. Acting Captain Merchant is authorized to grant you access to all our resources, and he'll be working alongside you," said the captain. "And though he is the acting bigshot, his own work comes first. Just means he'll have to make a few calls to authorize purchases of printer ink and toilet paper."

Merchant looked skeptically at the piles of paper on the captain's desk.

"I'm turning my phone off. Put the resumés submitted for your job in the washroom. They'll go to good use there. Two birds, one stone. I'm embracing it, Cap," said Merchant.

"That's the type of thinking that'll get you promoted, Merch. Now get to work, both of you," said the captain.

Chapter 3

Toronto

Cole stood, statuesque, arms crossed behind her back a few inches from the glass, as the elevator began its ascent.

Steele, standing to her right and slightly behind her, looked up into the night sky towards the top of a seventy-story office tower that rose above the others. Fifty-eight seconds later he was looking down at the roof of that same building as the attendant let the two of them out onto the observation deck. Once the tallest freestanding structure in the world, the CN Tower was undoubtedly an engineering marvel, and it remained an iconic stamp on Toronto's skyline.

"Look alive, Steele. It's been a long day, but stay sharp for what comes next," offered Cole.

Steele followed her around the observation deck, looking out through the tall, seamless glass, first northward, past the skyline to the lights of the city, then westward, as the shoreline snaked around Lake Ontario towards the point where light met darkness. The southern view was a shade of black alive with stars, as the moon peered back at itself on the still surface of the lake. They turned eastward to the opposite shoreline where the light was sparse and darkness seemed to have the upper hand.

Cole continued their after-hours private tour, leading Steele towards a glass floor and stepping out onto it. Steele wouldn't follow, but he peered down to the ground, over a thousand feet below.

"Scared? You know, a whole family of elephants could stand on this glass without breaking it," said Cole.

Steele just stared at her blankly.

"Suit yourself! Now, here we go." Cole led him up a narrow set of stairs that brought them to the revolving restaurant. There was only one person there, seated near the window.

Cole put her hands up. "Don't shoot me!" she mocked as she sat down across from Senna.

"Don't need to, you look dead already. Handling the jet lag well, I see. And how do I address that?" asked Senna, with a glance towards Steele.

"You don't. Look, I didn't travel across the continent for an exclusive chance to enjoy this late-night view with you. You've crowded 250,000 settlers into a repurposed Olympic village built for 20,000 people. I want custody of the settlement on behalf of Axiom Water so that I can ensure their well-being."

Steele looked out to the east and recognized now what the sparse light pattern was. The settlement was just below them.

"All those high-powered people you roll with must do things differently. That's not how it works here, Cole, with me. But thanks for the failure," said Senna, flippantly.

"It's impressive that River Enforcement has become one of the top private security firms in the world so quickly. You and your wardens got a good niche. What's more impressive, though, is your arrogance. Talking to *me* about failure when I got called in to clean up *your* mess in Vegas," replied Cole.

"I was the only one who could have saved them," Senna told her. "People never meant to be there in the first place."

Senna launched into a history lesson.

"Think about the early nineteenth century, about American territorial expansion. President Andrew Jackson sent explorers to what they were calling the 'unexplored' western frontier. To take advantage of it, they justified ethnic cleansing of the local Indigenous peoples. In time, the Colorado River basin was over-settled and there wasn't enough water to supply the land. It didn't help that so much of the land got converted for agriculture, which calls for the most intensive water use, depleting an already scarce resource. They were warned, you know, but they went ahead and did it anyway."

Cole tapped her finger slowly on the desk as she listened.

"The powers that be in Vegas had gone to the extreme, so I was ready to do the same. Set an example to everyone else who wasn't listening. We established strict water-use protocols and gave them legal force. And while I was filling community centers with violators, one sprawling mansion was consuming almost a hundred times the water of an average household. I proposed a termination. Do it to the right person, make them an example, and the rest will fall into line. Next time . . . I just won't tell them," said Senna.

"You think 'setting an example' justifies murder, Senna?" asked Cole.

"Please. You keep reminding me why we can't work together. We couldn't make it work in Cape Town. Why could *we* work here?" asked Senna.

"When you left Cape Town and stayed out of my way, Axiom Water averted Day Zero," countered Cole.

Senna stared at Cole. She let the silence linger, and waited. Then she took a long, deep breath.

"You'll keep stretching our water resources till the whole world is spent, Cole. Then we all die. You can't make the hard decisions. Las Vegas had reached their limit. But never mind, the settlement here won't be my problem for too long."

Cole listened as Senna made it clear that Toronto had no additional water for the sudden increase in people. The existing water treatment facilities were massive, and any improvement to expand the facility to support more people cost millions of dollars and normally took years to plan, design and construct. Senna told her that the development pressures for new high-rises in past years had been somewhat irresponsible. The city had been able to keep up its ability to provide enough water, for the most part, though there had been instances where downtown development stalled for years as the city expanded the treatment facilities.

Cole bowed her head knowingly.

"Everyone thinks that just because the lake is freshwater, Toronto can support unlimited growth. Freshwater still needs to meet strict drinking water standards. That's what the treatment facilities do," admitted Cole.

"Toronto wasn't counting on a quarter million settlers dropped in two months. Even if the city wanted to expand the water treatment, your talent to accelerate these big projects cannot help quickly enough. And as you also well know, no bulk water importation is allowed in any city where River Enforcement operates," Senna replied.

"But that care package of bottled water that has been cobbled together for the settlement won't last."

"The wigrants will run out of water in seven days."

"You're going to let them die?"

"They died in Las Vegas. They're a drain on my city. If you gave them any hope, that was your mistake. Who controls the water controls the world. And in this city, I'm in control. You have no place in the settlement," Senna declared coolly. "Stay out of my way."

Without another word, Cole stood up and left. Steele, close behind, could see she was fuming. She stormed back down the narrow stairs to the observation deck and over the glass floor, slowing her pace only as they neared the elevator. She withdrew her phone and dialed her assistant.

"Get a message to Robin Hood. I need him here now! Seven days to Day Zero for the wigrants!"

Chapter 4

Arius was standing on the foredeck of an ocean freighter, the *Neptune*, watching as objects that had started as just a glimmer on the horizon grew closer, when he got a call on the radio on his belt. He could barely hear it over the incessant surging of the waves below. He had been holding a small, familiar object, one that he carried with him always, but he quickly shoved it back into his pocket to take the call.

"We expecting company, Tao? How many?" he called into the worn device.

"Looks like two, Arius. Maybe they're bringing those Parisian croissants you were hoping for. But there's other news from Cole you'll want to hear," came the raspy reply.

"On my way to you."

Arius made his way from the bow of the freighter to *Neptune*'s bridge. There, the captain was conferring with one of the crew about the remaining distance and travel time to reach the port in France, but the crewman seemed to be distracted by another man on the bridge, who was looking out with binoculars. Arius followed the look to the broad V-shaped back of his accomplice. Tao's straight hair was pulled back into a warrior's bun, high on the back of his head. Had the crewman never seen an Asian before?

Arius borrowed the binoculars and focused in on the logo glistening on the sides of two high-powered vessels.

"I told Senna the blue 'R' in the olive branch was a bit tacky. Pirates probably have much better logos. Right, captain?" The captain remained engaged in giving orders to the crewman.

"You won't be in any position to argue with Senna if she finds out everything you've done for Cole," said Tao.

Arius shrugged with the binoculars still in his hands and a smile on his face.

"It's serious, Arius. She dropped a message to you. The settlement in Toronto hits Day Zero in seven days," said Tao.

The smile vanished from Arius's face.

He turned towards the captain. "What's on your shipping manifest?"

The captain lifted his head. "Nothing to worry about there. It's the guy on River Enforcement's watch list standing right in front of me that's troubling. You could land my crew and I in a River Enforcement detention facility in Paris, Arius. Doubt they serve croissants there," he said, glancing over to Tao.

"No need to give them cause for more rigorous inspection on our first bulk water shipment to Paris. I'd hoped to see it through myself, but I guess Tao and I should make a quick exit," said Arius, in a resigned tone. "Are we secure at the port in France?"

A crew member stationed by the navigation array nodded a confirmation to the captain.

"Ground source confirms the port is secure. Underwater pumps are set to offload," replied the captain.

"It's really that easy to pull off a bulk water heist?" Tao asked.

"Yes. It'll look like regular freighters just making regular deliveries. Hiding in plain sight. But their ballast, the seawater normally used to balance their buoyancy, is actually fresh water. It will be covertly offloaded underwater and then transported inland by tanker truck. While the water is offloaded, another pump intake will pull in seawater to offset the weight and maintain the ship's height above the water. River Enforcement always focus their attention on what's going on above the surface. Meanwhile, your friend Arius's associates will be casually extracting and delivering fresh water right under their noses."

A voice from the bridge chimed in, "River Enforcement, five minutes out, approaching port side."

"Time to walk the plank, gentlemen," said the captain.

The crew had spotted nine River Enforcement officers aboard two vessels. Arius and Tao made their way down to the stern of the freighter, where scuba gear was affixed underwater on the starboard side. They'd assumed any inspection would board port side, but if necessary the captain was prepared to make a slow turn to give cover.

One of the crewmen met Arius and Tao on the main deck amidst the rows and stacks of storage containers. There were a few narrow passageways between the container rows to navigate through in order to avoid the open area along the perimeter that was exposed to view from the water.

They stripped down to wetsuits and handed their clothes over to the crewman to be stowed somewhere safe. Next they each sealed a neoprene bag containing their personal items and strapped it over their shoulders. The crewman listened on a handheld radio for the all-clear, then gave a thumbs-up.

Tao responded immediately, made a dash and jumped overboard, but just then the crewman grabbed Arius's shoulder.

He held up one finger, and turned abruptly to face the bow over the starboard side.

"Uh-oh," sputtered Arius.

The crewman told him that two River Enforcement vessels had been preparing to board on the port side, but one vessel had split off to go around to the starboard side. The wake of Tao's entry into the water had cleared just as that vessel came into sight.

The crewman took off his hooded coat and handed it to Arius along with Arius's pants. Arius dressed quickly, and slung the neoprene bag carrying his personal things over one shoulder. With the hood pulled up to hide his face, Arius and the crewman walked as casually as possible along the starboard deck.

The River Enforcement crew cruised alongside *Neptune*'s starboard side in their vessel, scanning the deck of the halted freighter with their binoculars. Arius nudged the crewman, and together they ducked into the next narrow opening, just ahead of the gaze of the River Enforcement boat passing by on the water below. Through the passageway, Arius could see all the way to the port side, where River Enforcement was already boarding *Neptune*. The captain had come down to welcome them aboard, holding his radio behind his back.

The River Enforcement wardens flashed their credentials to the captain to begin the inspection process. Arius knelt down as if checking something on the deck, and the crewman followed his lead and pretended to look up at something on the container. One of the wardens shot a glance towards Arius and began to walk slowly in his direction. The crewman turned to block the view, and it was then that the captain realized what was up.

The captain jogged over to the warden to grab his attention, as though he needed to clarify some administrative matter. As he did so, the crewman dashed to Arius and grabbed him by the hood of his coat. The River Enforcement vessel had passed them but was still on the starboard side.

A short stream of signals sounded on the crewman's radio. The captain was tapping them out on the radio he held behind his back. Three letters in Morse code: *R-U-N.*

Arius had just risked a quick look back to gauge the position of the River Enforcement vessel when the crewman broke into a full sprint. The warden on deck signaled to his colleagues, who had just made their way around the stern of the freighter, and responded with a sharp turn to return to the starboard side.

"Coat!" Arius called ahead as they neared another midship passageway between the containers. The crewman grabbed it from him and turned into the passageway as Arius dove over the rail.

The wake from Arius's dive cleared in the waters of the Atlantic just as the warden peered down to see the River Enforcement vessel coming back around the starboard side.

6 DAYS TO DAY ZERO

Toronto

Chapter 5

When Senna proudly threw the front door open to welcome him to his own house, Arius stood silent for a moment beside Tao and abandoned the search for his house keys. Curious eyes peered from the garage across the street where his neighbors sat around the season's batch of tomato sauce slowly stewing. Then they lost interest and continued their own conversation in Italian.

"Surprised your cousin has time to welcome you home, huh?" asked Senna.

"Not at all, not at all. You know I'm always glad to see you, cuz," replied Arius as he shook off his bewilderment. He picked up his backpack and he and Tao followed Senna as she led them into Arius's house. Arius saw his teenage kids toiling in the kitchen down the short hallway as the fragrant scent of lentil soup welcomed them in. Senna explained that she'd had a small opening in her schedule and found out from Arius's wife that his return was imminent, so she thought she'd surprise him.

From behind Arius, Tao whispered, "You have to get to Cole. Make this quick!"

"Thought we could play a few quick hands before I go," shouted

Senna from the kitchen. Senna had set up a poker game at the dining room table.

Arius's wife came down the stairs and greeted Tao with a smile and rubbed his shoulder on her way to kiss Arius on the cheek.

"Dinner will be about another half hour. You've got time to play," she said.

Arius's daughter wanted to watch, and Tao offered her a seat beside him.

"Come and see what your Auntie Mira is about to do to these boys, darling," said Senna proudly as she dealt the cards.

"Detective Mira now! Tell them, Auntie Mira," said Arius's daughter. Senna explained how she'd been roped in to work with the police to investigate the murder of a wigrant.

"I thought 'settler' was the preferred term," offered Tao.

Senna shrugged as she looked at her cards. "Let's go, little boys. Time is money."

Arius rolled his eyes and made his bet. Tao cautiously showed the two cards he'd been dealt to Arius's daughter: the two of diamonds and six of diamonds.

"It's going nowhere fast, especially at this table." Tao tossed the cards in to fold his hand.

"Get used to seeing that, darling. Tao folds faster than a laundromat," Senna told her. Tao raised his hands in protest. Senna blew him a kiss in consolation, which Tao slapped away in the air as the girl chuckled.

When the first three community cards were laid on the table, the girl asked why it was called "the flop." Tao explained that it most likely came from the sound the three cards made when they hit the table. He went on to say that the name of the fourth community card, the "turn," probably came from the final turn in a horse race, and the name of the final card, the "river," might have come from the old riverboats on the Mississippi, where dealers who were caught cheating on the last card would be thrown in the river.

Twenty minutes later, Senna was sitting behind a large stack of chips while Tao and Arius held on for dear life. On the next hand Arius was dealt a pair of aces. Tao folded, and Arius stayed in for a final showdown with Senna.

The flop went down. Ace. Four of diamonds. Three of diamonds. Arius held his breath as Senna stayed in and placed a small bet.

At the turn, the fourth ace hit the table. Arius looked at the four-ace combination, then at the few chips he had remaining. He asked the others to wait a moment, and he left the table to go upstairs. A few moments later he came back down with a polished wooden box, about twice the size of a deck of cards.

Everyone looked at him oddly.

Arius opened the box. Senna pushed back from the table slightly, but his daughter was the first to speak.

"Are those almonds?! We learned about those in school! Where did you get them, Papa?" she asked.

"I did a favor for someone, and this is how they paid me. What did you learn about them?" asked Arius.

His daughter told them how California had once grown 80 percent of the world's almonds, but, as one of the most water-intensive crops, it was the first to go at the beginning of the great drought. She said each almond required a gallon of water to grow, and that the plants had to be watered even when they were not producing.

Arius handed her three almonds. "Here, my love. Take these and share them with your mother and brother," She took her prize and ran into the kitchen.

Tao looked down as Senna shot lasers at Arius with her eyes.

"I don't want to know where those came from, Arius. I've turned a blind eye to whatever you're doing because we're blood. I've tried to look the other way, but every day you're making it harder, and someday I may not be able to," Senna said, keeping her tone low and even. "Don't let that day come."

"These cost way more than that stack of chips you're sitting behind," said Arius. He pushed the small box towards Senna, indicating he was all in. Tao took a deep breath and shook his head.

"Call," said Senna, without hesitation.

They turned up their cards to show their hands.

Senna held the two of diamonds and the six of diamonds. Arius looked at the cards, feeling certain of a win as the final card was placed. His victory vanished as the five of diamonds completed a straight flush for Senna, beating Arius's four aces.

"You caught a lucky break on the river," declared Arius, throwing his cards in the air.

"Never feels like luck when you're this good, darling," said Senna.

Chapter 6

Senna made another visit to the police. She knew that Merchant would rather have hand scrubbed all the toilets at the station than be partnered with her, but she'd reviewed all the files, and now she was going to do everything she could to vindicate River Enforcement in this business of the termination.

Senna could see Merchant working in the captain's office. When she knocked, he waved her off, so she took a seat and waited. But after ten minutes of impatient observation, she decided to invite herself in.

"If I throw a shoe, will you go away?" asked Merchant.

"With my good luck you'd miss, break the wall behind me, and expose a trunk of gold doubloons," replied Senna.

"Really . . . doubloons? Anyway, way I hear it is you don't believe in luck, good or bad. Some crap about hard work," said Merchant.

Since the promised shoe hadn't come, Senna took a seat in front of Merchant's desk, displaying as much confidence as anyone could while expecting a projectile to be launched at her head at any moment.

"If you know that, then you know I'm not the type to sidle over to rub it in, *acting captain*. I want to go over something with you," she said.

"Let these clowns around here dress me up as captain. You stick with sergeant. And see that funny-looking thing with a dial pad on the corner of the desk? Sometimes people use it to speak to one another to, oh, you know, save time, avoid pointless face-to-face meetings," said Merchant.

"Yeah? See, at first I thought it was just a decoration. You know, a throwback to set the mood. But then it rang. In fact, in the ten minutes I spent watching you in this palatial office, you let three calls go. And have you seen this funny thing that I keep in my pocket? It's what people have used for the last thirty years instead of that thing." Senna waved her cellphone in Merchant's face.

"Are you here to talk about the victim's criminal history?" he asked, calmly.

Not what Senna was expecting. Merchant seemed almost . . . reasonable. That wasn't going to last, she guessed, after she asked her next question.

"This termination," she said. "You know it happened off the settlement, right? I want you to go to the scene with me."

Merchant sat back in his chair and eyed her coldly for a long moment. "Get the hell out," he said at last.

As Senna turned and walked towards the door, she saw, then heard, a size-eleven boot hit the wall beside her.

"No doubloons. Meet me at HTO Park at 9:00 p.m.," Merchant said.

◊ ◆ ◊

Senna was there at 8:45, and the summer sun setting against the clouds painted the sand with an orange glow. The HTO Park was on the city's lakefront, a beach oasis at Queen's Quay, just south of Toronto's commercial downtown. It was bustling, a popular destination for families, even at that late hour, and it struck Senna that it made an unlikely setting for a termination.

She found Merchant sitting on the beach in a red Muskoka chair. His police cruiser was parked nearby.

"Sure you didn't want to park your car on the beach, sergeant? There's an empty patch over there by that kid's sandcastle," said Senna.

Merchant, in response to her judgmental tone, casually glanced up.

"You're now standing on the spot where the body was left. The victim got through your River Enforcement perimeter after curfew and somehow made his way almost two miles from the settlement to get here and end up dead," he said plainly.

Senna looked around. "Why did he leave the perimeter after 8:00 p.m.?" she wondered aloud. All the basic necessities of life were available to the wigrants on the settlement, and while they could go out during the day, everyone was supposed to be inside the fence between 8:00 p.m. and 8:00 a.m. Wigrants all received a coded marker stripe on their right hand. It looked like a short white paint strip, and it contained a code that helped identify them, for ease of food rationing and other administrative protocols. If they were offsite during curfew, they risked consequences.

"Maybe he knew Geppetto was coming for him?" Merchant explained that they'd found a string at the scene that made him think of a marionette, so he'd named the assailant after the fabled puppet-maker.

Senna scrunched her eyebrows quizzically. So, maybe the victim knew the assailant? She took a deep breath and slumped into a red Muskoka chair beside Merchant's.

"Hmm. A string, huh? I'd have named him 'The Hangman,' then," she offered.

"You're no good at this sicko. Leave the naming to me. So, how did he get out? I thought your mandate was to keep the perimeter tight at night?" said Merchant.

That was an uncomfortable question, and Senna was keen to change the subject. "You know, there's a lot of hostility directed towards the wigrants here. Nothing serious yet, but my wardens report a lot of jeering, honking, and they've even seen some garbage thrown at wigrants from the perimeter. Keeping them on the settlement at night is for their own protection."

"But, somehow, the victim was lured out and got past your perimeter. Possibly worse— someone chased him out," said Merchant, his voice trailing off.

"Which could mean that the assailant easily broke in and out through the perimeter." Senna closed her eyes as she completed Merchant's line of reasoning. "And, of course, the easiest way to do that is if the assailant was with River Enforcement."

For the first time since they'd met, they stared directly at one another as partners.

Chapter 7

After being a ghost for so many years, Geppetto quite enjoyed the new, playful name he'd been given. It felt oddly endearing.

And here he was, practically settling down in one city for a while. It was rare that he worked repeatedly in one particular part of the world. It was riskier, for sure, increasing the odds that a law enforcement agency might finally close in on him. And he really wanted to avoid the cliché of the career criminal who manages to evade the hotshot officer assigned to chase him, but ends up getting pulled over for a broken taillight.

Like any professional at the top of their field, selecting clients and projects was crucial to him in order to sustain his success. He exercised vigilance in client selection, to ensure that his marks blended well in terms of cover and rate of return on risk. But as chance would have it, a number of his clients had marks strewn throughout one city, as a result of the wigration. In the ten years he'd been in practice, a string of marks had never lined up that way. Some might have called it an omen: time to pack up shop and leave the game. He didn't see it that way at all. Maybe if his work had been more like a hobby . . . but when it's your passion, the writing on the wall takes on a whole new meaning. It no longer speaks to you saying, "Be cautious . . . imminent danger." Rather, it inspires you to new heights.

It wouldn't have been so strange if it had been a large European or Asian city, but a relatively small city of 3 million like Toronto offered both challenge and opportunity. The decisions then became: which files in particular to capitalize on, and what specific methods to employ.

It was an inspired moment, a chance to get creative. The majority of practitioners in his trade were subtle in completing their work, unless expressly instructed otherwise, usually to make a point. Most of the time they would remain a shadow, for example, in the wake of a heart attack. After all, who would search for an assassin when no assassination had taken place?

Art blended with science to craft a suitable demise, and each practitioner had his own particular stamp. One of his colleagues, dubbed "The Cipher," was a suicide specialist. Even among the most skilled practitioners, The Cipher's methods remained mysterious. Whether it was some form of chemical contagion, mental suggestion, personal threat, or combination thereof, no one knew, other than to say there wasn't a mark that didn't fall to The Cipher's methods.

For Geppetto, his signature wasn't one particular finish. Yes, the ending was the same. But the short road to the finish line was what made the difference for him. When he once pursued a mark, it was to exact an ending that would display irony. Humiliation wasn't the goal. Not at all. It was to make a statement about their deeds, and how they were ultimately undone. His clients sought something that his colleagues didn't provide. Other practitioners could track and execute with precision and efficiency, and he left the bloodier, more violent, vengeful jobs for other specialists. His clients wanted justice.

The Toronto dossier, taken as a whole, might have called for what he thought of as his "special delivery." But unless he could have contrived to have them all on a bus at the same time, that approach was risky, not to mention the lamentable collateral damage to innocents. That many incidents, at the same place in a short time span, would draw attention. And no one seemed to be moving out of the settlement where several of his marks now resided.

At first, he thought that casting suspicion on a police officer would be the appropriate way to conclude his business, but it was evident that the existing tension in Toronto surrounding the policing of the settlement by River Enforcement wardens would lend its own smoke and mirrors.

His first victim in Toronto had gone from riches to rags just before Vegas fell. He'd run a high-end escort service with little regard for human dignity or life. On the avails of prostitution, he'd accrued gambling debt beyond his means, and he'd barely survived when the underworld's collection agency came for their money. The wigration may very well have saved what little was left of his pitiful life. Geppetto's client, a sibling of one of the deceased escorts, wanted the victim to know what was coming. Geppetto apprehended him in his shanty dwelling disguised as a warden. Under the pretense of upgrading his decrepit abode, he escorted the mark beyond the settlement's perimeter, declared his true intent, and told him it was no use asking anyone for help. The victim lugged his plump physique for two slow, painstaking miles as poison coursed through his body, before he finally collapsed from fatigue. It was there, in the dead of night at HTO Park, that Geppetto said farewell on behalf of the deceased, showing him a photo of her, before silently delivering three appropriately placed bullets.

Of the names still on his list, four potential marks remained in Toronto. One of his clients had suffered an incident in which their young child was taken advantage of. A house call was in order.

For him, this trademark, this matching of punishment to deed, was what had lured his clients. It was what they would wait for. Justice was his service. And Geppetto would deliver.

Chapter 8

"Knees out! You're not a wobbly baby giraffe!"

Cole held her gaze slightly upward and corrected her leg position as she swung the kettlebell over her head. She'd asked Steele to find her a personal trainer with free time and a private space where she could burn off some energy while she waited for Arius's arrival. Now Cole was getting yelled at in a converted retail space amidst pull-up rigs, dumbbells, and climbing ropes.

Steele watched from just inside the doorway.

"Faster! You're off pace. Stop wasting my time," shouted the trainer over the rap playlist blasting through the speakers.

Cole's skipping rope, so fast it was barely visible, whipped through ten "double-unders," where the rope passed under the feet twice on each jump. When she was finished, she picked up the kettlebells again to complete her lunges.

"Faster!"

"Turn it up," said Cole, calmly cutting her off. "Loud."

The trainer fell silent witnessing what came next. Cole's movements were liquid power. The burpees were fast and aggressive. The double-unders were just a flash. Trainers rarely worried about someone at this level hurting themselves, but this might have been the exception.

"COUNT!" yelled Cole as she began her last ten pull-ups.

"One, two, three, four, five, six, seven, eight, nine, ten!" the trainer yelled back over the music.

"Time!" hollered Cole as she bent over, her hands on her knees, sweat rolling from her brow. The trainer nodded as she recorded the time. She turned off the music and winked at Steele, whose jaw was frozen open, as she left.

About thirty seconds to an eternity later, Steele unfroze his jaw and walked over to hand Cole her water bottle. Cole was in a runner's stretch. He pulled up a bench close by and pursed his lips patiently, widened his eyes, and looked around at nothing.

A few minutes later, a chime sounded on Steele's phone, and he checked it.

"He's here. Outside."

Cole nodded and threw a hoodie on over her sweat-soaked workout clothes. Steele put on his sunglasses.

The sunshine welcomed them onto Yonge Street alongside the bustling pedestrians who dove in and out of the many retail establishments and eateries that characterized this part of the longest road in the world. Cole spotted Arius waiting at the Gould Street intersection and followed him around the corner, where he perched on a wide set of stairs leading to the university student center. She sat down near him below a canopy of iridescent-blue metal panels twenty feet overhead.

Steele stayed behind at a calculated distance, never more than ten feet away. He scanned the vicinity and spotted someone on the other side of Yonge Street, leaning up against a convenience store window. No doubt this was Arius's man.

"That thing following you looks as if it was raised in the gym, when it wasn't modeling high-end casual wear. Why the handler?" Arius asked Cole.

"Axiom Water's board got worried when I put myself in the middle of the wigration. Its name, *his* name is Steele, and he's former SAS, turned private security," Cole explained.

"A bit of privacy, if you don't mind?" asked Arius, glancing over at Steele.

Cole immediately turned to wave him off, but as she did, Steele dipped his sunglasses slightly and directed her attention across the street. She nodded, waved him off, and he paced back to fifty feet.

"Will you oblige me as well, Arius?" Cole asked solemnly.

Arius swallowed his pride as he looked across the street and gave a nod. The man outside the convenience store stood up straight and walked away.

Arius told Cole he was unplugged, that his associate held his electronics, and Cole acknowledged the same. She leaned back, braced by her arms, watching the students come and go.

"Your cousin Senna has locked me out of the settlement," said Cole. "I sent the wigrants from a bad situation into a worse one. There's no municipal water for them. Too many people arriving at once—apparently the city can't accommodate the sudden increase."

"You have no control over water here?" asked Arius.

"Axiom Water runs the water distribution in cities around Europe where they felt—well, we convinced them—that a private company could do a better job than the public sector. They handed over control to me there. But not here in Toronto. The city runs the water network under oversight from River Enforcement, so I have no say. Not yet, anyway," said Cole.

"Senna is watching me. I can't be seen on the settlement or it might raise red flags. It needs to be you," said Arius. Cole pursed her lips skeptically as Arius dug into his bag, searching for something. He pulled out a thin folder and studied a picture he'd extracted from it. Arius showed her the picture of the individual Axiom Water had assigned responsibility for the settlement. Cole's expression went blank as she stared at it.

"If I didn't know better, I'd say you two might be related," Arius offered with a slight smile.

Cole sighed slowly.

"Tight timeline, but I may have a broker with access to enough bottled water to solve the problem. Got to warn you, though, he's shady. What about you getting control of the settlement?" asked Arius.

Cole took a deep breath before locking her gaze on his green eyes. "Remember what you did for me in Seville?"

Arius winced as his muscles tightened. He sat upright, looking away from her.

"That was a desperate situation, Cole," he said at last.

"Arius . . . in six days, people will die. And the deaths will only stop when they're all gone," said Cole.

He closed his eyes and nodded slowly.

"Those other operations could have landed you in jail, Arius. If you're caught by River Enforcement this time, it will be much worse," said Cole, looking into the distance.

Arius stood up, closed his worn messenger bag, and threw it over his shoulder and smoothed out his waist length peacoat.

"Higher the stakes, higher the satisfaction. Two nights from now. Be ready. You'll know if anything changes." He gave Cole a quick thumbs-up and a wink before walking away.

Arius walked south at a brisk pace for another block and sat down at one of the tables in Dundas Square. The surrounding supersized billboards and screens rained down a storm of visual imagery on the open-air plaza. As he so often did when he needed to think, Arius pulled from his pocket his familiar talisman and rubbed it for luck. It was a polished, black marble chess piece, a pawn.

The man from the convenience store caught up to him and pulled up a chair.

"Are you just bad at looking normal, Tao?" asked Arius.

"No such thing as normal. It was Steele," Tao replied. "We trained together just over ten years ago on his home turf, at the end of my service. I bet he recognized me. And we know better than to assume coincidence, so he must have flagged me to his client."

"Fancy that. Guess you'd better not find yourself on the settlement, then, because that's where Cole is headed next." Arius stirred uneasily in his chair, and returned the pawn to his pocket. "Time for me to disappear."

Chapter 9

L ooking into the makeshift settlement was like looking at a fight gone bad.

Just moments earlier, Cole had instructed Steele to go eastbound on the Gardiner Expressway so she could see the entire settlement from a good vantage point before they entered. The drive on the elevated highway overlooked a sea of tents, numbering in the thousands. And what wasn't too pretty from far away was very far from pretty up close.

Cole pointed past the tents. "See those high-rises? They were built on industrial land to accommodate the athletes coming for the Olympic Games. The plan was to convert them for residential use, but now they're being used to house wigrants."

"Sounds like a perfect fit. Shelter and a fresh start in a new city, no?" asked Steele as he watched the road.

Cole explained that about two-thirds of the people who'd lived in Vegas had been able to find their own way outside Vegas, whether on their own or by staying with people they knew elsewhere. "But a third of the people had nowhere to go. So they came here."

"Okay. So, the athletes' village accommodates, what?"

"Twenty thousand people."

"And how many came?"

"Two hundred and fifty thousand."

"Ouch. That's … that's a huge problem," Steele replied.

"D'ya think?"

Now an eight-foot-high chain-link fence enclosed the decrepit makeshift city within the city.

To the south of the settlement was a waterfront that was in reality a shipping channel, and beyond that the vastness of Lake Ontario. The settlement itself was bordered by a wide basin that freighters used to offload shipments.

At the center of the settlement, a block of nine high-rises stood in three rows of three, like glass soldiers on an asphalt battlefield. The luster of these gems had faded amidst the tents that surrounded them on three sides. A narrow band of mustard-yellow tents had been established on the north side, but the majority sat brazenly on the west side in three large clusters. A field of portable toilets separated the largest two.

East of the high-rises sat two large warehouses. While the larger one was actually a warehouse with supplies, the smaller one seemed to be housing people. South of the high-rises was another collection of tents, but these appeared to have been set up in a much more orderly manner.

When they pulled in to the settlement at the western edge, Cole asked Steele to lower the tinted windows. The warm breeze that poured in was flavored with sweat. Even with a light summer breeze off the lake, the congested air in the settlement suggested a hog farm. They got out of the car and walked towards an access gate, where two River Enforcement wardens were contending with a small group of people inside the perimeter fence.

"My friend is missing!" yelled one man, who had clearly been wearing the same clothes for days.

"And my sister hasn't arrived!" yelled a mother holding her daughter's hand. She was at the head of the small group.

Cole and Steele both froze at the voice of the mother. The mother from Las Vegas, with strawberry-blond hair, stood beside the smaller version of herself.

"Cole?" asked the mother in a surprised tone. The crowd settled slightly at the mother's pause.

Cole approached her from outside the gate and listened to her explain that one of the buses had never made it to the settlement.

"How is that possible?" Cole wondered out loud.

One of the wardens interrupted to ask Cole her business.

She snapped back into character. "I need to speak with Gus. Right now," she demanded.

The wardens looked curiously at Cole, then eyed up Steele. "Get lost."

"No. Get on your radio and tell Gus that Cole is here to see him. Do it now!" said Cole plainly.

The wardens looked at one another before one took a few steps back, picked up his phone, and conveyed the message. Then he repeated it. And then there was nothing. The warden held the phone up to his ear, waiting for something. He looked at it to make sure it was still working, then put it to his ear again. Nothing. He hung up.

"I don't know who you are," the warden said then, "but it looks like you'd better stop wasting my time."

Steele took a small step closer to Cole and coughed lightly, an indication to her to get back to the car to formulate a new plan.

Cole walked right up to the fence, within an inch of the warden's face.

"Call again, or hand me the phone," she demanded in a deadpan tone.

The crowd on the other side of the fence fell silent as a lean, taut figure in a tan River Enforcement uniform passed through. He was a tall, dark-skinned man, and his bald head glided above them. The wardens stood to attention in their black, gold-trimmed uniforms, reassuring the man that they had everything under control. He dismissed them with a wave of his hand.

"I hope you pay good money to your security, Gus," said Cole.

"'Dad' would be fine. 'Papa.' Even 'Pops' if you'd like," replied Gus.

Chapter 10

C ole's father chuckled gently as they stood in front of the settlement gate. When the wardens opened the gate for him, he came out and acknowledged Steele with a simple nod. His smile vanished as he approached Cole.

"It's been made abundantly clear to me by River Enforcement that your presence is intolerable here," he said, and his familiar deep voice reverberated in Cole's ear.

"Those words are not surprising from you at all," replied Cole, crossing her arms rebelliously.

"Not *my* words. Senna's words to me, just yesterday. I'm the only one standing between you and my wardens right now. Literally. Why are you here?"

Cole turned her back on her father and walked a few yards away from the fence, putting some distance between herself and the wardens. Gus followed after her, and Steele positioned himself between Gus and the fence.

Cole turned to face her father. "Same Gus. New crew. Nothing changes."

"Looks like it. Just as judgmental as you ever were. And you want into my crew again, just like you did twenty years ago," he said.

Cole clenched her fists tight, her arms still crossed over her chest. "You think that's why I'm here!? Sure, to rekindle your glory days. Oh, sorry you're not carrying a weapon. Oh well, too bad!"

Gus bit his lip and shook his head.

"Let me in," Cole demanded.

Gus raised his eyebrows, turned to walk back towards the gate, and ran up against Steele. He looked directly down into Steele's mirrored sunglasses.

"Young man," Gus said, warningly. Steele had to fight off a reflexive urge to salute. Instead he took off his sunglasses and leaned around Gus to make eye contact with Cole, seeking instructions. She just sighed loudly.

Gus locked eyes with Steele for a moment, then turned back to talk to Cole.

"Do these people know about the status of your water supply?" Cole asked.

Gus hesitated. "What are you talking about? I've been told our supply will be replenished by the end of this week."

Cole let his statement twist in the breeze.

"Would you like to hear what Senna said to *me* yesterday?" Cole asked Gus.

Gus pursed his lips. He began to walk back towards the gate. Steele looked to Cole for direction, but she had turned to face away from them, so Steele stepped aside this time to let Gus pass.

Gus entered through the gate and looked over to the wardens. "They're with me," he said, and the wardens nodded obediently.

Cole turned and walked casually through the gate, with Steele following close behind her. As she walked inside, a little hand tugged at Cole's sleeve. The little girl with the strawberry-blond hair looked up into Cole's brown eyes.

Cole smiled into the girl's brilliant hazel eyes, but she had nothing to say to her. As Cole pulled away gently, the group began piping up again with their complaints to the wardens.

Chapter 11

In the grocery store, three teens noticed something different about the brightly dressed man going through the checkout: a white stripe on his right hand. One of them elbowed another to point it out, and they started whispering among themselves. They followed him out of the store.

As the man walked quickly along Queen's Quay, the teens opened a carton of eggs and started lobbing them across the street in his direction. The first egg landed far in front of him. The second flew a foot over his fashionable purple beret before bursting on the sidewalk beside him. He hoped that the teenagers couldn't see the sweat that was beginning to soak through his red rayon shirt.

"Fancy colors, wigrant! You come here to steal our water, but you got enough to buy your own groceries, eh? You're a scammer, wigrant!"

"Hey, Colors! Need some eggs for breakfast?!" One of the teens threw another egg that fell far from its mark. Just then a police car happened by and the teens scattered.

"Colors" thanked his good fortune and picked up his pace to get back to the settlement. He felt lucky to have got a place in one of the high-rise buildings. Even though he, his wife and child had to share the two-bedroom unit with another family of four, this was home now.

He walked past a small play structure that had survived the speedy erection of the tents on the Olympic village site. Next to it, he noted, a sweaty man sat smoking a cigar. When he got to his building at last, it was reassuring to see Gus, the man overseeing the settlement, who greeted him with a gentlemanly nod as he entered his residence.

◊ ◆ ◊

Gus was giving Cole a tour of the settlement, with Steele tagging along. They had already walked through the largest cluster of tents, not far from the gates. Now they were passing the play structure. Steele recoiled at the smell of cigar smoke and tapped Cole on the shoulder. She saw the direction of Steele's glance and nodded approval. Steele approached the cigar-chomping sweat bomb.

"Sir, can I ask that you put out the cigar since you're so close to the children's play area?"

"Smoke" let his wide-eyed gaze drift from the play area all the way up to Steele's sunglasses. He held the cigar in one hand and shot Steele a Cheshire Cat grin. In a lazy Southern accent, the man said, "Want to help me, son? I'm a mite thirsty. Can you find one of those there wardens?" He exhaled a thick fog through his nostrils. And no sooner had he exhaled than a sleek, taut flash of tan uniform appeared. Gus smacked Smoke's hanging wrist so hard that his arm almost snapped at the elbow, and the cigar fell to the ground.

"Found one," said Steele, as he stepped on the cigar. "Thank you for your cooperation . . . son."

Gus took the lead again to continue their walk as Cole followed behind, never saying a word.

They walked past the high-rise buildings, and for just a moment a gentle breeze off the lake cleared the looming odor of all the clustered tent dwellers. Cole scrunched her nose as the breeze settled and the odor descended once again.

Her attention shifted to the orderly group of tents that sat to the south, between the high-rises and the shipping channel. Cole noted that the tents were guarded, and she looked to Steele inquisitively with a glance towards them.

Steele shrugged his shoulders, as if to say, *I'm supposed to know?*

Now Cole motioned with a glance towards Gus, but Steele's reply was an unimpressed flat gaze.

Cole shot him a stern look. He rebelled, hands in the air, shrugging his shoulders. The look he got from Cole then was sheer ice.

Steele craned his head back and rolled his eyes, with a slow, deep breath of exasperation.

"I wonder, sir, if you could tell us what the function of these tents is? Do they serve some sort of . . . administrative purpose?"

Gus simply called back, "This is a security compound, for any problems on site." And he left it at that.

Eventually they reached the warehouses at the eastern perimeter.

"These buildings went up really fast," he explained, "within weeks, to accommodate the massive influx."

One of the warehouses was being used as a hostel to shelter people without a residence or tent. The other housed food handouts and supplies, including the water stockpile.

Inside, forklifts skittered around, moving pallets and supplies between the tall racks. They walked around a food stockpile waiting to be loaded on to the racks. Beyond that was the water stockpile, set up as a large pyramid of unlabeled cases in one corner.

Gus checked in with the warden in charge of supplies, who confirmed that there were six days of water remaining, but he became uneasy when the warden could not confirm any pending shipments for more supply.

"Does that include the emergency reserve?" Gus asked.

The warden nodded, pointing to another smaller room that included supply for just over a day.

Gus looked suspiciously at Cole as he picked up his phone and walked away from her. He worked to keep his deep voice hushed as he questioned someone on the other end of the line.

When he'd hung up he came back to Cole. His lips were pressed tightly together. "I'm sure it will be fine," he said. His voice was trying for an air of confidence.

"Go ahead. Just wait till the bodies start piling up later this week," said Cole.

"It doesn't make any sense. Senna can't allow that to happen," said Gus.

"You think I want to believe it? I'm not here for a family reunion. This is going to be a disaster, and it will have your name all over it. Glad I changed mine," she said.

"Ha. Not such a far cry from your real name, Ms. *Coltrane*," said Gus wryly.

Cole winced at the reminder of the name she'd excised from her life years earlier.

Steele interrupted to show Cole a new text from Arius.

She stood, pensive, working out in her mind how she could use the information on her own. Cringing at the inevitable conclusion, but resisting every instinct she had, she told Gus.

"We have a lead on a water broker at the edge of the city," she said.

The words hung in the air. Gus smothered a smile: she needed his help.

The three of them stood together in a silent showdown as forklifts whirred past them. Gus was the first to speak.

"You shouldn't even be here on the settlement, you know. You're *persona non grata* around here. And now you want me to work against Senna and everything she believes in by helping you go behind her back to get water from a broker?"

"Worried your boss is going to yell at you?" Cole asked.

The color drained from Gus's face. "Yell. If only."

Cole was puzzled. "Do you trust her that much? Do you believe she's right to refuse to import water? And what if she's wrong, if you're wrong? What then? What happens when the water runs out?"

Cole took Gus's silence as acceptance.

"I'll text you the location and time tomorrow morning," said Cole.

"No, you can't. Never by phone. Our phones belong to River Enforcement and they're strictly monitored."

The supply warden approached to tell Gus that Senna wanted to speak with him, and she'd be there soon.

Cole's eyes widened as she understood that Senna was just moments away. She grabbed Steele's phone, put it in front of Gus's face to show him the location, and yelled out a time.

Cole and Steele made a dash for the door they'd entered through, but a forklift unloaded a pallet of supplies in their path. They quickly turned to hide behind a tall food stockpile just as Senna entered.

Gus's deep voice carried in the warehouse. They heard bits and pieces of the conversation: Senna said she couldn't stay long, she had to get over to HTO Park, and she reassured Gus that the water supplies were well in hand.

Cole tilted her head and shot a doubtful look back at Steele's skeptical stare. The footsteps and voices got louder as Gus and Senna closed in on their hiding place. Steele led Cole around the stockpile to a rear wall and they walked along it slowly. They peeked around one of the tall racks to see Gus facing them, and Senna's back. Luckily Gus spotted them and led Senna towards the food stockpile, and Cole and Steele moved in the opposite direction to sneak out the way Senna came in.

Chapter 12

After Cole and Gus were out of sight, Geppetto approached "Smoke" and presented him with a Cuban Cohiba cigar. He consoled Smoke on the "radical ignorance of the authorities in this place" and told him that guys like the two of them had to stick together to get through this mess they put them in. Smoke nursed his sore wrist and invited the stranger to sit with him by the play structure.

No one ever sees a criminal.

In Toronto, many years earlier, Geppetto had seen a man on the subway with a long, grizzly white beard, disheveled clothing, and a perplexingly unpleasant aroma. Geppetto wanted to think he was better than the people who shied away with no concern for this poor homeless man's health and safety. He knew it was only good fortune that separated him, and everyone else aboard that subway car, from this poor soul. He dropped a dollar coin into the homeless man's coffee cup before getting off at his stop.

Fifteen minutes later Geppetto was in class, looking at the same man teaching advanced computational mathematics. Fortunately, the professor hadn't choked on the dollar he'd dropped into his six-dollar cup of coffee, which Geppetto had thought was an empty salvaged from the trash. He was sitting before one of the premier mathematicians on the planet, a man who simply focused his very capable energies on his work, not his hygiene.

No one ever sees a criminal, because everyone reads the world as though it's their own storybook. They look for the suspicious, devious type. In Geppetto's storybook, such a thing was a rarity. Hiding in plain sight was far easier than staying concealed. If he'd seen Geppetto on the subway with the appearance he'd taken on, Smoke may very well have dropped a dollar in Geppetto's coffee. A simple cigar had broken through that barrier of prejudice.

Smoke had a record in the River Enforcement database for water trafficking. He was, in effect, a connoisseur who brokered water like wine, from sources around the world. He sampled various types of water—spring, tap, distilled, filtered. Could the region be discerned in the flavor? How did the varying concentration of dissolved solids, typically minerals, affect the taste? His highest-value product was glacial meltwater that sold for $10,000 a bottle.

Smoke had served short sentences in River Enforcement custody, but continued with his entrepreneurial pursuits when he was free. It was his other pastimes, however, that put Smoke in Geppetto's crosshairs.

Geppetto had been approached three years earlier, in the usual way, to contend with Smoke. Finding Geppetto was a simple matter of speaking to the right people, and being directed to the appropriate website with instructions to contact him through coded email. The code was simple: a subject line referring to any random ailment, with the body of the message containing contact information. First, though, Geppetto needed to vet the client. Intuition played a considerable part in determining whether he was willing to make his services available, especially when it came to sniffing out undercover law enforcement agents hell-bent on entrapment.

Geppetto set up a meeting with this prospective client downtown at Dundas Square, after an evening concert. Some oral inserts, tinted eyeglasses, cap and otherwise grubby garb assisted the meeting as he observed her through the crowd for thirty minutes before approaching, even though he'd been tracking her from the time she left her home. The most important test came next. He dropped her a look in passing, and she followed him right back to her home. He asked if she'd let him in. The panicky look in her eyes suggested fear, not avoidance. It was the next tick on his checklist.

She asked if they could go to a nearby café, and compromised on his suggestion of a hotel lobby. Her agreement and silence were consistent with the reluctance he'd expected to see. He wasn't out to convince her to hand over her money. If anything, he'd suggest she reconsider altogether and forgo hiring him, or anyone else.

Though he served justice, humanity, he felt, was best served by forgiveness. Only love, he told himself, could conquer hate.

But if clients were determined to go ahead with the commission, he would be certain to meet their requirements. And she was determined.

To confirm his acceptance of the file they discussed terms of payment, including fee and logistics. She'd stated that the money she could spend was limited to cash on hand. It was less than he usually asked, but in this situation he was willing to accept. The man she wanted him to terminate had once run a charitable organization organizing events for children, during which children were sexually abused. Allegations had been made, and the client had watched other parents try and fail to prosecute this man for his many misdeeds. Even with the help of a journalist from a local newspaper, they'd succeeded only in having his business accounts frozen pending further investigation.

Payment in full would be made following an agreed upon protocol in the next day if she decided to retain him, giving her more time to change her mind.

Finally, Geppetto communicated his most important parameter to the client. The assignment would take place anytime from the next month to within ten years.

5 DAYS TO DAY ZERO

Toronto

Chapter 13

Senna's morning started in a cordoned-off parking lot in the city's historical Distillery District, not far from the settlement. There was some sort of trouble at a coffee house there, and Toronto Police and an ambulance were already on the scene, along with a River Enforcement vehicle. The Victorian-era industrial buildings overlooking the scene were home to boutique retailers, art galleries, and restaurants, but it was too early for any of them to be open yet.

Senna was walking the brick-paved lane towards the nineteenth-century pump house turned coffee roaster when Merchant's car hopped the curb behind her. He killed the engine and got out.

"You like to make a dramatic entrance, don't you, Sergeant Merchant?" Senna said.

"Can't you just call me Merch, like everyone else?"

Merchant took the lead and pushed his thick frame through the front door of the coffee house. Two police officers were already inside arguing with a couple of wardens. Meanwhile, a young man sat handcuffed on the floor, propped up against the exposed brick wall. Another young man was about to be carried out on a stretcher by the paramedics.

The wardens came over to Senna, and the officers spoke to Merchant.

"This was a break-in and an assault on the coffee house employee, captain! The collar belongs to us. It's our jurisdiction," shouted one of the officers.

"Senna," a warden said, "this man is a wigrant who was caught red-handed trying to steal water from this establishment and load it into small flasks to sell on the settlement. This is a water crime!"

When Senna asked if they'd scanned his marker stripe, they told her he was a single occupant here on his own from Vegas.

Senna pursed her lips, trying desperately to contain her anger in front of Merchant. She walked away from them all and stood over the young man in handcuffs, whose head was bowed down.

"Who are you, wigrant!?" she shouted, so loudly that everyone in the room jumped. Senna knelt down and put one finger under the young man's chin to lift his face so she could look into his eyes. Merchant watched, carefully.

Senna lowered her volume and sternly asked, "Young man, how did you get out of the settlement before lockdown was lifted?"

"I jumped the fence this morning when there were no wardens around. It was about 6:30," the young man replied.

Senna stood up and addressed the wardens. "Bring him back to the settlement."

The police officers shook their heads at one another and stood back as the wardens lifted the young man to his feet to escort him out. Resigned to the outcome, they followed the wardens and perpetrator outside.

"There's no way our victim jumped the fence," Senna muttered to Merchant, with one eyebrow raised.

"Uh-huh. More likely I ran a marathon than that guy jumping a fence."

Senna led him outside to the brick-paved laneway towards their cars, past a thirty-foot-high steel sculpture that looked part alien relic, part corkscrew.

But Merchant wasn't done. "Officers. Take custody of the wigrant from the wardens. Bring him to the station instead," he ordered.

The officers and wardens froze.

The blood rushed to Senna's face. What the hell was Merchant thinking? But the tightness overtaking her body was interrupted by the ringing of her phone.

Chapter 14

T he ten-year provision was common to all Geppetto's contracts and was non-negotiable. This was to ensure clients understood his manner of working and, perhaps more importantly, to help them appreciate the value of retribution.

Only twice had his services been terminated without delivery. The first time was early in his career. A client who had requested Geppetto's services for his boss had canceled the contract just a week after retaining him, leading Geppetto to wonder whether this was something he could expect to happen often. On another occasion, he'd been retained by a client to terminate an ex-spouse; five years later the client had a change of heart following a spiritual awakening. These clients walked with their pockets a bit lighter and a huge weight off their guilty conscience.

In the three years since he'd had Smoke on his roster, the man had continued to travel between Toronto and his home in Vegas.

Now Geppetto sat with his new friend inside Smoke's tight quarters, a two-bedroom corner unit on the top floor of the tallest high-rise, which he shared with a young couple. A Cuban cigar was the flare for their friendship, but Geppetto's refined knowledge of illegal water products intrigued Smoke even further, and he couldn't resist the temptation to proudly show his new friend the contraband water products from around the world that he kept locked in his bedroom, including his prized bottle of Canadian Arctic glacial water.

That was Geppetto's cue to reach into his bag and bring out a present that he'd mocked up for his new friend.

"From Scandinavia!" He'd poured distilled water with some added features into an antique glass soda bottle, sealed it, and labeled it "Fjord."

Smoke's hands shook as he carefully put down his cigar, took custody of the present, and walked over to the bedroom window to hold it up to the light. His eyes teared up as he held it high.

"It's absolutely crystal clear. What do you think?" Smoke asked hopefully. "Do you think we should sell it, or . . . ?"

"I can't imagine wasting something this fine on some thirsty wigrant. Can you?" Geppetto replied.

A box in the corner was popped open and two small glasses were filled with the liquid. They clinked their glasses, and Smoke savored his shot. Geppetto then turned his back and quickly added a special coagulant into the bottle that would cause the microscopic glass shards he'd added to the water to quickly coalesce together. Geppetto held his glass high and insisted that Smoke continue to drown his sorrows.

Geppetto handed him the bottle. As they laughed their troubles away, Smoke guzzled the water like a swine, ingesting all the minuscule particles that would almost instantly become razor-like stones inside him.

Minutes later, Smoke slumped to the bedroom floor, wincing in agony. Geppetto estimated that his target would succumb within the hour to internal bleeding. He injected a chemical cocktail to paralyze Smoke's speech and limbs while keeping him alert. He showed Smoke a photo of his client's son as a reminder, and read a small note saying simply "Farewell" before leaving it in Smoke's pants pocket.

He had just finished wiping the scene down when he heard a key in the front door lock.

Smoke's roommates, who he'd been told were out looking for work, had obviously returned home much earlier than expected. Geppetto heard them talking in the kitchen, probably making themselves a late breakfast.

Geppetto stepped over Smoke to look out the bedroom window at the straight drop, then stepped back over him towards the bedroom door. He made a hushing gesture to Smoke with his index finger as he listened to the couple talk about their job prospects over the clang of pots and pans. Geppetto reached into his bag for his phone and opened the app he'd designed to track the whereabouts of all of River Enforcement's wardens. He switched over to the notes he had on Smoke's file that included cellphone numbers for the couple, as well as the interview details previously extracted from their e-mail accounts.

The ping on their phones went off a moment later. He heard their surprise and they reveled in the surprise text message asking them for a follow-up chat immediately. They turned off everything in the kitchen and went back out.

Geppetto gave a thumbs-up and a wink to Smoke and made his way to the front door of the unit. He waited five minutes before calling River Enforcement to report that someone in Smoke's unit had contraband. When he heard nothing outside the door in the hallway beyond, he made his exit, leaving the front door unlocked as he ducked into the adjacent stairwell.

As the wardens approached Smoke's unit, he applied a voice mask on his phone before calling.

"Put this call on speaker, Detective Mira. Sergeant Merchant, the wardens have done it again," Geppetto said before hanging up. He exited the stairwell directly outside and felt a light breeze on his face.

Chapter 15

The SUV crept up the long estate driveway towards a blindingly white building that suggested a transplanted Southern plantation interpreted with a modern architectural flair. Lake Ontario framed the building from behind. Steele scanned the waterfront property as they pulled in, comparing the exterior layout to the schematics he'd memorized.

"We're early," said Steele, as he surveyed the secluded surroundings.

"We'll wait in the car, then."

Steele recognized an opportunity to push for a few more answers. "What exactly does this guy do, this water broker?" he asked.

Cole explained that where River Enforcement operated, they outlawed every water source except the city's own water supply and then restricted demand. "It was Senna's belief that importing water to a drought zone would only deprive other regions and prolong the inevitable. When the settlers arrived in Toronto from Las Vegas, Senna reluctantly allowed the city to commit its entire disaster stockpile to the settlement for that unique emergency situation. The criminal underworld seized the opportunity to sell water to those who could afford it."

"And where are they getting the water from?" Steele asked.

"Does it matter?"

Steele would not take a hint. "This contact of yours who set up this meeting—why the Robin Hood act?"

"I don't really care. As long as he helps me get water to those who can't afford it," replied Cole.

Steele could see that the wall of plausible deniability that Cole had erected was about to be destroyed. Not much point in pushing on that.

"So, Senna . . . she's a real piece of work, right? What about her?" When Cole began to describe Senna's demeanor, he interrupted. "No, I mean . . . not what she's like. I saw enough at the CN Tower. How does she operate?" asked Steele.

Cole paused, and squinted as if thinking hard. "Gus would know," she blurted, finally. Then, "I see that smirk on your face, Steele. Stop trying to be my therapist," she snapped.

He knew enough about warfare to leave the battle for another day.

Not long after, Gus arrived with a driver in a similar black SUV.

"Two cars is good. We'll have a safe secondary egress in case anything goes sideways," Steele told her solemnly.

Gus walked over to the car at a slow, casual pace.

Cole blinked. She rolled down her window to talk to him.

"Why are you here?" she asked.

"Didn't you tell me to meet you here?" asked Gus.

"Not here. *Here!*" said Cole, tugging on the arm patch of Gus's tan River Enforcement uniform to make her point clear.

"I think she hired me to piss you off," replied Gus.

Cole remained silent.

"Listen, if you really understood, you'd never expect an apology from me," attempted Gus.

Still silence.

"But you don't. And that's my fault too," Gus added. "I'm sorry."

Waves crashed against the shoreline wall in the distance, filling in the void of Gus's silence. The lake reached to the horizon in three directions. So vast you'd mistake it for the sea.

Suddenly, at the top of the white marble staircase that led up to the house, the oversized double doors swung open. A man with disheveled black hair stood in the threshold wearing a full-length dark blue trench coat over a banana-yellow suit with a neon blue shirt.

Cole left the car and walked up to the house with Gus. Steele followed.

"Yikes. I think I have an extra uniform in the trunk," Gus whispered to Cole. Cole's head dipped, perhaps to hide her smile.

"Welcome!"

The broker led them through one vast, empty room to a cavernous, sparsely furnished living space. Cole and Gus sat together on a low, gray leather couch set beneath a spherical chandelier. They faced the floor-to-ceiling windows that looked out onto the manicured grounds at the front of the property. Steele, assessing the best vantage point, took up a lookout position to the far right of the windows.

On either side of the oversized glass panes sat what seemed like the only other pieces of furniture in the house: two black, steel-framed, high-backed, red-cushioned stools. The broker pulled one up and sat.

"I'm accustomed to meeting with your errand boy, Cole. I assumed you wanted to keep your hands clean. But I suppose some things are so important they must be done yourself. Is this one of those times?" asked the broker. His right leg twitched restlessly as he spoke.

Cole got straight to the point. "Are you going to be donating the water we need to make up the deficit at the settlement?"

The broker nodded knowingly, eyes squinted, one hand on his chin. Without hesitation he tore a scrap from the notepad in his jacket pocket and handed it to Cole with a pen.

She smirked at him as she scribbled a dollar figure on the page and returned it to him.

Now the broker put on a pair of excessively thick, yellow-framed wooden bifocals. He nodded knowingly again and made a scribble of his own for Cole and passed it back.

"That's exorbitant," declared Cole.

"And what price do we put on human lives?" said the broker, his arms spread wide above his head.

Cole sat pensive for a moment. "Show me some good faith—a donation to keep the settlement going—and I'll see what I can do," she said.

This time the broker looked thoughtful. The twitch in his leg ceased, and he sat eerily still.

"There is something even more valuable you can give me, Cole," said the broker.

Gus shot lasers with his eyes. The broker noticed.

"Oh please, we're gentlemen here." The broker got up and stood next to Cole. "May I?"

Gus grunted his displeasure but yielded his place on the sofa to the broker.

"Your errand boy sent you here because you're tight on time, and he knows I'm the only one that can deliver," said the broker.

Cole was determined to hide her disgust—at the broker's behavior, at his glasses, at his overbearing cologne. It was all perfectly too much. But he was her only chance.

"What do you want?" she asked.

He took the scrap of paper from her hand and chuckled as he crumpled it.

"That was a want. My source is ready any time to meet your needs. What I *need* is to have my suppliers unblocked by River Enforcement," said the broker.

Just then Steele called from his position by the window. "Cole. To the car. There's movement on the perimeter!" He motioned everyone to get down and jammed himself against the edge of the windowpane to maintain a safe vantage point.

If there was ever a top ten list of "People Most Likely to Question Authority," it would have been a hard tie between Cole and Gus. But neither hesitated to follow Steele's directions. They began to crawl past the window as the broker sat idly. Then a shot cracked in near the top of the window.

Gus and Cole made it past the window and got up to bolt through the door and to the vehicles as the broker dashed the other way.

"I need the broker, Steele!" yelled Cole.

"To the car. Now, Cole!" Steele yelled back, even louder.

"Is your driver a warden or civilian?" Steele asked Gus as they ran down the stairs bent forward so the high marble railings covered their exit.

"Warden," yelled Gus.

Steele instructed the driver to go up the driveway as a decoy, while Gus ducked into Cole's vehicle with her.

Steele drove away from the entrance towards a gravel road at the back of the property. Another shot rang out.

"Was that for us?" Cole turned to see if she could see anything through the back window of the SUV.

"We're not waiting to find out," said Steele coolly.

Cole kept looking as the SUV bounced down the gravel road. And then, for an instant, she saw a ghost, a face she'd thought was ancient history, lurking in the bushes.

"Couldn't the shooter intercept us wherever this road comes out?" asked Gus.

Just as the SUV entered a stand of trees, Steele took an abrupt turn towards the water. They dove down a slight ridge onto a short rocky beach, where a Zodiac awaited them.

"Out," ordered Steele.

The three of them quickly moved from the SUV onto the Zodiac. Tao pushed off, fired up the engine and turned towards the open lake. They kept their heads down as Steele kept his eyes fixed on the shoreline. As they made their way out, Steele turned for a quick fist bump with Tao.

"Wherever, whenever," Tao said to Steele.

Chapter 16

Back at the settlement, Senna was still seething over Merchant's heavy-handed move with the wigrant arrested at the coffee house. What business did he have taking the suspect from the River Enforcement wardens and putting him in police custody? It was such an obnoxious power move! But she kept remembering the ultimatum from the mayor: without police cooperation, her ability to vindicate River Enforcement in the matter of the termination of the wigrant at HTO Park would be in jeopardy.

And now, there was another wigrant fatality. She'd had a call from an anonymous informant who blamed it on River Enforcement wardens. Another public embarrassment on River Enforcement's watch. And Merchant had listened to the call as well. Great.

Already the news was out. Sitting in her car, Senna was scrolling through social media.

"Disgraced Philanthropist Terminated by River Enforcement."

"Wigrant Slain Before Settling."

"Death Linked to Rogue Warden."

"Settlement Marks Another Loss."

She could see Merchant outside, in her rearview mirror, deep in discussion with one of his officers, who handed him some pages from his notebook. Turning her attention forward, Senna could see one of her wardens being escorted towards a police car by another officer. She bit her lip, closed her eyes, and tried to take deep breaths for what seemed like an eternity. Then came two loud raps on her passenger-side window.

Merchant opened the door to let himself in, and his stocky presence filled the front seat.

Senna sighed an uncharacteristic sigh. The biggest uncertainty troubling her, at this moment, wasn't the array of headlines. It was the heavy force of authority beside her.

Finally, Merchant broke the silence. He told her what his officer had explained to him about the young couple who were staying with Smoke. Merchant handed Senna the pages from his officer's notebook. The couple had left the apartment after receiving a text message about a follow-up to a job interview. But when they arrived, no one knew anything about it.

"They got that text about ten minutes before River Enforcement arrived on the scene," Merchant explained, "and only a few minutes after that, you got that weird anonymous call. I've developed a healthy suspicion of coincidences," he said.

"I don't get it. I don't see how these terminations keep getting pinned on our wardens. For one thing, every warden uniform has a GPS tracker chip in it. We know where they go. How would they end up at a crime scene without being tracked? Especially if they have to go off site?" asked Senna.

"They take off their uniform? Or, they take their chip out?" suggested Merchant.

"Yeah, but why would a wigrant follow someone in plain clothes? Would be like an off-duty officer making demands on a house call. I don't think so. Then, when the victim was found at HTO Park, Gus made all the wardens inventory their uniforms. Nothing came up. Everything was intact. And it's not easy to take the chip out and put it back in without leaving evidence of tampering."

"But if someone could do it, every warden would be a suspect," Merchant suggested. "Do they go through any kind of background check or psychiatric screening when they're hired? I mean, do you have a way of weeding out anybody who might be hostile to environmental issues?"

"Because they might have a motive to make River Enforcement look bad?"

"Well, something like that, sure," Merchant replied.

"Yeah, we do, in fact. We don't make it known, but we screen for that. And also for anyone who is way over on the radical environmentalist edge, too."

They both fell silent for a while.

Then, "How easy is it to impersonate a warden?" Merchant asked.

"Not nearly as easy as impersonating a police officer, I'm sure."

Merchant squinted his eyes in agitation at the assertion.

"But anything is possible, I suppose," Senna conceded.

"Can we work on another assumption? What if someone infiltrated River Enforcement?" asked Merchant.

Senna stopped and took a long, deep breath.

"Then you walk me through why this isn't a warden, and we build the profile to get this guy before he hits again," said Merchant.

Senna glanced at Merchant. He met her eyes with an awkward glance.

"Or girl," he said.

"Let's go with guy," said Senna, with a half-smile. "You're calling him Geppetto, right?"

"Okay, so let's say this is Geppetto again," said Merchant. "Look at the mode of operation. There is no standard MO. The first victim was chased and shot. The second was found in his room, paralyzed, and he died on the way to the hospital of internal bleeding, with a 'Farewell' note in his pocket, to make it look like a suicide, I suppose. There's nothing to link the victims, so we're lost on a pattern."

"But for a second, let's assume there isn't one . . . Could it be that Geppetto is a serial killer?" asked Senna.

"Doesn't put out that vibe to me. Is there a psychological game at play that we're not seeing? The only people I see getting caught up in a game right now are us . . . That phone call to you, Senna. How did the caller get your cell number?" asked Merchant.

"That number is on my business card so its public," replied Senna. Lying to Merchant didn't bother her. The implications of the truth did. "You're wondering, why call at all? If he's taunting us, why give us any direction? Why single me out?"

Merchant asked her to repeat the words from the phone call she'd received.

"He said, 'Put this call on speaker, Detective Mira. Sergeant Merchant, the wardens have done it again.'" A chill went down her spine.

"Wouldn't happen to know his first name too? You know, if I were to believe River Enforcement's innocence, that's two terminations that could be linked to one person," said Merchant.

"Yeah, there's nothing coincidental or heat of the moment about any of this," Senna agreed.

Merchant knew she was right. This was no rogue.

As the police car carrying her warden pulled off, Merchant pointed to it, then waggled his finger. The finger waggle was then directed at Senna.

"These years, everything I've seen about River Enforcement. Never liked what I saw. I never trusted you. But, something is . . ." His voice trailed off as the accusatory finger waggle transformed into a pensive prop for Merchant's lower lip.

Just as Senna settled back in the driver seat, Merchant snapped back.

"That stunt at the Distillery District, Senna. You're on thin ice," he boomed.

With that, he threw open the passenger door and lugged his hefty frame out. Senna hollered to ask where he was going.

"We have an assassin," Merchant called back. "Follow me."

Senna followed Merchant back to his division office. There, he checked in with the unit that had been gathering evidence on the allegations against Smoke, his charitable events, and the abuse of children. They started by reviewing the investigative report done by the journalist that had broken a year earlier. Then Senna pulled out an incident report from the file, from three years before that. When Merchant saw her scrutinizing it, he came around the table and read at the same time. Their eyes widened at the end when they read about the mother's bitter disappointment that the alleged assailant continued to run free, despite all the parents who had tried to prosecute him.

Merchant stood back and took a deep breath before questioning what he sensed Senna was contemplating.

"We're gonna shake down a distraught mother on the basis of our suspicion? Even if it has only an outside chance of making sense to us, we're going to go and ask her if she had her child's assailant killed? I'd like to rewind an hour to a simpler time when I was just worried about you terminating wigrants," said Merchant.

"If you haven't noticed, Merch, I'm good with people," said Senna.

"Whatever. Before you talk to her, give me a chance to pull on my bulletproof vest," pleaded Merchant.

The address on the incident report was about thirty minutes away, and as they pulled up to the home, they saw a young woman walking out with her son. She froze instinctively when she saw the police car and scooted her son inside. They casually got out of the car as she waited in front of her home. Merchant stayed back as Senna went to speak with her.

"Good evening, ma'am. My name is Mira Senna, and I'm from River Enforcement. I'm working alongside Toronto Police on a murder investigation. I understand you filed a report relating to an assault some time ago," she said.

"That's right. Is there something you'd like to discuss with me about the case? I hadn't heard anything at all until the investigative report a year ago, but there's been nothing since then," replied the mother.

"I do, ma'am. And I'm terribly sorry for what you've gone through." The mother looked a little less defensive now, but Senna could quickly lose control of the situation. It was time to reassert her position.

"I just wanted to make you aware, ma'am, that there was an incident involving the alleged perpetrator," said Senna.

And the mother went as pale as a ghost.

Chapter 17

"You in here, Arius?" asked Tao, as he entered the garage from inside the house. The door was in the corner of the double-car garage and, since everyone always parked on the driveway, Arius had put a long wooden bookcase beside the door, creating a short corridor as you entered his workspace.

As he closed the door behind him, Tao heard hustled shuffling on the opposite side of the bookcase.

"Arius? The kids said you were here . . ." As he approached the corner of the bookcase, he noticed one of the garage doors was slightly open, and he detected a faint odor.

"Hey, I was just telling your kids about your favorite Bruce Lee quote. 'Be like water, my frie—'" He stopped abruptly as he turned the corner.

The stench of gasoline hit him in the face. Strewn on the tables in the garage were empty beer bottles, pieces of cloth stripped from old shirts, funnels, and various bottles. A large bucket full of liquid sat on the ground between two heavy wooden stools.

Arius stared back at Tao wide-eyed. He was standing in front of a gathered-up pile of rolled-up sheets of paper. Tao walked slowly over to the table and looked directly at Arius.

"What are you going to do with Molotov cocktail bombs?" he asked.

The sweat on Arius's forehead glistened under the fluorescent garage lights as Tao pushed past him towards the rolled-up sheets. Arius relented and went to sit on the stool farthest from Tao as the sheets were unfurled.

Tao looked in utter astonishment at blown-up aerial images of the settlement. He flipped from one to another, noticing notes on the large sheets in Arius's chaotic cursive. Tao gathered and stacked them again, leaving the sheet with the most notes on top.

"These are blown-up photos taken by your drone. Say the words. What are you going to do?" Tao asked again.

"What needs to be done!" Arius finally declared, unconvincingly.

Tao took a sharp breath and pulled the other stool up to sit and listen.

"Cole needs to get some control over the settlement, right? Otherwise, how can she ward off the disaster that's coming when the water runs out?" Arius took a deep breath before continuing. "Setting a fire on the settlement will give Cole the opportunity to save the day and demonstrate her authority over Senna."

Tao shot back a puzzled expression. "River Enforcement will put out the fire. So what then? Senna has a guy on site looking after it all the time. Well, almost all the time. I just ferried them away from a shooter. That's what I came here to tell you about," said Tao.

"They *can't* put out the fire," said Arius. "There's no water."

Arius told Tao that when the Olympic village was built, watermains were installed to provide water to 20,000 people. The design of the water system was always based on providing both a suitable pressure for regular water use, such as showers and toilets, and additional pressure for emergency use, like fighting a fire.

If 20,000 people lived in the Olympic village, everything was fine. But there were 250,000 people squeezed into the settlement. The little water that was provided to the buildings was stretched well beyond capacity, and furthermore, the new makeshift warehouse buildings and the tents that had been erected were far beyond the coverage area and the ability of the water system to manage.

Tao closed his eyes as he listened. When Arius had finished explaining, he opened his eyes and reached over to pull the top sheet off the pile. He threw it on the table so they could both see it. He pointed to the markings on the sheet along a corner of the settlement in a mass of tents.

"If a fire started here, River Enforcement could not put it out. They'd call the fire department for help, and *they* wouldn't be able to put it out," said Tao.

"That's correct," Arius answered plainly.

Tao held his finger on the sheet and waited to hear Arius say something, anything, that would vindicate him. The smell of gasoline lingered between them.

"How does the fire stop, Arius?!" Tao finally said, his voice escalating.

"Cole looks after that," Arius immediately snapped back.

"How?!" asked Tao, louder than before.

"I don't know," said Arius.

"What? Those tents will go up in flames like a tinderbox. That much fire and smoke is going to injure people, probably kill some. And you don't know how it's going to stop!?" yelled Tao.

"Cole will look after it. And when she does her part, she'll leverage the win to get control over the settlement," said Arius.

Then he put a finger to his lips and pointed to the house, to encourage Tao to lower his voice.

Tao's eyes nearly popped out of his head. "Listen to yourself. You're out of your mind!"

"Let's the two of us not play the judgment game, all right?!" replied Arius with a tone of finality.

Tao broke eye contact and turned his head to the wall.

"I can't sit here while you do this, Arius," he said. He threw the stool down as he got up to walk away. "Two days ago, I was with you in the ocean watching the work you were doing, the personal risk you were taking to do good for the world. I wanted to see how you'd been helping Cole right the 'natural imbalance,' as you call it. But that was just a snapshot. This is the real picture right here. Take a good look and see what it looks like." With that, Tao stormed out, slamming the door behind him.

Arius slumped on the stool and dropped his head in his hands.

Chapter 18

Three hours after speeding over the lake in the Zodiac, Cole was relaxing with Gus in a safe house in Greektown that Steele had taken them both to. The aroma of grilled souvlaki permeated the second-floor duplex unit from the restaurant below. They sat quietly in out-of-date furniture as Cole's mind lingered on the face in the bushes at the broker's estate. Had she really recognized someone, or had it all been in her imagination?

"I need to see the broker again," Cole said to Steele, snapping herself out of the trance.

"Can we get what he wants?" Gus asked.

"Don't you worry about it. This," Cole pointed to herself and then to Gus, "was a bad idea. I'll handle it myself from here."

"Surely you don't think I had anything to do with that shooter showing up," said Gus. "And remember, even if you get the water, you'll still need my help to handle everything on site."

Cole sat quietly, looking past Gus and the dusty curtains out the window to the rooftop patio across the street. The crowd of people there gave her an idea of where to meet the broker once she had the money together. She told Gus she'd find a way to handle it, then nodded to Steele, and they stood up, a sign to Gus that it was time to go.

"Look, aside from the water, I'll be your shield from Senna's fierce loyalty to this city. I just want a bit more time to talk," pleaded Gus.

"In a minute or less . . . what do you want from me?" asked Cole.

Gus sighed, then gathered himself as he leaned forward on his seat and looked up to Cole.

"To show you I'm not the man you think I am. Not anymore. What happened can't be undone, but I can redeem myself. I've been trying for years, ever since I left. I want to do right by you," said Gus. He waited for any kind of response from Cole, but none was forthcoming.

"Time for us to go our separate ways, Mr. Coltrane," said Steele.

"My way is wherever she is," said Gus, making a final attempt.

"Not anymore, sir," said Steele. He escorted Gus out of the safe house and watched him start eastward along the Danforth on foot.

Gus went from worried to very worried when he turned his phone back on. It had been turned off since early morning, and now the chimes pinged relentlessly with messages and texts. He jumped in a cab and began to read the unbelievable accounts of what had happened during his short absence.

Cole's worries were also escalating. She'd turned on her phone to find one critical text message.

"*RE probing Robin Hood,*" said the text from her assistant at Axiom Water. She reached her assistant in Paris, where it was nearing midnight.

"*Oui?*" came the surprisingly sprite response.

"Must be a good night," she said.

"*Ah, oui,*" the assistant said, with just a hint of a yawn. "*Et tu?*"

"Well, I sent 250,000 people to imminent doom. Recruited my estranged father. I'm negotiating with a style-challenged water broker. Been shot at by a mysterious assailant. Escaped in a Zodiac. Landed at a safe house in Greektown, but no Greek food . . ." Cole started.

She looked at Steele. He slow-blinked back disapprovingly.

". . . kicked my father to the curb. Called you," Cole finished.

"What!? No Greek food in Greektown?" her assistant asked.

"Right?" said Cole.

Again, the look at Steele. Again, the disapproving slow blink.

Cole instructed her assistant on how to access and send the money she needed, saying she'd deal with the board if any questions arose. Then she asked about the text message. Her assistant explained that River Enforcement had tasked someone with pulling together everything they could find on Arius. Her office had received a package containing a file of allegations arising from his activities on behalf of Axiom Water, right up to the Paris bulk water heist.

"Who's on the file from River Enforcement?" asked Cole. Her assistant said he'd go back to look at the package and text her the name.

After she hung up, Steele removed the SIM card from Cole's cell and his own, then destroyed them both. He did a full sweep on himself and Cole for bugs of any type. He grabbed a burner cell and his go-bag with fresh supplies and cash from the safe house. And they left.

Out on the Danforth, the lively street once brimming with Greek ambiance now offered a more diverse blend of cultural fare.

The evening would set in soon and, with it, the dinner crowd would appear.

Cole asked Steele to text her assistant with the burner cell number and awaited a response from Paris.

"You're doing pretty well, for someone who was shot at this morning," Steele told her, with a hint of admiration.

"To tell you the truth, it didn't feel like that. It was tense, sure, but the shot came in so high," said Cole.

"Not that I hope to run into that shooter again, but let's not bank on the likelihood that he's near-sighted," said Steele.

"You were in the SAS, Steele. I'm guessing shooting people and getting shot at is nothing new for you?"

"Can't talk about it. Classified," he told her.

"Yeah, but, hypothetically, if you ever killed anyone . . . do you think it would bother you?" Cole asked.

"Hypothetically. It wouldn't be my place to judge," replied Steele without missing a beat.

"I asked if it would bother *you*," said Cole.

"Yes. I mean, if I was ever called to do that, I'd just assume they must have deserved it. Hypothetically, of course. If I helped stop a person from doing evil in the world, I'd sleep just fine at night," said Steele.

"And how do you define 'evil'?"

"That's above my pay grade, Cole. But for what it's worth, I'd much rather pull the trigger than be the person calling the hit," said Steele.

As they walked by a mirrored storefront, Cole caught her own eyes in her reflection. "I wonder if both parties aren't just as guilty, though. You know?"

They walked a full block in silence.

Families, couples, and friends squeezed through the crowds on the sidewalk in both directions. Steele expertly watched the faces, studying risk, identifying patterns, and predicting potential threats. He watched a woman approaching them reach into her purse as she neared, but he didn't bat an eye. In his peripheral vision, he caught sight of two athletically built men running up behind them. No threat. They ran right past.

He saw. Everything.

At one point, the crowd squeezed them closer, and Steele's arm brushed up against Cole's for an instant. That's when a surge of heat ran through his body.

And then there was only Cole.

The faces and movements he had studied only a moment earlier all faded to background. No families. No couples. No friends.

He saw. Nothing. But her.

Steele steadied himself.

"Is there something else you'd like me to look into for you?" he asked her, trying desperately to bring his mind back on task.

Cole pondered a long moment.

"Just reach Arius, please. Get the broker's number from him, and once you have it, get the broker on board for a meet," said Cole.

As they turned down a side street to catch a cab, Steele got a ping on the burner phone and turned it so Cole could see. It was the response from Axiom Water's Paris headquarters to her question about who at River Enforcement had been tasked with investigating Arius.

"*Gus Coltrane*" read the message.

20 YEARS EARLIER

Cape Town, South Africa

1

Cole moved her knight to prepare an attack on her father's queen, her gaze hungrily fixed on the board, anticipating victory.

Gus just sipped his hot chocolate. "You become so invested in your strategy, you're blind to my attack," he said. Then he took her pawn with his bishop and declared checkmate.

As he got up from the table, he said, "Start by knowing yourself. Someday, you'll win . . . to truly engage in battle you must know *yourself.*"

Weekend chess games were an important part of their family routine. On Saturday mornings, Gus would move the kitchen table from the center of the room to a spot closer to the window and slightly to the right. It was an awkward place, and it made his chair so hard to get into that he had to sit sideways the whole game to be comfortable.

Cole's mother found the furniture rearranging pointless and annoying. Then, one sunny Saturday, she walked through the kitchen to see Gus sitting sideways, holding his hot chocolate, and gazing raptly at Cole as she leaned over the table studying her next move. The beams of light illuminated her young face, holding it, as if time were standing still. She never complained about the awkward table location again.

Cole respected the fact that Gus never let her win. He'd give her all the time she needed to make her move.

"Earn the win. Until then, suffering is your best ally. In those moments when you think you'll fall, that is where you grow," her father told her.

◊ ◆ ◊

Cole heard her parents having a heated conversation upstairs.

"You think you're teaching her? All that talent she has . . . for what? To be a member of your crew?" her mother asked.

"She's nineteen. She'll find her way, like I did," said Gus.

"You treat her with privilege that you didn't have growing up. And all she does now is hang out with you and those boys at the social club. You want to teach her? Then teach her what she can do. Being is nothing without doing," her mother said.

◊ ◆ ◊

Cole grabbed the keys to one of the family cars and her three "friends" from Gus's crew jumped in for a drive around town to check in on their businesses.

She listened as the young men spoke proudly of their various tasks. One guy floated the idea of tailoring their private protection services to specific businesses. Another talked about a money-laundering operation he was running. The third one talked about a gambling ring that was bringing in big profits.

Today, the view to Signal Hill was blocked by smoke, the serenity of the brilliant pastel façades of the local homes marred by haze. Cole peered down the cobblestone street that was so familiar to her to the billowing smoke that seemed so alien.

"The fire must be near the water distribution station," said one of the guys.

She pulled over, and they got out to see if they could get a closer look.

The neighborhood they were in now was called Bo-Kaap, meaning "above the cape." Many of the homes in this part of Cape Town had been built in the mid-eighteenth to early-nineteenth centuries. Their brilliant pastel façades were painted by the residents in celebration of their freedom and individualism. It was a post-apartheid tribute, set above the business district she knew so well, and below the majestic Table Mountain formation.

Walking against the crowd, Cole was startled when someone reached out and tugged at her arm.

"Big girl! Surprised to see you in these parts again. Tell me, is your father doing anything about this rationing?" The woman's face was familiar: it was someone who had been a neighbor when Cole was just a child, before they'd moved into a bigger house in a wealthier district.

"Auntie! It's nice to see you! But my dad? Of all people, my dad wouldn't have any sway with the government. Anyway, there's not much anyone can do here after three years of drought," replied Cole, with uncertain certainty.

Auntie held on to Cole's arm and she held her eyes in what felt almost like an angry glare After a moment, though, she politely softened her gaze, and offered a sage, knowing nod.

"One people. One people with a twenty-five-liter water ration," Auntie said slowly before offering another knowing nod. "A three-minute shower will finish that, big girl. Two grandchildren with me here, you know. The smallest almost got trampled at that water distribution point yesterday. The crowd was so upset at the conditions that they set one of the government buildings on fire.

"I got used to fifty liters, big girl. The children got used to catching their shower water into buckets. We used that to flush the toilets. I showered every other day, but kids . . . Well, you know . . . I hope the water comes back in winter," Auntie said.

Cole told Auntie she'd read that the water levels in the reservoirs inside the dams were below 20 percent. The government said they'd need years of regular rain to get everything back to normal.

Cole and her friends walked back to the car and she drove them next to the water distribution point.

On any other day, the vibrancy of the people and bustle of the area would have been heavenly, with neighbors and friends greeting one another, stepping away from their work and errands to join the modest lineup for their daily water ration. Today, though, the line snaked into the distance as far as she could see. Portable toilets produced a terrible stench. People aged five to eighty-five—men, women, and children—all exhaustedly waited for their ration. Her passengers urged her to head back to the social club.

As she readied the car to turn back, Cole saw a slim man with his two young children waiting patiently in line. He carried the younger boy while the older walked beside him, holding his hand. The man was possibly in his early thirties, but conditions seemed to have aged him well beyond his years. They had fruit in the car for snacks, and Cole stopped and got out so she could give it to the children.

When others in the lineup saw her generosity, they started coming to her, asking for help. The man put down his son to hug

Cole gently, but he was almost immediately dragged away from her. Cole's friends had jumped out of the car to "rescue" her, and they were now roughing him up.

"You don't touch her!" one the guys shouted.

The onlookers were aghast and started yelling at them. As soon as Cole came to her senses she tried to call the guys off.

"Stop!" she shouted at them. "I'm fine!"

One of the guys dragged her to the car, and they drove away.

In the rearview, Cole watched the two children tending to their father as he slowly got up, leaning on the older boy for support, as the younger son picked up the food she'd given.

"One people. . . ?" Cole said, as the image imprinted in her mind forever somehow coupled with Auntie's haunting words.

II

One day, in the middle of a chess game, Cole jumped off the chair and out of the light that framed her. Gus sat upright. At first, he thought she was about to leave in a huff, but then he realized something else was happening.

Cole paced alongside the table slowly. Her hands were locked gently behind her back and her gaze was fixed on a point slightly in front of her, but never on the table.

She paced for fifteen minutes straight. Then she stopped, sat back down, and looked at the polished marble chessboard.

She moved her knight. This time, rather than lean forward on her arms, she pushed back and sat cross-legged on her chair, looking at the entire board.

Gus forced his chair back in the tight space and squeezed himself to face forward. He leaned forward on his arms and made his move.

Three moves later, Cole declared checkmate with a final move of her pawn. She sat up and looked at her father's ear-to-ear grin. He leaned forward to carefully pick up the polished black marble pawn that had besieged him in the endgame. He held it up to the light and examined it as she watched him curiously.

"To look at, it is easily underestimated. It earned victory today because of what it did, not because of what it was," said Gus as he handed the pawn to her proudly. "Victory lives inside you."

◊ ♦ ◊

Cole was lying on her stomach on her large canopy bed, reading a tattered copy of *War of the Worlds*, by H.G. Wells. She heard footsteps approaching, and then two light knocks at her bedroom door.

"Come in," said Cole.

It was her mother. Cole sat up, wondering what the reason for this visit might be.

"What did your friend have to say about you borrowing her book?" her mother asked. Cole was quite certain this was just a conversation-starter.

"It's fine. She's read it already. I have to keep yelling at her not to tell me what happens, though," she answered.

"I'm really just wondering if everything's okay, honey. You haven't been going out as much lately, and your dad told me you were very quiet the last time you were out with him. Did something happen?"

Cole receded slightly as she quietly turned a page. It had been two weeks since the visit to Bo-Kaap. She let out a small sigh and sat up to explain what was troubling her.

She told her mother about seeing Auntie, and how she was living with her grandkids. She described the smell in the air around the water distribution station, and the sight of children lining up for hours to secure a bit of life's most basic necessity. Then she told her mother the story of what happened when she tried to share a bit of food with a man and his children.

"I'm sorry that happened to you. Was it very scary?" her mother asked.

With her eyes, Cole told her mother she had it wrong.

"It was infuriating. And those are our old neighbors in Bo-Kaap. A 'nice' area! I've been driving around since then, and it's like that and worse every day in the settlement areas where the poor people live.

"I've been talking to some people in the government since then. The numbers I get are different depending on who I talk to, but it seems like more than 20 percent of Cape Towners live in settlements. Most of them don't have access to clean water, sanitation, or electricity. And we live here like royalty, doing not a damn thing about it," Cole continued.

"Then what?" ventured her mother cautiously, her shoulders tensing.

"What does Dad say about time?" Cole asked.

"'No one owns time. We borrow it and spend it the way we see best,'" her mother quoted.

"And most people just waste it. What does Dad's crew really do? Anything of value to help anyone?" said Cole.

"What they do might seem fleeting. I understand why you might say that. It looks like action without direction. But some action is better than no action at all," her mother replied.

Cole reminded her mother how well she knew the crew. She told them they could do more, if they were led with purpose.

"Don't look at me like that. I don't mean Dad is doing a bad job. I mean I can help. We can do something to help people, rather than just this nonsense that makes their bosses more money," said Cole.

Her mother sat still on the bed, until they both heard shuffling downstairs. It had to be her father, Cole thought. And next, she heard someone stumble, and fall. They ran downstairs to see Gus lying on the ground, blood seeping through his shirt at his shoulder as one of his crew members knelt over him.

Her mother sprang into action, retrieving a first aid kit that Cole had never seen before. She held a compress to Gus's shoulder and told Cole to apply pressure. Then her mother ran to the phone and made a call.

It was five long minutes later when another two of Gus's crew showed up with three large objects that looked like heavy suitcases.

In minutes, their foyer became a makeshift operating room. There were medical supplies, and a small cooler with blood packs, which they fed into Gus through an intravenous drip. Gus seemed to drift in and out of consciousness, but he didn't speak. When he was patched up, one of the crew declared that Gus was stable and would need to rest. Soon they would take him somewhere else for more medical attention.

She watched her father sleep on the floor. Her mother propped his head up on a pillow, then went to get cloths to start cleaning up.

"Can't you bring him to the hospital?" asked Cole.

Their look back answered her question.

|||

For a full week after Gus came home bloody from a gunshot wound, Cole searched for answers about who shot her father.

Her mother wouldn't talk about it. Cole tried asking the crew, but she got nowhere with them, either.

"Everyone is stonewalling me," she complained to her mother. "But how can I be sure he's safe if I don't even know what happened to him?"

She went to sit at her father's bedside and watched him rest. "What don't you want me to know?" Cole asked gently as she stroked his hair. Part of her wanted to shake him awake and yell, but her better judgment prevailed and she left the room quietly.

She found her mother in the kitchen. "Can you at least tell me why he never went to a hospital?" Cole asked her.

Her mother stared long and hard into Cole's eyes.

Cole sat down at the kitchen table, the same one she and Gus played chess at every Saturday morning.

"Tea?" her mother asked.

"Hot water with lemon, please."

When the drinks were ready, her mother sat down with her at the table.

"Your father's business is a private matter," she began. "What I *can* say, though," she continued, "is that a public hospital, or even the most private facility, might not be the safest place for him right now."

"Right now?" asked Cole.

"You asked me a question. I thought I could at least answer that one. After your father was stable, he went to rest at an old friend's house. His friend's son is a doctor, and the house is very comfortable. They were able to look after him properly and safely there."

"I don't know if you really answered my question," said Cole.

"It's the best answer I can give you now," she replied.

A few days later, Cole went out with the same three young men from the day of the Bo-Kaap incident. They were quiet this time as she drove them to their various stops, until they reached a store where they were to pick up protection money. Cole pulled up in front of the establishment as she'd done many times before, but this time the proprietor ran out to the car.

The back passenger-side window rolled down and the proprietor leaned in. "He's over there," he whispered.

A man sat by himself at an outdoor café table, reading a newspaper. Cole guessed he was in his thirties. He wore an impeccable, classic, gray pinstriped suit that fitted him well, even sitting down, paired with a white silk shirt and gray vest. His clean-shaven alabaster face carried a salmon patch birthmark on the right cheek.

"Who is it?" asked Cole, a bit agitated.

There was an immediate tension and silence. The proprietor stepped back, then bent down to look into the front seat.

"Are you kidding? You brought his daughter here with you?!"

Cole threw the car into park and jumped out. The other three doors immediately flew open as the guys tried, unsuccessfully, to gather her back in. She pushed the proprietor into his establishment. One of the guys remained outside to keep an eye on the man seated at the café, who had noticed the kerfuffle and looked over to doff his fedora. The other two went inside with Cole.

All of the patrons inside the small store left when they saw what was happening. Cole had pinned the man up against a wall, insisting he tell her what he was talking about. The two guys who'd come in with Cole were shaking their heads "no" most convincingly.

"It's the man who shot your father," said the proprietor anxiously.

Cole stormed over to the front door to look at the alabaster man again.

"Why did he do it?" she asked.

"He was hired," said the proprietor.

"Hired?! By who?"

"By the family of the man Gus eliminated," said one of the guys, finally.

The proprietor breathed a sigh of relief and went back behind his counter.

Cole turned to the two guys who had come in with her. "What?"

They explained to her something she already knew: that Gus's business interests were sometimes outside the limits of the law, and he had no interest in drugs or prostitution and the problems that came with them. Then they told her what she didn't know: he saw the future.

"Your dad has an idea about the big picture, you know? He saw how the world goes to war over oil, and he heard about places where water is becoming scarce, too. So, years back he made some investments. He talked to experts and bought land where water reservoirs might be needed. He invested in the future. Get it?"

Gus, he explained, was well connected to some big decision-makers, and he'd been able to convince governments to buy his land. He made a huge profit, then turned around and reinvested a lot of his money in the infrastructure that supported Cape Town. In effect, he was a silent partner making a big profit in a public venture.

Only one competitor ever really challenged Gus's dominance. Another private business owner, a guy with ties to the criminal underworld, made a pitch to the government that he could build a better system to serve the public's interest. He was threatening to steal Gus's business and cut off his steady, reliable income stream.

"Then Gus and this creep went out for dinner one day. And Gus was the only one to leave the restaurant," said the other guy.

She squeezed her lips tight, but it was impossible to hide the tears that streamed down her face.

Their crew mate from outside ran in. "He's gone," he announced.

One of the guys used the proprietor's phone to call Gus's house. He spoke with Cole's mother and told her everything that happened before he hustled them out to the car to leave.

At home, Cole's mother ran up the stairs and woke Gus. She told him what happened at the store, and that the shooter could have identified Cole with the guys.

"You need to tell me, right now." She stared into his eyes, looking for traces of honesty or deceit. "Are family members off limits?"

Gus nodded yes. A tear rolled down his cheek.

"If you're telling the truth, then why are you upset?"

"She's in the crew. She's not family, to those who're looking," said Gus.

His wife slapped him across his tear-streaked face.

Gus sat up and told her what she already knew had to happen. She immediately phoned her brother in Paris.

Cole arrived home to find packed suitcases at the door. The moment she understood they were for her, she was shuffled out with nothing but a jacket in her hands.

Gus didn't have a chance to see her leave his life. He would only have his memories of the sun gracing and illuminating her young face at the kitchen table.

4 DAYS TO DAY ZERO

Toronto

Chapter 19

Cole was pushing through the crowd at the St. Lawrence Market. Steele trailed right behind, keeping a close eye on her backpack, which they'd neatly packed with the broker's cash.

Inside the nineteenth-century market building, people clamored as they shopped at the vendors' stalls. Some stopped to linger over twenty varieties of handmade pasta, while across the aisle the fishmongers yelled out the specials of the day. They found the water broker in the southwest corner, dressed in bright red pants and an impossibly outlandish gold-trimmed polo shirt. He sat at a table for two, halfway through downing a calamari Po Boy sandwich. He turned to sit sideways to size up Steele. Then he looked Cole up and down over his sandwich.

"No dad today?" he finally asked. With a head tilt, he invited Cole to sit on the vacant chair beside him. Unable to squeeze herself and the backpack into the chair, she sat sideways as well, and stared at the stack of fried seafood overwhelming his grip.

"Would you rather we pump the oil right into your arteries? I need you alive long enough to deliver my water," said Cole. "I have what you want." She turned slightly to showcase the lean bulk of her backpack.

The broker took two more greasy bites. Unable to bear watching him eat any more, Steele took two large steps over to hug a corner close enough to hear them.

"What I want, Cole," he finished chewing and put the last quarter of his sandwich down on the table, "is irrelevant. Getting shot at helps you put your life into perspective. In this high-stakes game, it's all about what I need," he said, with a greasy smile. "I thought I was clear about that."

"Look. People's lives are at stake, so stop playing games," said Cole. "You know I need what you've got. And you know getting Senna and River Enforcement to look the other way, or approve your contraband water suppliers, is not going to happen. I have your money. That's what you get. What time today does my goodwill package arrive at the settlement?"

The broker raised his eyebrows as he dabbed a corner of his mouth with a napkin.

"I don't think he recognized me. Gus. Of course, it's been a long time, and I was barely a teenager then," said the broker.

Cole squinted her eyes at the comment. But then, abruptly, the broker's face went pale. Steele was leaning against the wall, but he stood at attention as the broker jumped up from the table and walked away briskly without turning to look back.

Cole leapt to her feet, but when she turned to follow him, she saw the ghost, the man she'd seen at the broker's mansion. He was walking towards the south exit door wearing a navy blue suit jacket and light denim jeans. The salmon birthmark on the face of the alabaster man was unmistakable.

"Steele!" She pointed towards him.

The alabaster man glanced back in the direction he'd come from and then sped towards the exit. The broker had completely disappeared into the crowd of shoppers.

Cole and Steele took off in pursuit of the alabaster man. They pushed past the crowd and through the exit to see him running westward. Cole tried to keep her voice down. "He was the shooter at the mansion!" she told Steele.

They chased him through the summer heat along The Esplanade, zipping past street-side patios. The noises at street level were outdone by the roar of the Snowbirds air formation flying low in the sky above. Cole answered Steele as they ran, telling him the end of summer air show was on. They barely kept up with him as he made his way towards Union Station. Cole expected him to duck into the entrance to the subway line, where he could easily be on a train and out of reach before they could catch him. But instead, oddly, he ran through the Front Street entrance and straight into the Great Hall.

In the center of the hall of the train station, under the spectacular two-story vaulted ceiling, was a circular ticket kiosk, with a ticker board displaying arrival and departure times. And on a bench facing the kiosk sat the alabaster man.

Cole and Steele approached him cautiously, Steele in front, and he flung his arm back protectively over Cole when the alabaster man opened his jacket slightly to display his weapon.

"Why did you shoot high at the mansion?" asked Steele. He had a hunch it was no accident that the shot was fired harmlessly.

The alabaster man closed his jacket and smiled. "I saw someone moving on the second floor, coming towards you. That shot kept them upstairs and gave you all time to get out."

Cole came around to stand beside Steele. At a nod from Steele, she sat on the bench beside the alabaster man. Steele stood idly in front of them, as if watching the ticker board.

"You think I shot Gus back in Cape Town?" the man asked.

Cole nodded. Then the alabaster man nodded as well.

"I did it to protect him. I was employed by his enemy. The other family, his business adversary. But I was really working for Gus. He had me keeping an eye out for him, from the shadows. When they were moving on him, I stayed one step ahead to keep him safe. But there came a moment when they had their sights on him, and the only thing I could do to remove him from harm's way in that instant was fire a non-lethal shot before I got the shooter," he explained.

"But he nearly bled out on the floor in our house. How was that saving him?"

"If I hadn't shot him in the shoulder, he'd have been dead in the street in Cape Town," the alabaster man countered. "Would that have been better?"

"What are you doing here now?" Steele asked.

"Still protecting him. His marriage fell apart after she left," he said, pointing to Cole. "But his ex-wife still wants him safe. I needed to disappear from that world—there was a lot of suspicion cast on me—and I've been looking out for him at a distance ever since."

"And why did the man we were meeting with run when he saw you?" Cole asked him.

"His uncle was Gus's business rival, the man that Gus killed. He was just a boy when that happened. But he remembers me. He must have got spooked when he saw me there."

Fifty feet away, a man in a checkered hoodie composed a text as he hovered around a small group of tourists discussing directions. The group moved towards the Front Street exit, and he stopped as if to tie his shoelace.

"Your father's life is in danger now that he's on the broker's radar. He wants to avenge his family. But at least you're here for him." The alabaster man patted her knee.

A text message alert sounded on his phone. He extracted the phone from his jacket pocket and opened it.

"You could've told me this at the market," Cole said. "Why did you run from us?"

"I wasn't running from you," he replied.

Steele glanced at the text: a one-word message, "Farewell," with a photo of the broker below it.

Steele's muscles tensed as he picked up on what the man had just said, just as the roar of the Snowbirds shook the building. Cole reflexively looked up to peer to the skies through the windows, while Steele's eyes instinctively looked down to meet the alabaster man's serene gaze. Then he saw the red laser dot illuminate the man's jacket pocket.

The alabaster man's last sight was the muzzle flash fifty feet away from a silenced weapon.

There was no commotion right away—gunshots, even when they're not silenced, are really not as alarming as TV and movies make them sound. Geppetto casually tucked the weapon inside his checkered hoodie, zipped it up, and walked out of the Great Hall into the open air.

Chapter 20

S enna's favorite dining spot bustled at lunch hour with the crowd from the financial district. The indoor market restaurant offered a buffet to suit all palates. Senna and Arius sat quietly side by side, waiting for their final musketeer to arrive. Arius rubbed the back of his neck and looked down at the table, while Senna watched the world go by from their corner table by the window.

"Third year in a row here celebrating my birthday," Senna said, filling in the dead air between them.

"Uh-huh," said Arius, nervously. His tension broke and rose at the same time when Tao arrived. He carried a restaurant tray with a plate of food on it.

No one got up to greet him. He put the tray down at the place next to Senna, by the window. When he was sitting, he used his sleeve to wipe sweat from his forehead.

"Run here?" Senna asked bluntly.

"Sorry. My previous appointment ran a bit late. I assumed you'd start without me, so I grabbed my stir-fry," he said.

Senna left to go select her food.

The distant sound of clattering plates and cutlery from the buffet serving stations was the only sound at the table by the window for a long time. Tao dug into his stir-fry. Arius hung his head.

"Still set on lighting a fire tonight?" Tao asked quietly, his eyes focused on his food.

Arius took a breath to gather himself, then asked, "If someone were bleeding out and you had no bandage, wouldn't you burn the wound to stop the bleeding?"

"Maybe. If I knew what I was doing. If I didn't know, I'd worry about killing them," replied Tao.

"Huh. Ironic coming from you, of all people," said Arius.

When Senna returned, she put her tray down and made a point of laying both her phones on the table. "In case I get any urgent calls," she said.

"Who'd call your personal cell, Detective Mira? Half the people who know the number are here, and your parents are vacationing in Rio," said Tao, staring into his half-finished meal.

Arius lifted his head to look at each of them with scrunched eyebrows. "Are you two . . . dating now?"

"Nope," they said at the same time.

Arius shrugged and left them to go find something appetizing.

Tao spilled a spoonful of rice and picked up a napkin to wipe the front of his checkered hoodie.

"Who are you working for?" Senna asked, once Arius was far enough away.

"That's a complicated opening question," replied Tao. He eased back in his chair, arms crossed, and slumped slightly, which pushed the hoodie farther over his forehead.

"Fine, then. Who are you?" asked Senna, leaning in to him.

"'Geppetto' works. But I have to say, I did like the 'Hangman' suggestion," said Tao.

Senna flinched at the response, remembering her private conversation with Merchant. She put her hand on the River Enforcement phone. "Our corporate security protocols are top tier."

Tao replied by simply patting her personal cell.

Senna closed her eyes and inhaled deeply. Then she shook herself alert once again.

"Why are you doing this, Tao? This is no game," said Senna.

"It certainly isn't." Tao tilted his head slightly to his left, towards their friend. As Arius approached the table, Senna and Tao began eating again in silence.

"Lover's quarrel all sorted out?" The chime of utensils on plates was the only answer Arius got. He put down his tray and walked away again. "Dessert it is!"

Arius was out of earshot when Senna put her chopsticks down and sat back with her arms crossed.

"So that's it. You want Arius vindicated from what my investigation will inevitably turn up," said Senna.

Tao shrugged with his mouth full, head down, and eyes focused on his food. Senna stared back at the top of his hoodie, then paused.

"Can you get him to stand down?" she asked.

Tao stopped chewing and looked up for a moment to confirm what she already knew.

Senna closed her eyes again and slowed her breathing. Then she chuckled lightly and opened her eyes. Tao finally put his utensils down and folded his arms on the table.

"You think you can hold me for ransom. Me. To allow him to keep going outlaw around the world and undermine me?" said Senna.

Tao fixed his gaze on Senna's eyes, unflinching.

"Maybe you think he's a small problem. What your probing ears don't hear is how he emboldens those he helps. Whether it's for Cole, or otherwise. Every time he steals from the water-rich and gives to the water-poor, he erodes what I'm doing to wake people up and save humanity from themselves," Senna declared.

"One man is undoing the work of thousands of River Enforcement wardens around the world?" challenged Tao.

Senna raised one eyebrow. "Don't forget. People used to use their common sense and build their communities around essential natural resources. Look at Las Vegas—now they expect resources will be built, grown, planted, created, and shaped wherever a road can be put down. They want water merrily carted to them across a freaking desert, if need be. And see what's happened because of their terrible decisions? Anybody who stands a chance of being saved needs to listen up, right now," said Senna.

"To you," stated Tao.

"Of course! Who else?! Cole?! Who continues to make the same mistake and tries to stretch our limited resources across the whole damn planet, like a rubber band pulled to its breaking point? And where she hasn't been chosen to work, she calls in her Robin Hood to keep these places hobbling along," said Senna.

"You've looked the other way, until now . . ." said Tao.

"That was my mistake. And now you think you can risk everything I've built. I'm forced to let a quarter million people succumb to dehydration. Nothing stands in the way of River Enforcement. You think two deaths will stop me? Just wait. I don't have the evidence yet, but I'll get what I need to put you down and clear my own name," said Senna.

Arius approached the table again with another tray.

Before he got within earshot, Tao said, "Good luck, sweetheart. You'll never catch me."

Chapter 21

A rickety fan in the corner of the makeshift warehouse office whirled away as Senna slowly flipped through the pages of the two-inch-thick file Gus had compiled on Arius. Sweat ran down Gus's back as he stood, patiently waiting for her conclusion. He looked longingly through the small office window at the long shadows cast by the late-afternoon sun, and the lake beyond.

"Do we think this is everything?" Senna finally asked.

"No," replied Gus.

"Was afraid you'd say that," said Senna, closing the file and sitting back.

"So, do we get ready to take this guy into custody?"

She was about to reply when a call came over the radio for Gus. It was from a warden at the front gate.

"Boss. That lady who was here with you the other day is back."

Senna narrowed her eyes. Gus gulped quietly as the clarification came a moment later.

"It's Cole," shouted Cole through the radio. "I need to see Gus right now! It's urgent."

Gus grimaced. *Urgent?* "Bring her here."

The guard acknowledged the message, explaining, "I'm on my own. I'd have to leave the front gate unmanned."

"The gate's just been closed for curfew," Gus replied. "It's okay. Just bring her."

In the few minutes it took Cole to arrive, Senna read Gus the riot act.

"I told you, unequivocally, that your daughter is *not* allowed on site. What part of that did you not understand?" Before he could open his mouth to answer, she went on. "We trusted you here. You were a rising star in this organization. But this? This makes us genuinely doubt your commitment. And considering your history, I don't know why you're being so generous to her."

Gus stood silently and took it.

Then Cole walked in.

Cole stood beside Gus as Senna circled them both like a shark around its prey.

"I demand an explanation!" Senna shouted.

"An explanation for right now, or before?" asked Gus, innocently.

Senna let out an exasperated breath. "I'll take whatever you've got! Why are you here, Cole?!" Senna demanded.

"I need to speak with Gus privately," Cole replied. She had spotted the thick file on the desk in front of her.

"No," Senna shot back. "You want to speak with him, you're welcome to do so right now."

Cole chose her next words carefully. She said to Gus, "I met someone recently who assures me your life is at risk. An old friend of yours. Salmon birthmark on his face," she said plainly.

Gus stopped breathing for a moment. Senna looked up to Gus and waited for a response.

"Where is he now?" asked Gus.

"He died a few hours ago. Gunshot wound," replied Cole, pointing to her heart.

Then a call came over the radio—a panicked voice from the front gate.

"Fire! Fire!"

◊ ♦ ◊

The next ten minutes felt like hours.

Word came that several tents were on fire, and Senna promptly called the Fire Department. While the gate was unmanned, vandals had thrown in Molotov cocktails, targeting an area where Gus had ordered the wigrants to temporarily move out for maintenance. The fire was spreading from tent to tent quickly. Senna, Gus, and Cole ran out of the office and collected Steele, who had been waiting outside, on the way there.

Cole let the three of them run ahead of her as she made an urgent call.

They ran towards the fire, against the crowd of screaming wigrants running away from it. By the time they arrived, Toronto Fire was on the scene with four trucks, but the blaze had already engulfed a large group of tents. The firefighters finally found a hydrant to connect to in the old industrial area, but the pressure was inadequate for their hoses.

They switched to hand-held fire extinguishers from their trucks and began dousing the flames. When it looked like they were having some success, the captain directed the others to get closer and circle the flame to contain it with their equipment. The firefighters moved in and tried to encircle the blaze, but they soon came back out, saying the tents were spaced so close together that the fire was jumping too fast for them to keep up with.

The captain polled his team for ideas as the fire raged on. As the summer sun descended towards the horizon, the sound of propellers grew louder and louder overhead. Everyone looked up as the captain called his team back.

"Clear out! Clear out!" he yelled. Toronto Fire backed away from the blaze as water poured down from the clear evening sky.

The first load from the water bomber knocked down most of the blaze, to cheers and applause from Toronto Fire. A few minutes later the plane circled back and doused whatever remained with its second mighty load. The captain ordered his firefighters in to check any flare-ups as he waved the bomber off.

Gus asked Senna, "Did you order any maintenance on the settlement? Did you give an order for these tents to be evacuated?" She shook her head, no, and he pursed his lips in thought.

The two of them approached the captain to thank him, but he declined their commendations. He wasn't the one who'd called in the water bomber, he said.

Now Senna turned angrily to Cole. "Am I expected to believe that it's just a coincidence that you picked this time to show up?"

As Senna and Cole had it out, Gus walked outside the fence, looking for the most likely place from which the vandals could have thrown the Molotov cocktails. He surveyed the area and leaned down to pick up something familiar, then held it up to the light, examining it. Frowning, he dusted it off, exhaled slowly, put it in his pocket, and walked back inside the settlement.

In the distance, Arius watched the scene play out through binoculars. He finally breathed a sigh of relief when the action had died down and the water bomber passed overhead.

Arius searched for the artifact that reminded him of victory. He searched one pocket for the black marble pawn that Cole had given him, the token of her trust. Nothing. He searched the other pocket. It was gone.

Part Two

The Turn

3 DAYS TO DAY ZERO

Toronto

Chapter 22

"If I see any more dead bodies in our headlines, rest assured I will see to it that neither of you ever again has enough clout to be a primary school hall monitor," said the mayor.

The mayor's boardroom looked out over the city's main civic square, site of every kind of gathering, from protests to celebrations. Three concrete arches spanned a glistening reflecting pool that the mayor had refused to drain, despite Senna's insistence that the city set an example. The city hall structure itself was composed of two large, curved, space-age towers, separated by an overturned saucer that housed the City Council chambers. The iconic buildings had helped unlock the city's future in the middle of the twentieth century, but today they were just one big principal's office for Cole and Senna.

The mayor shook his head as he reviewed an incident report in the large boardroom. Cole sat quietly opposite Senna on the other side of the cherrywood boardroom table, while Steele leaned against the wall behind Cole.

"It's a miracle none of the wigrants were injured. And I'm none too pleased to see you here again so soon, Senna," said the mayor.

Senna gulped hard as she told the mayor she was making progress with the police. She also claimed to have a suspect in the settlement fire.

"Two deaths inside a week, and now you're telling me an arsonist wrecks . . ." the mayor glanced at the report, "20 percent of the tents. That settlement is like a ticking time bomb under your watch, Senna."

Cole self-consciously coughed at the sentiment.

"And you, Cole. I've been getting calls from your board about your involvement here. I'm sure you know they're asking a lot of questions about what you're up to."

Cole was ready for this. "What I've been 'up to,' as you put it, since I arrived here is engaging in valuable, firsthand, on-the-ground research. And now that I'm up to speed on how everything here operates, I think I can make a strong case that Axiom Water should be a partner in managing the settlement." It was more or less a lie, but it was one that Cole could easily justify. "There will be no more troublesome headlines once I'm involved, Mr. Mayor."

"Promises, promises," said the mayor, rolling his eyes.

Senna immediately went on the defensive.

"Mr. Mayor, I can't prove that Cole is connected to all the untoward incidents that have been causing you concern, but consider the facts of the most recent events. She arrives on site—which I had expressly forbidden, by the way—at the moment when my wardens are changing shifts. The front gate is left unattended so she can be escorted in, and that's when the vandals start the fire. And then, just when it looks like a complete disaster, Cole happens to have a water bomber at the ready. Do you know how long it would take a water bomber to get here? She obviously knew it was going to happen!"

"That is a hefty allegation you're leveling, Senna," the mayor said. He paused for a moment in thought as he watched her.

"Air show," replied Cole simply. All eyes turned to her.

"Anyone who had done any infrastructure research would have realized that the water supply at the settlement would be problematic should a fire break out. Looking into the resiliency and weaknesses of the water distribution system at the settlement was just a small part of my research."

The mayor leaned forward and nodded slightly.

"As for the water bomber, Senna is right. A water bomber could have taken an hour to get here on a normal day. But you've all been hearing the planes fly overhead these last couple days for the air show. Turns out an old friend was flying a water bomber in this year's show, so when I saw what was happening on the settlement yesterday, I was lucky to reach him for an urgent drop," she explained.

"Lucky," said the mayor, as he stroked his chin.

"Very lucky," said Senna, scrunching her nose.

The mayor turned away from them to look out the window towards the city. Senna peered fiercely at Cole. A minute passed, and one of the mayor's aides got up to look out the window while another picked up her phone.

After ten long, uncomfortable minutes of silence, the mayor finally swiveled his chair back around.

"Then it's settled," he said. Cole and Senna turned to face him. "Axiom Water will provide support on the settlement."

"Mr. Mayor!" Senna cried.

"This is *my* city, Senna. You work for *me*. And you'll agree that Cole here has clearly demonstrated she is capable and ready to respond to complications. River Enforcement still has operational control, for now, but you'll fully cooperate on site." The mayor got up to leave.

Senna sat tightly, her arms wrapped around her chest and her legs crossed, while Cole beamed silently, sitting across from her.

"No more messes. Both of you. Senna, if I don't hear some real news on your investigation of the termination at HTO Park by the end of the day you'll be removed from the case." And with that, the mayor left the room, followed by his two aides.

The room was dead still after the door closed. It was as though even the dust particles dared not move. Senna took a deep breath and uncrossed her legs and arms.

"Why didn't you tell him about the water?" Senna asked, looking out the window from where she sat. "If he knew I'd allowed us to fall to three days' supply . . . forget the settlement, he'd have kicked me right out of the city. You'd have had complete control."

Cole thought carefully.

"I'd have gladly done it. If I had all the answers. But I don't. I'll come back to you later today with something to think about. Keep an open mind," she said.

"Let's hope this goes better than Cape Town," Senna said with a sigh.

"Well, we're both older. And I'm wiser," said Cole.

TEN YEARS EARLIER

Cape Town, South Africa

After ten years of exile in Paris, where she'd disassociated herself from her father's name, she came back as an employee of Axiom Water. River Enforcement was in charge of water in Cape Town then, and the legacy of their mismanagement was obvious. Everything that had previously been lush had withered. Without sufficient irrigation, all the greenery in Bo-Kaap was brown and dying. A local market had been turned into an outdoor medical facility. The stench of inadequate sanitation was ripe in the air as she cruised the cobblestoned street with the windows down.

She stopped briefly for a private visit on her way to the Axiom Water office.

There were bars on the door this time. One of the grandkids opened the door slightly when she knocked. She explained who she was. The teenager told her to wait, and locked the door again. A few minutes later, the chain was removed and the door opened again.

"Grandma says come upstairs."

She tried not to hold her nose as she entered, but the smell was gut-wrenching. Auntie was lying in her bed. Cole could see at once that she was weak and likely dehydrated. The old woman slowly turned her head to give Cole a smile.

"Big girl. All this time you're scarce. You came back to rescue us," Auntie said.

There was no blame anymore, only resignation in the small room. Cole knelt beside the bed and held Auntie's hand.

"Why the bars on the front door, Auntie?"

Auntie closed her eyes to gather her strength to speak. "Not everyone's set up nice like me. Those silly street boys. All they had was washing cars to make some money. River Enforcement would put them in jail for a bit when they caught them. But when they got out there was no more car washing, no money. No money for them means problems for us. The bars are to keep the grandkids safe."

Chapter 23

Toronto, 3 Days to Day Zero

Cole felt as if a month had gone by since she'd met the broker at the St. Lawrence Market, but barely twenty-four hours had passed. She'd returned to the exact spot they'd met a day earlier and awaited his negotiated return. Steele took advantage of arriving early to secure a calamari Po Boy sandwich.

"Aren't you supposed to have eyes on me? Or were you just looking at his sandwich the whole time?" asked Cole.

Steele's eyebrows rose for an instant. "Seriously. Barely know what the guy looks like. You can look after yourself, right?" he asked, chomping down on the fried goodness.

Cole smiled her answer back.

"You're certain you want to deal with the likes of him? I'm surprised he agreed to meet you again," Steele said, through a mouthful of food.

"We have mutual interests, he and I. There's nowhere else he'd rather be," said Cole. Her smile grew bigger still. "Besides, Steele, I'm sure you'd resist the 'I told you so' urge if the need ever arose."

"Living with the Brits, I grew fond of their expression 'right then.' You lead, and I follow," said Steele.

After a while, Steele caught her eye and tilted his head. "He's comin' at you, and wow," he said, pointing to the broker, who'd just turned a corner about fifty feet away. He would have been hard to miss—he was wearing a blue velvet short-sleeved shirt, tight brown short-cropped corduroy pants, and brown brogues with no socks. "Careful. He might be off—something actually matches!"

The broker sidled up and pulled a chair beside Cole's as Steele, as usual, stepped back. Cole told him bluntly that Gus was off-limits.

"It's nothing personal. Well, sorry, it's actually *very* personal. I mean it's nothing personal between me and you," said the broker.

"I have a hard time not taking it personally now that you and I are in business. Truth is, even though you hate Gus, you might actually like him more than me. But I don't want him dead," said Cole.

The broker turned his head slightly and squinted, struggling to comprehend the father-daughter dysfunction. He offered his own woes to Cole in return.

"My uncle, he put everything he had, and a lot he didn't, into his business venture, the one that he was going to take your dad down with. He was the only one who understood how it was all set up, and when he died suddenly, there was no one to pick up the pieces."

It was as if Gus had singlehandedly pulled the rug out from under this family's life, Cole thought.

"On top of that, River Enforcement moves in then and imposes the most severe restrictions Cape Town ever saw. What little water was left was rationed for hospitals, schools, and food production," he explained.

Cole had seen for herself what that did to people.

"Then, ten years later, Axiom Water comes in to construct the very same system my uncle proposed, processing salt water from the ocean into drinking water."

"Your uncle was proposing the desalination plant I built?" Cole asked.

The broker nodded. "Felt like it almost killed me, too."

Cole then explained that River Enforcement had fought her every day in the almost two years it took to get approval for the plant. Senna was adamant that conservation was the only solution that made sense, and conservation measures were the only solution that River Enforcement allowed. They insisted on no importation of bottled or bulk water, and no desalination plant. It was just digging one hole to fill another, Senna always said, and she would not listen to reason. But Cape Town was going to die. So the Cape Town government made an arrangement whereby Axiom Water helped pay for the plant with outside money, to be paid back over time.

"When the desalination plant was fully functional, we kicked River Enforcement out," Cole explained. "No one had any more patience for their severe water restrictions when the taps could readily flow. That was when River Enforcement demanded that cities choose: it had to be either them or us."

"I understand that you want to avenge your family," she went on, "but let's get down to what you need here and now. You need to sell your contraband water. I'll convince Senna to allow it. You'll be free to make your deals without fear of punishment," stated Cole.

"And I'd be the only one brokering water," he confirmed. "But wait, you've been saying all along that Senna can't be convinced," said the broker, with his fingers tented. "So . . . what's changed all of a sudden?"

"I'm going to make the impossible possible," Cole told him. "The past is the past. We can't bring your uncle back. Cancel the contract on Gus, and I can make this come true for you. After all, a man of your impeccable style needs his livelihood protected. Think of it. No more sneaking around."

The broker stroked his chin. "There's no contract on Gus," he said.

Cole took that to mean that he had intended to resolve this very personal matter by his own hand. Better still, she thought. No third party to worry about, especially one capable of a precision daylight hit like the one she'd recently witnessed.

"I'll have your down payment delivered to the settlement by this evening. Once I see I'm working with impunity, you have my word, I'll let the past go," said the broker. He stood up, but he must have noted the skepticism in Cole's eyes. "Look past this beautiful exterior, Cole. What's beneath it is a businessman. I'm nothing without my good word, so trust me when I tell you this—when you make good on your part of the bargain, you'll be free to dislike your father again."

With that, the broker walked over to the takeout line and ordered a crab sandwich to go.

After the broker had gone, Cole heard a slow clap.

"'I'm going to make the impossible possible'?" Steele said with a smirk.

"No judgment from you, Steele," scolded Cole.

"Right then," said Steele, with his hands up.

20 YEARS EARLIER

Paris, France

For two weeks after Cole arrived in Paris, she said not a word. Nothing her uncle said or did elicited little more than a fleeting glance. At whatever hour she dragged herself out of bed, she would leave his artist studio in the prestigious fourth arrondissement of Paris and walk.

Her wayward travel took her up and down the walkways along the banks of the Seine River, and often to the Jardin des Tuileries. The pristinely groomed hedges loomed over her as she wandered through the centuries-old manicured maze.

Being inside the garden dulled the city noises, but Cole could not escape the noises in her head.

At a small pond with a fountain, a father and his teenage daughter had pulled up four lawn chairs and were using two to sit in and the other two as footstools, reclining to savor the urban oasis. The daughter spoke without pause as her father listened peacefully, smiling all the while. Every so often when the narrative slowed, the father would ask a one or two word question and the narrative re-ignited. Cole glanced momentarily at the scene, turned and walked back from the direction she came.

Despite being immersed in the ambiance of the Parisian surroundings, Cole looked, but never saw. She listened, but heard not a thing. Nothing registered. She barely ate. Upon her return ten hours later, she would flop down on the bed in a fetal position, and, sometime in the wee hours, fall asleep.

And the next day, the routine repeated itself. Day after day: rise in a stupor, walk endlessly, see nothing, collapse.

Like a shark, Cole never stopped.

Unlike a goldfish, Cole did not forget. She refused to.

After two weeks, her uncle received a phone call while Cole was out walking. Gus told him he was coming for Cole.

They arranged to meet at the iconic tea room Angelina, on Rue de Rivoli. When Gus arrived, Cole was there with her uncle. She was seated with her back to him, but he gasped quietly to himself at the reduced, sunken silhouette of his daughter. He turned away momentarily, catching his breath, as he was still recovering from his injury, and he mustered up the nerve to approach them, having rehearsed his greeting to his daughter repeatedly in his head.

Gus was standing near a glass case where exquisite patisseries were on display for storefront customers, and just then, a clean-shaven, impeccably dressed gentleman with alabaster skin came up beside him, got the attention of a shop clerk, and casually pointed to a delicate chocolate croissant.

The clerk packaged the croissant in a small box, handed it to the gentleman, and moved on to another customer.

Gus kept his eyes fixed on the display case, but his nerves were on fire. "Are you here for me?" he asked the man with alabaster skin.

"I am," the man replied plainly.

Gus turned to face him now, rising to his full height to peer down into the man's eyes.

"Do what you like," Gus told the man, "but I'm here to bring my daughter home." He explained explicitly that his wife had told him to get out, bring their daughter back, or never come back home.

The two locked eyes silently for a moment.

The alabaster man considered his deeds to that point in his life, what he'd done for his employers and how it had stained his soul. The lives he had taken. But the one thing he knew he would truly regret in his life would be this moment.

Of all the things alabaster had done, he'd never had to break a man's heart.

"If you bring her back, she'll never be safe," the alabaster man said.

Cole's uncle peered intently at the exhausted man he had once respected. He watched that man age twenty years as he spoke to the pale stranger. He saw him getting increasingly agitated, while the other man was coolly replying with short responses and slow shakes of his head. And then he saw Gus, slumped and defeated, walking away from the man towards the door.

Cole lifted her head, and she saw the distress in her uncle's eyes. She turned in her chair to see what he had just seen, and she saw her father's back as he walked away. And in that instant, she saw, too, the ghost that haunted her, just a glimpse of alabaster skin and a salmon patch birthmark. It was in that instant that all hope fled from her.

That moment would catapult her from the depths of despair into a cauldron of anger.

Chapter 24

Toronto, 3 Days to Day Zero

Among the charred remnants of tents and scattered belongings on the settlement, a makeshift hospital was emerging. Senna had her wardens clear an area of the detritus to allow for a large tent to be erected. The fence near the front entrance of the settlement had been partially taken down to allow ambulances and medical supply vehicles to back in.

Underneath that large tent were several rows of beds, many of which were already occupied. Cole and Steele were helping to set up beds and equipment when they saw Gus bringing a woman in a wheelchair. Colors followed behind Gus and his wife, holding their young child in his arms. As Gus settled the woman in, Colors watched helplessly at her bedside, cuddling their child over his shoulder. His gaze was focused on his wife's face as he held her hand tenderly amidst the other bedridden wigrants. The woman's face reminded Cole of Cape Town and Auntie—she'd had the same lethargic, colorless expression when she was suffering from dehydration.

"What happened to the wigrants who were living here?" Cole asked Senna.

Senna told her the wigrants whose tents were destroyed had been piled into the hostel. It was already difficult to manage the temperature there in the summer heat, and the overcrowding had exacerbated the harsh conditions inside.

"Heat exhaustion, heat stroke, and dehydration are spiking. Thanks for helping clear some space for a medical setup," Senna said to Cole sarcastically.

Cole pulled Senna aside. "You said I have no place on this settlement. And now I'm empowered to support you. You told me to stay out of your way. Well, now, wherever your way goes, you can be sure I'll be right beside you. Accept it, Senna. We're in this together." She stood with her hands on her hips.

"Do you expect me to consult you on all my decisions, my Queen?" Senna asked.

Cole took in the scene around her. It wasn't the sickness that tore at her. It was the sheer sense of abandonment and loss that she'd seen at the Bo-Kaap water distribution point. Where was anyone's sense of dignity to treat other human beings this way? Corralled into a tent, looking out at a civil society from behind a fence while you live on rationed food and poisoned water. The cauldron of anger that had fired her twenty years ago was getting ready to boil over again. She struggled hard not to slip over the threshold, into that dark place. If there was any chance of saving them, she knew she had to keep her cool. Order was necessary.

"The wigrants deserve better than us fighting over whether to use carrots or sticks to change the world. Neither of our methods on their own were enough to help them. But now that they're here, thousands of miles from their homes, let's play the hand we've been dealt and find a solution that works for them?" Cole suggested.

Senna puffed a breath of exasperation, shook her head, and smirked.

"The more I get to you know you, the less I like you. Let me tell you something, Sister Cole. With me, you may not like what you see, but what you see is what you get. You, on the other hand . . . you want to look pure and clean while someone else does your dirty work. You have these people set on fire, then you sidle up to me to tell me how we should save them?" Senna's eyes narrowed.

Steele was wiping his hands on his khaki pants as he approached Cole and Senna to see what was going on. Cole seized the moment to tell Senna about the bottled water shipment that would arrive at the settlement that evening. She got as much information out as possible within the shortest time. Telling her she'd got shot at while negotiating the bailout delivery. Telling her how it would provide much needed relief. Telling her it would spare her further rebuke from the mayor. Then she hunkered down for the response.

Senna took a deep breath, and walked away.

Gus was walking towards where they stood, clapping the dust from his hands and watched Senna past him as he joined Cole and Steele.

"Aren't you supposed to be after someone?" Cole asked her father.

"I am, actually. You might like to see an interesting piece of evidence that recently came into my hands." Gus dug into his pocket and produced the black marble pawn.

Cole held herself together when she saw it in his outstretched hand.

"I remember like it was yesterday. I remember how this little soldier besieged me all game," Gus said, with an air of nostalgia.

She peeled her eyes away from the pawn and looked up at him with an intense focus. "And do you remember what you told me then? Victory lives inside me. Well. Now I win every day. And I'll keep coming at you, and her," Cole said fiercely.

Gus closed his palm and pocketed the pawn. He asked her where he could find Arius.

"Are you ready for the end of Axiom Water? Once Senna has him in custody to validate the information I've compiled, there is simply no way your firm can survive. Certainly not with you involved, anyway. All that good work, undone," said Gus.

Cole could still see the pawn in her mind's eye. She looked up at Gus, who was waiting for a response.

"Any 'informal' arrangement around the globe that may have hinged on you or Arius would stop," he went on. "Think about it. Think about Paris. Where is Arius?"

"How do you know that was in his possession anyway?" Cole dared to ask.

"You were right beside me when the fire happened. I'm sure you didn't drop it when we last met in front of the gate. And you almost certainly just told me with that question," replied Gus.

"I've no idea where Arius can be found. Do say hello for me if you find him," said Cole.

Chapter 25

At the police station, Merchant sat beside a computer terminal as Senna barged in to claim a seat in his office. She clenched and unclenched her fists before meeting Merchant's expectant gaze.

"Just got reamed by the mayor. Again. I'm telling you, Cole is working me, but whatever we have, we need to report progress to the mayor today," she said to Merchant.

"I miss the days of being suspicious of everybody. Hey, Senna, know who really shot JFK? Me. Ha, you knew something was off about me, right?" said Merchant with a wink.

Senna looked down. She knew that, despite Merchant's initial misgivings, she'd made a good first impression. But she was on thin ice now. His playful, boisterous tone could revert to a bulldog demeanor in a blink. And he was her ticket to clearing River Enforcement in this business of the terminated wigrants, so whatever rapport she'd built had to be risked. She met his expectant gaze once again.

"I haven't been honest with you, Merch," she said.

Merchant leaned forward in his chair with a dead-serious expression. "It was *you* who shot JFK, wasn't it? Damn, you look good for your age."

"I know who—" Senna began.

A police officer intruded just then, demanding the acting captain's attention. At Merchant's request, Senna left to wait outside his office, and closed the door behind her. She watched curiously through the glass wall as Merchant listened intently to the officer. The expression on Merchant's face changed in a blink.

The bulldog.

There was no talking for a minute. Senna saw Merchant fall back into his chair, and his eyes widened. Merchant waved the officer to put the material he'd brought on his desk, and they reviewed it together, as Merchant's shoulders slumped a little more with every minute that passed. He rubbed his head and turned a circle in his chair.

Merchant looked to the officer and nodded. Senna's curiosity was piqued by the icy glare the officer gave her as he shut the door behind him. She turned to see Merchant staring down, his elbows on the desk and his head in his hands. She looked back at the officer walking away down the hall. And waited.

She could hear police officers discussing both business and personal matters in the background as she waited. She overhead one conversation about a bank robbery, and another about a family trip to Centre Island. She reached for her corporate phone, having abandoned her personal cell, and was about to check her messages when Merchant yelled.

"Senna!"

Every conversation in the station stopped. Every officer looked towards her.

She closed the door behind her on her way in and sat in front of Merchant's desk, feeling the stare of every officer on the back of her neck.

"You probably heard of a brazen execution at Union Station yesterday. We didn't have much to go on at first, but a report came in from someone on a walking tour about a suspicious man in a checkered hoodie. Fair-skinned, athletic build, about five foot ten. My officer just shared with me that someone else from that same group independently reported seeing a man of the same description shortly afterward," said Merchant as he dropped a blown-up cellphone image on the table.

The photo was taken from the street looking inside a restaurant. It was clearly taken on the move, but it showed the back of someone wearing a checkered hoodie, arms crossed, with a portion of the facial profile visible. What was very clear in the photo was the person sitting across the table.

"Merch, I came in to tell—" Senna started.

"Tell me why I shouldn't arrest you right now!" Merchant shouted. He got up from the desk and slammed it with both hands. Papers went flying, and it was a miracle that all the glass in the station didn't shatter.

Senna looked down. Merchant looked around his office at the papers strewn everywhere and walked around his desk to pick one up. He put it in front of her.

"This was the image on the victim's cellphone when he died," he said.

Senna looked down at the unfamiliar image, and the very familiar word: "Farewell."

"I wanted to believe in coincidences again when I saw that," Merchant said, standing directly behind her. He didn't have to remind her of the message in Smoke's pocket that now potentially linked one person to all three deaths.

"Tell me everything you know."

Senna gave him the highlights of her long history with Tao. She spoke of his ability to speak multiple languages and mentioned his armed forces experience, along with his academic credentials, which included a master's degree in Human Behavior and a Ph.D. focused on data encryption.

Merchant sat on his desk so that his heavy-set frame loomed over her. He swallowed hard before asking the next question.

"Look at me, Senna. Look at me. When did you know?"

Senna explained the phone call after Smoke's death, this time elaborating on the relevance of the caller's use of "Detective Mira." She clarified that the call had come to her private cell number, which was known to only four people.

"The tiny problem with my conclusion is that I have no evidence to substantiate that Tao is actually the assailant," said Senna.

"The exact same problem I have tying you formally to any of this mess. Where is Tao now?" asked Merchant.

Senna very delicately pushed her chair a foot back from him, cleared her throat, and tried to offer a light chuckle.

"Funny story. We've had a bit of a tiff, he and I," she said. "Not exactly on the speed-dial list anymore."

Merchant stared at her. "Is there anything else you're not telling me?"

Senna shook her head slowly.

"Senna?"

"No. No. That's it."

Merchant continued to stare. "I could hold you with what I have, but there's not enough to arrest you. You're a liability as a witness and dead weight as a partner. Get out of my station," he said plainly as he rose from his desk.

Senna shot up immediately and opened the door to the silence on the other side. Everyone in the station was very consciously looking anywhere but at Merchant. She turned and, with half her body behind the solid wall that separated the threshold of the door and the glass wall looking into his office, she lobbed in a whispered question.

"Merch. Any chance I could ask you not to say anything to the mayor?"

She quickly ducked behind the solid wall, covering her head as a size-eleven boot came crashing through the glass wall beside her.

20 YEARS EARLIER

Georgetown, Ontario

I

"That man at the back literally has a pitchfork," Arius whispered.

"*Tranquille, tranquille,*" said the mayor. "Calm down, calm down." Or maybe it was more like, "Shut up and stay quiet."

The high school gymnasium was packed, as if families from the township had decided to make an evening of it. Three people faced the crowd from the stage. Arius was one of them, sitting beside the mayor of his family's township of Georgetown, while Senna was fielding questions at the microphone.

"Did I tell you I'm not Italian?" Arius muttered.

"French," said the mayor.

Arius started to lean over to whisper to her again but the mayor turned to face him. "Son, keep leaning over to me like that. The audience will think you're either farting or you have some dark secret to keep," she cautioned.

"Madam mayor, the well at my farm has gone down so much that I hardly have water for the crops. If it stays like this, I don't know if we can last another season. We'll have to move, but I don't want to go. This is our home!" The man at the microphone looked back to three small children seated a few rows behind him, then to his wife, who gave him a nod to confirm that he was representing the family proudly. The audience rose in support, cheering him on and echoing his concern.

"I can't leave my farm either! I don't know how else to support my family."

"We have nowhere else to go!"

Putting a microphone at the front and asking people to line up had initially helped to preserve order, but now the lineup stretched all the way to the back of the room. Everyone felt a genuine need to tell their story.

Senna raised her right hand, palm facing the crowd. The tension remained but the voices began to quiet. Then she turned her palm downward, and made a small patting motion in midair. Hushing could be heard around the room. At last it was quiet.

"To echo the mayor's earlier comments, I want to make it clear that we're very concerned for your well-being, and we understand why you're worried. Mayor Warby has been working with us for some time to review what's happening with your water, and she asked us to come tonight to share some of our findings," said Senna. She had been making eye contact with the gentleman at the microphone initially, and then proceeded to make eye contact with other residents, including children in the audience. As she non-verbally worked the crowd, she dug down deep to disguise her disdain at her next comment. "We understand there has been some confusion about our neighboring township taking water. They too, like us, are facing a challenging situation."

She took the microphone from the stand, gathered up some of the cord, and stepped down from the stage to address the audience more directly. A projection came on the screen behind her that showed the water cycle. Senna explained that there was essentially the same amount of water on the planet now as in prehistoric times. And, if undisturbed, the water cycle would continue endlessly, from lake, to clouds, to rain, to runoff, and back to lake. She directed the laser pointer at a spot on the graphic where the runoff was coming off the land into a river.

"And I want to point out to you that when water runs off the land, the river takes back to the lake whatever we've put on the land. That means fertilizer, pesticides, and dirt. All of that goes back to the source of our drinking water."

When the hands went up to point out that there was no lake nearby, as she'd anticipated, she gently patted the air again with her hand and advanced to the next image.

"You see on this photo there's a community like yours, and underneath it's like an underground lake. When water doesn't run into a river, what doesn't go back into the air through evaporation goes into the ground, towards the groundwater. That's the same groundwater your wells take water from. It's the water you drink, and the water you use to irrigate your crops. It's fed from snowmelt and rain that seeps into the ground."

She faced the crowd the entire time, walking slowly from one side of the audience to the other. The man at the back had brought his pitchfork and slowly made his way up the side aisle along the wall, with his pitchfork, to get a closer look at the screen and her presentation.

Senna explained water scarcity to the crowd with an example that had them imagine the world was flat.

"If you flattened the Earth and covered it with a stack of all the available water from the oceans, lakes, and groundwater, it would make a tower almost two miles tall. But only a small part of that would be readily available fresh water. How tall do you think the fresh water part would be?"

"One mile!" shouted one resident.

"Quarter of a mile," came another guess.

"Just six and a half feet," she told them. And she paused for a moment to let that sink in. "If you want to look at it another way, if all the world's water were enough to fill a gallon jug, our available fresh water would be just a teaspoon of that. The challenge, my friends, is that we're drawing water faster than it is being put back," said Senna.

Her last words hung in the air.

"How do we fix it?" came the question from somewhere deep in the room.

Senna hesitated. She turned to look back briefly to Arius, and she felt that her eyes very likely betrayed the despair in her soul.

"How do we fix it?" came the haunting question again, like a ghost from another part of the room.

"It can't be fixed," was her answer, in a faint whisper.

Senna waited for the challenge. Waited for someone to point the finger, or to object to the truth. She waited and watched the audience so intently that she didn't notice the pitchfork man getting up and approaching her from the side until the last moment.

She turned to face him as he embraced her in a big, awkward hug, sobbing on her shoulder. Senna turned the mic off, dropped it, and put both arms around him as her eyes welled up.

❙❙

The sound of pots and pans banging in the background was as familiar as the lingering scent of ground cumin being parched on the stove. The scents were wafting from the kitchen to the nearby living room. Arius's mother was preparing a comfort-food meal after the community meeting.

"Can one of you lazy children come and help me in the kitchen?"

Senna volunteered Arius. "Auntie! Your son would be only too happy to help. River and I are gonna play cards," she said as she grabbed some candy from a nearby table.

Arius rolled up his sleeves and went to the kitchen to help, defeated. Senna snuck into the small blanket tent that her younger sister had built in the living room.

"Blackjack is the game. I'm the house," River commanded. She wagered two candies, Senna anted up, and the cards were slapped down. A six and a nine in front of Senna.

"Hit me," said Senna. She glanced at the four, and stuck at nineteen.

River looked at her cards and tapped her chin. She dealt a card to herself and looked at it. Then she tapped her chin again. She shifted her gaze from her cards to Senna's, and then looked her right in the eyes. Senna shifted uncomfortably as the seven-year-old's hazel stare bore into the recesses of her brain.

River held the stare and nodded to Senna with a Cheshire Cat grin as she dealt herself another card. Senna's gaze moved between River's eyes and the blue *R* cut out and taped to her shirt. It was drawn to look wavy, like a running river, and it was surrounded by a brown arc that she said represented the Earth.

"Don't you want to count it first, Ms. Twenty-Nine?" Senna joked.

"Girl, I've been adding for four years now. Count 'em yourself," River jeered.

Senna peered at her three-card total, showing nineteen. Then Senna glanced down to River's four cards: ten, four, five, and two.

Twenty-one to her nineteen. River racked up the candies like a Vegas high roller and stuffed them in her pajama pockets.

"Dinner!" came a yell from the kitchen.

River emerged from the tent victorious, with her arms thrown up, then slapped the *R* with both hands.

"Yeah! *R* stands for 'Romp.' I own you, baby." And with that she marched into the kitchen, her makeshift blanket cape floating in her wake.

Entering the small kitchen was like walking into a banquet hall. As Senna sat down around more food than you'd expect at a royal wedding, she jokingly whispered to Arius how her sister had just hustled her.

"Ma, are you taking River to the casino?" asked Arius as he reached for the roasted lemon chicken. "Who hits at nineteen after taking two low cards? Someone is teaching her."

"Boy, you think Ma got time for nonsense like you," Ma said with a mischievous grin.

"Check the cape, son. *R* stands for 'Rogue,'" River jeered. A high five from Arius to River.

The dinner conversation started with family talk, moved through world affairs, and circled back to the meeting with the farmers in town from earlier that evening. Senna walked Ma through her explanation and pitchfork man's surrender. Then Ma brought the conversation right back to family.

"When are my son and my niece going to move back from that big city? It's time you two stopped stroking your big brains and put your arms and legs to work around our community."

Silence followed. And gulps.

"What we're doing in Toronto helps everyone," Arius tried.

"Protests. Championing policy reform. Don't look surprised,

boy, I listen. What's it all amounting to? How has it helped people's crops here, in your hometown? How has it helped Mr. Whalen? That man is so nervous now he walks everywhere with his pitchfork," Ma said.

"Isn't that a bit unnerving, Ma?" asked Arius.

"It's unnerving when people don't make small talk in the grocery store anymore. Might not make sense to you, city boy, but people here don't know what to do about their real problems. While you're trying to help everybody, you're helping nobody," said Ma.

Arius looked to Senna for a life preserver. She rolled her head and finally jumped in with him.

"Be fair, Auntie. Change takes time! We're doing what feels right in our hearts, and that means years of education and policy change."

The truth in Senna's heart, though, was very different. It was why she knew she couldn't sell her aunt on this point. She didn't believe it herself. This was not about taking time. To her, it was clear there was something fundamentally wrong with the way people behaved.

Ma had said it herself. People didn't even know what the problem was. It started with Senna and Arius trying to influence the government in order that sound decisions would be made about how to manage water . . . but that would all be too little, too late.

Ma seemed to see right into Senna's soul. She spoke up again.

"I've told him since he was small: the heart achieves what the mind only dreams of. Yes. But your intentions need to be watered with action, to bloom the flower of your efforts. While you're talking, people are looking to pack up and move their homes. Do you understand having to pick up your family and move somewhere unfamiliar to you because you can't support yourself?" asked Ma.

"It's like she's been saying, Ma . . . we are taking action!" Arius tried, as Senna's head hung progressively lower.

"Says you," Ma countered, before turning to Senna. She conceded a smile before offering, "I'll give you this though, girl. What you've done with the mayor to allow our neighboring township to take water from us is truly noble."

Senna bit her lip hard. It was true. She'd convinced the mayor that they couldn't leave their neighbors in the lurch. But what had felt right to her at first was increasingly feeling like the worst decision she'd ever made. She couldn't put her finger on exactly what it was. Was it right? Didn't they always say on planes that you needed to look after yourself before those in your care? How was it that she'd sold out the people she'd grown up with? Maybe this was her opportunity to bare her soul.

"Auntie," Senna started, and she swallowed hard. "I don't know if that was the right thing I did. All I did was get our water used up even faster. For all I know, I'm the one who killed Mr. Whalen's crops."

"Whatever happens, we don't put our neighbors to the curb. We're in it together. We look after one another," Ma concluded.

At the end of it all, it was River who had the last word. She'd watched the whole ordeal and kept score in her head.

"*R* stands for 'Roasted,'" she declared, with a glance to Senna and Arius and a snap of her fingers.

The night sky was like a love letter from the universe. As Senna and Arius walked off their dinner, an ocean of stars welcomed the cousins who were as close as siblings. They took a dirt path to a clearing that opened up to the skies above.

"There's an opportunity I've just been made aware of. I've been approached by the City of Toronto. They've agreed to allow a small task force to enforce water use in the city. It's a proactive measure, to be sure. But, the city does not want to take the lake for granted."

"What exactly is the opportunity?" asked Arius.

"They need someone to shape and direct the task force," she replied.

The words hung in the air.

"What latitude is there in shaping this role?" he asked.

"Anything within reason."

"And what about things beyond reason?"

Senna just shrugged her shoulders.

"Turning the clock back is impossible, no matter what dream world you're living in, Senna. Know what happens if you try to beat everyone into submission. They'll want to beat you back. Maybe it works for a few years, but it's doomed to fail."

"You see the same world I do," Senna shot back. "The main groundwater source for the western coastal United States is collapsing. In South Africa, Cape Town is projecting a 'Day Zero' when they actually run out of water. And a billion people around the world already have no access to clean water. How can you possibly think it's not time yet for swift and severe action? We've tried enough 'carrots.' Now we need more 'sticks,'" she said.

Arius wasn't so easily convinced. "We can't remake the map the way you want and put everyone where water is. We're not going to move a billion people. Our only choice is to bring water to them."

"Bless you, Arius," said Senna, forcing out a breath and shaking her head. "I badly want to live in the world you dream of. But that's not the world we live in."

Chapter 26

Toronto, 3 Days to Day Zero

Gus was called away from the hospital tent to the supply warehouse. There was good news.

He arrived to a flurry of activity in the main area of the warehouse. Two forklifts were being directed by two wardens on the floor as they stacked up cases of unlabeled water. The main water stockpile had dwindled down, but the supply warden was now happily sorting it with the shipment that had just arrived.

Gus put a hand on the supply warden's shoulder and breathed a sigh of relief. "How much water do we have on hand now?"

"With all of this from the new shipment, plus the reserve, we're good for at least a couple of weeks. We're just putting everything together for the best use of space in here."

"Excellent. Let's get it distributed right away. Start with the medical tent as a priority, then the hostel, and so on from there." Gus crossed his arms and looked on with satisfaction. "Hmph. I knew she wouldn't let it happen."

"Do you know where it came from?" the supply warden asked.

Gus shook his head. "Senna must have found a reliable supplier."

"If anyone could, it would be her, I suppose. Not easy these days. Even when bottled water was in vogue years ago, you could never tell what was in it. I remember reading once, during the height of commercial bottled sales, that a quarter of the products on the market were just tap water. It was never classified as food, so it wasn't subject to the same safety checks. Most of it was safe, though," said the supply warden, patting the hefty stockpile.

◊ ◆ ◊

Just over an hour later, Senna radioed Gus to come to the medical tent urgently.

When he'd left to visit the supply warehouse earlier, about twenty of the hundred temporary beds had been in use. Now, almost half of them were occupied. Large industrial fans blew cool air in from the corners of the tent.

Gus heard something completely unexpected: the sound of a human being retching. Multiplied by almost every bed in use.

The patients were suffering from painful spasms as they threw up. The smell of vomit permeated the air. Senna and the medical staff were running from one bed-ridden, dehydrated wigrant to another. What the hell was going on?

He walked over to the bed where the woman he'd brought in the wheelchair was lying. Colors had put their child down on the scorched grass while he tended to his wife, and the young child was looking up at him with a tear-streaked face. The breeze from the industrial fan provided a momentary reprieve as he walked past it to Colors family, but moments later the overpowering smell of regurgitation hit Gus once again.

Colors stood beside an intravenous setup, holding a plastic bag to catch the vomit from his wife. The medical attendants had started IV drips of a mild saline solution to try to rehydrate the wigrants. Colors was putting down the vomit bag when he could to help his wife sip from a water bottle to supplement the IV.

Gus did a double take on the water bottle. He scanned the area and saw a stack of open cases from the delivery he'd ordered just over an hour earlier. He looked through the commotion to spot them. At almost every bed, he saw one. Open.

He wanted to vomit too.

Gus ran to the opposite end of the field of beds and dragged Senna away from the wigrant she was tending to.

"They have to stop drinking the water!" Gus declared quietly.

Senna stared blankly at him. She looked around at the open bottles being used to supplement the IV drips and back at him.

Gus ran madly along each row telling every patient and the medical attendants to stop using the bottled water. Gus grabbed bottles from the hands of patients and their caregivers, collecting them as he ran. Water spilled all over his clothes.

He dumped all the bottles he'd collected by the open stack, and the uncapped bottles spilled their contents into the parched ground. He returned to Colors. Someone arrived at the bedside and injected Colors' wife with an anti-nauseant. Her pale figure settled in the bed as Colors applied a cold compress to her forehead.

Senna was standing casually in the breeze of one of the fans when Gus returned, panting from the hustle.

"You vetted the source of that shipment, yes?" It was the only logical question Gus could think to ask.

"Shipment?!" Senna retorted, shaking her head. "Cole said that wouldn't get here till the evening. It arrived early!"

Gus went wide-eyed as he connected the dots, the recognition of his daughter's grand failure dawning on him. He closed his eyes and swallowed. He told Senna everything about the visit with the broker. Senna asked if Gus thought this was where the bad water came from. He nodded, and Senna looked pensive.

"What does he look like, this broker?" asked Senna.

"Style gone bad," Gus replied.

"The South African?" asked Senna, doing a double take. "You know him?"

"We don't all know each other," Gus said plainly.

Senna gave him a side-eye. She walked a slow circle around him, arms crossed behind her back.

"This house of cards could collapse. On us. This is Cole's doing, and she needs to take responsibility for it. It's time for her to claim what she always wanted," said Senna.

"Where are you going?" asked Gus.

"To track down an old friend. If I'm going to take Axiom Water from her, I've got to clear my good name first," she said.

Gus took a couple of steps to put an arm on her shoulder.

"One last thing, Senna. About the water stockpile . . ." Gus began.

2 DAYS TO DAY ZERO

Toronto

Chapter 27

What could historians write about an invisible man? Tao wondered. Someone who worked in the shadows. It was something the operators would occasionally talk about on their missions, during his time in the SAS.

Tao's Special Forces unit, and units like his, had often been tasked with exterminating despots and tyrants. Sometimes those decisions came after weighty political debate, albeit among a small cast of characters from the greater political realm. Sometimes those decisions came from covert branches of government, away from the failings of the political arena.

Special Forces operators nudged events that affected history. But outside that sphere, never once had he received such a grandiose request from a private individual. The referral in this instance came from a trusted source, which made it that much more intriguing, but that was not enough to dissuade him from doing his due diligence.

He vetted the client to ensure there was no risk of entrapment. He conducted a deep search of their internet fingerprint to establish any pattern that raised concern for his safety, the privacy of his identity, or his professional capacity. If people knew each other's Google search history, he thought, no one would ever speak to anybody else.

Tao made his way to High Park in Toronto's west end, their prearranged meeting location. There, the symphony of cicadas felt like electricity on his skin. He watched other people enjoying the lush vegetation and walking trails. High Park had a small zoo and historic buildings, and today it had one additional attraction: the wigrants' last hope for survival in the world. He was meeting someone with enough influence to remake the fabric of history.

Tao discreetly watched Cole for an hour after she arrived. She had wandered away from the more regularly traveled areas, as he'd directed. His scan confirmed that she had no devices on her whatsoever. That last requirement of his in particular made people feel very naked. No one knew how to be alone anymore, he reflected.

They sat on the grass and looked out over Grenadier Pond, and the scent of flowers reached them now and then on the wafting breeze.

Cole told him how a fire had been started at the settlement, nearly killing many wigrants, and that she knew Arius was responsible. She admitted her role in asking Arius to do for her what he had done before in Seville. On that occasion, Arius had set fire to vacant dwellings that burned to the ground as the fire fighters had inadequate water supply. The stir caused by the incident rallied the Spanish city to action with Cole at the helm.

Cole decried Arius as a loose cannon. She told Tao that Arius's care for the cause now overrode caution. Tao would have liked to hold Cole responsible, but he had seen firsthand how his friend was going off the rails. He himself knew about Arius's plans, about the Molotov cocktails.

She openly corroborated Tao's information. Arius held information about illegally sanctioned bulk water movements that jeopardized her company. If he was caught, Axiom Water would go down in flames. The wigrants' only champion would be powerless. There was no point targeting Senna, since Gus could easily succeed her. River Enforcement could live on beyond Senna, and they were on a life-or-death timeline in which, Arius's fate also hung in the balance.

Cole ended her proposition with a simple statement.

"I hear you have a reputation for seeing that justice is done. Justice is your thing. Well, this is a moment in history. Judge yourself on what your role will be."

Tao thought back to a trip he and Arius had taken to Cape Town, years earlier. On that trip, on the cable car to the top of Table Mountain, Arius had told him how severe things had been there, and what Cole had done to resolve the water crisis.

"What she did reminds me of that quote from Stephen Richards," Arius had said, "'When we have reached the depths of despair, only then can we look up and see the light of hope.'"

The day had been clear, and the view from the top of the overlook was breathtaking. They could see out to Robben Island, the infamous prison island that had housed Nelson Mandela for so long. It made Tao think about what Mandela had learned during his twenty-seven years there. How, even in captivity, there was disagreement among the prisoners concerning the best way forward for humanity. How one person can choose to be better, for themselves and for others. How humanity shows itself in kindnesses to others and oneself, even in dire predicaments.

He picked up a stone and walked to the shoreline of Grenadier Pond. He looked down at himself in the stillness of the water, the reflection of the invisible man, and skipped the stone across it. This was a decisive moment. He was being called on to work in the shadows to nudge history. His failure or inaction in this moment could lead to the death of countless innocents.

To the light of hope, he thought to himself, as the ripples faded back to stillness.

He knew what needed to be done.

Chapter 28

"Y ou've thought this through, Senna?" Gus asked over the phone.

"Tao might not want to speak with me. But as Geppetto, he must have a digital footprint. I've got to get in his head if we want to clear River Enforcement. And I think I know what thread to pull to do that. Did you look after those wigrants I asked about?" Senna asked as she pulled into Guild Park.

"It's looked after. I'm just amazed you got that young lady to meet you again. Let's hope she doesn't find out you got kicked off the case. Cole is expecting to meet with you in a couple of hours. You've got time for this?" asked Gus.

"Take care of the minutes, the hours will take care of themselves," Senna said before hanging up.

Senna drove to the Scarborough Bluffs, an escarpment on Toronto's east side that towered almost twenty-five stories above Lake Ontario. Monuments and sculptures dotted Guild Park, many of which were relics rescued from the demolition of buildings in downtown Toronto, arranged here to resemble ancient ruins.

A Greek-style theater had been built from the remnants of an old Bank of Toronto building. Senna looked through a marble arch and admired the eight repurposed columns that served as the backdrop to the stage. And in the distance, she saw the young woman she was to meet. She was standing towards the edge of the park, looking out over the water.

Senna walked towards the young woman, and when she turned, Senna saw more calmness in her face than the last time they'd met one another.

"It's quite a view. I've never come out here," said the young lady.

"I was here once, on a date. It was a summer night. We set up a blanket on the grass towards the edge, like where we're standing now. No one else was around, and we watched the moon come up till its reflection in the water was all you could see, as if it was the only thing that existed. It was majestic. Honestly, felt like another world," said Senna.

"I'll have to remember to come back, then," she said to Senna.

"There's something else I want you to remember right now. And please, let me assure you again, you're really helping me on this. This is not about you at all," said Senna.

The young woman shared a knowing smile.

"I'm sorry the police aren't working with you anymore, Senna. It's okay. I knew who you were when we met. It was actually the police officer who made me nervous, and I'm sure he'd be here with you if you were still working together," said the young lady.

Senna bowed her head as a show of apology and thanks.

"You're after him, aren't you? The assassin. He's the one responsible for the other termination, the one at HTO Park? You want to know how I decided to hire him to terminate the cigar-smoking man," she suggested to Senna.

"I'm sorry, I can't tell you why I'm asking." Senna paused for a moment and thought about the young woman's last question.

Senna explained that she and her little sister had spent a lot of time with family growing up, as her parents traveled for work. She had a cousin she was very close to, and she was moved by her cousin's passion for water. It was what made her want to save the world too. She admired him for that passion and wanted to emulate it.

"It's ironic that the same passion would drive a wedge between us," she said, turning towards the lake.

"Your twenties are like an adult childhood," Senna went on, "another formative time in life. One of the things I learned is that just because I admired someone, it didn't mean I had to do what they were doing. I opted to save the world in the way that felt right to me. In my heart, I knew the world I wanted to live in, but it's hard when people can't see simple wisdom. After we started the water policing task force in Toronto, before it even had a name, I stood up and took notice when my cousin aligned himself against me. Especially after what happened in Georgetown," said Senna.

The young lady gave a curious glance. Senna told her what had happened in Georgetown, where they grew up. She said it imprinted on her the importance of protecting and using water so carefully.

"Did you try to change your cousin's mind?" the young lady asked.

"I started asking questions. A question is one of the most potent forces in the universe. Questions open minds. And open minds change the world," said Senna.

She went on to tell her how she'd spend her spare time questioning every conventional assumption and approach that had been taken to try to make things right. She'd chased every expert and individual willing to answer her questions. She swore if she hadn't worked as hard as she did, they'd have found a reason to get rid of her just for some peace and quiet.

"You see, I get you. I know what's it's like to want to look after family. So, to your question, I don't want to know how you decided you could hire him. I need to know how you *actually* hired him," said Senna.

Chapter 29

"I give up," Senna declared. "You win, Cole."

Senna sat at the edge of the seating area in the hotel lounge, next to floor-to-ceiling glass that wrapped the side of the building, under a twenty-foot-high, cloud-white ceiling. A jazz quartet had set up across from the large-scale fireplace and were starting their first evening set as people returned from dinner. As night fell on the city, Senna could see across the street to the city's chic opera house.

"What did you do?" Cole demanded. She focused on Senna's eyes, tuning out the activity at the front desk.

"Not a thing you wouldn't have done yourself, I'm sure," replied Senna, betraying nothing with her demeanor. She told Cole that, effective immediately, Axiom Water was the lead agency, with custody of the settlement, and River Enforcement would operate in a supporting role only.

Steele, who had been hovering behind Cole, took a step forward, leaned in to tap her shoulder, and pointed past the front desk to the portico beyond. Cole now saw what had caught his eye. The valet had opened the passenger door of a sleek sports car, painted as if it were a kid's toy from the 1970s. The water broker emerged in a salmon tuxedo and matching top hat, carrying a gaudy, silver-tipped walking cane.

Two of the broker's associates had pulled up ahead of him, and another exited the driver side of the oversized plaything. The whole circus act entered through the large revolving lobby door. One took up a position near the front of the hotel, another walked around to stand near the band, and the largest of them accompanied the broker into the lounge.

The large escort snapped his fingers as they approached. Two of the serving staff rushed past an elderly couple admiring the wall of crafted tea urns to bring the broker a chair. He sat just as the chair was placed between Cole and Senna, and his brutish escort stood behind Senna.

"Ahh. Friends. Such a pleasant surprise to see you here. Cole, you're looking well. And Senna. What a delight," said the broker cheerfully.

Cole and Senna sat silently. The three of them remained in that awkward triangle for several moments until a drink was handed to the broker by one of the servers. The broker raised his glass in a toast to a bevy of stainless-steel doves hanging from the ceiling.

"My ladies. Sometimes I spend the hour it takes to get here only to sit in this very spot and admire that art installation just outside, even for five minutes. Do you know what the artist was telling us with it?" asked the broker as he leaned forward with his drink.

They turned their heads to follow the doves suspended overhead to the home of their stainless-steel flock. There, outside the side entrance to the lounge, stood the stainless-steel dragon. Its body, made to look like twisted tree branches, was covered by countless doves.

Cole and Senna caught each other's quizzical expression as they turned back to the broker.

"The doves are the international symbol of world peace, but they rest cautiously on this mythical beast who is bound to nature. He is reminding us of the fragile conditions facing our planet. He is encouraging us to protect the delicate harmony between humans and nature. I toast you both for this tonight." He raised and then downed his drink.

Cole bit her top lip as Senna shook her head briskly and briefly. The broker turned around and called for a round for his friends.

"Come. Come. Drinks are on their way. We drink to our new partnership, yes? With the access you've granted me through the good faith delivery today, we can restore the imbalance of water that exists. *One People, One Water*, yes!" the broker said, raising his empty glass with a beaming smile.

Senna was the first to react. "Your brain is as polluted as the product you push!" she said. "That shipment Cole snuck through under my nose is liquid poison."

"Snuck through?!" Cole shouted.

"Trust me, sister, it's all on you," Senna said, pointing accusingly.

"Cole. You told me you'd make the impossible possible. Am I authorized to deal or not?" the broker now asked.

"Every wigrant who drank your water ended up puking their guts out," Senna explained. "We had to put them on a saline IV to save their lives."

Cole's grip tightened on the armrests of her chair, and she had a panicked look.

"One thing is for certain. Cole may have custody of the settlement now. But River Enforcement looks after this city. You're the worst of a bad lot, and I don't want to see or hear from you ever again. Good luck to you, Cole. When that water was brought in, it got mixed in with our stockpile. There's no telling which bottles are contaminated. It's all unusable now," said Senna.

Cole's eyes widened as she sat forward. "The reserve?"

Senna nodded. "One day left," she said, with a wave of her hand.

The broker threw his empty glass to the ground between them and watched it shatter. The room went silent.

"Fine, then. We'll make it a father-daughter package deal," the broker said, jumping up from his chair. His brutish accomplice moved forward and slid his right hand inside his jacket.

From nowhere, Steele moved in like lightning and delivered a solid blow to the accomplice's nose as he held the big man's hand in his jacket. The broker's eyes bulged wide and he made a dash for the front lobby door, along with the associate who had positioned himself by the jazz band.

The lobby crowd, which had at first fallen silent, now became hysterical. At once, everyone got up and scattered in all directions.

As the hulk in Steele's custody reached to nurse his broken nose with his left hand, Steele moved behind him and manipulated the man's right hand like a puppet to withdraw the weapon. He turned the man towards the broker, who was weaving through the crowd, blocking any clear line of sight. Steele took the weapon from the hulk's hand and knocked him cold with his fist.

Senna watched the huge man crumple to the ground in front of her. Cole and Steele ran together to the revolving door, where the broker and his two remaining associates were clambering into the toy sports car. The passenger door was still closing when they came out, and the car began to drive away.

Steele exploded into a runner's stride.

Cole called out after him. "Forget him, Steele. At least for now."

1 DAY TO DAY ZERO

Toronto

Chapter 30

The clouds from an early-morning thunderstorm had cleared, but the Don River was still swollen from the rain. The morning sun had begun drying out the leaves as Arius navigated his way off the beaten paths towards the shore of one of the city's main rivers.

As requested, he found their old meeting place, a particular spot in the ravine system right beside the river, where they had hung out in their youth. It was nestled away from the bustle of the surrounding urban core, downstream of hundreds of acres of urbanized development, and it was hard to realize that it was just a ten-minute walk from the chaotic city traffic.

Arius sat on the banks of the mighty Don River, gazing past the muddied waters that looked like chocolate milk after every storm. He studied a maple tree perched on the opposite bank. The tree stood strong for its age, though its base was dangerously exposed along the river. The roots poked their thirsty fingers through the riverbank like a dozen thick straws into a glass of milk.

There was no one around. Until there was.

Tao was very somber on his approach. He thanked Arius for meeting him, to which Arius replied with a friendly grunt.

"Do you remember that week, we were in our twenties, and I came home on leave from the forces? We just chilled and hung out like this, caught movies, hit up some restos?" asked Tao, sitting on a rock beside Arius.

Arius nodded thoughtfully, smiling.

"What was that line you liked from that movie about William Wallace?" asked Tao.

"'Every man dies. Not every man truly lives,'" Arius said, after another moment's thought.

"What do you think you'd do with your final hours . . . if you knew?" asked Tao.

The Don River seemed to get louder.

"I suppose it would depend on what I'd done last and how old I was. Twenty years ago, more movies, more bars. Huh. Sorry to say. If it was now, though? Probably stay right here, just like this."

Tao nodded, and looked down. He curled one leg up as he sat, throwing his arms around his knee as the other leg dangled over the river.

"'Few will have the greatness to bend history itself; but each of us can work to change a small portion of events, and in the total, of all those acts will be written the history of this generation,'" said Tao.

"Robert Kennedy," Arius replied instantly. "I'd dare to dream that I was in that first group, Tao. But it's the contrary. I'm the invisible hand. Helping make change with all the other invisible hands."

Arius leaned forward and looked over to see Tao smiling his acknowledgment.

"Here's to the invisible hands," said Tao, holding up an invisible glass to an invisible audience.

They bumped the backs of their fists to seal the toast. Across the riverbank, a branch from halfway up the mighty maple tree broke off and fell into the water.

"Let's hope everything we've both done moves the needle in the right direction," said Tao.

The water's wavy surface smoothed out as the Don River's flow seemed to subside.

"Moved." Arius corrected Tao to the past tense. His lower lip trembled as he held himself together. He dared a look over, trying to peek inside the unzipped checkered hoodie Tao wore. He took a deep breath and steadied himself, tracing the movement of the maple branch as it floated down the river. He decided if this was where judgement arrived for him, then this was where he would present his final case.

Arius cleared his throat and asked Tao, "Do you think Dr. Martin Luther King, Jr., set out to bend history or get his name in a history book?"

Tao shook his head, no.

"So . . . was it for recognition . . . money . . . love?"

Tao's eyes focused on the soft ebbs and flows of the Don River as it undulated around its banks, constantly competing with the hard edge of land and rock. The river always overcame it, wearing away rock with its constant persistence, shaping the land to its will.

"He was driven by purpose," said Tao, with firm resolve.

"'Not everybody can be famous, but everybody can be great, because greatness is determined by service,'" Arius quoted.

"Arius, I only joined you on the one mission to Paris. It helped me see. It made me understand. But when do you cross a line in serving that purpose?"

Arius told Tao about one of his biggest water thefts for Axiom Water. It had involved drilling underground to tap into a water system near the border of Canada and the United States. Water was being sent from Canada into the States right past an Indigenous community that was suffering with no access to clean water. It took almost a year, but Arius's operation covertly tapped in to provide clean water to that Indigenous community on an ongoing basis.

"To this day, no one is any the wiser except for the beneficiaries. That community survives because of the risks I took. I don't see a line when it comes to doing my part, Tao," said Arius.

"That's the problem, though. Your risk is not just your own. Everything Axiom Water has done around the world can be undone if your exploits and risks become known. And the settlement is different. If I hadn't intervened and impersonated Gus, telling them to clear the area of the settlement you targeted, people would have died," said Tao.

Arius offered a deep, gracious nod as he put both his hands on his chest. He blinked his eyes dry as they welled up, and steadied his breathing again.

"I went seeking what they all sought. To follow my purpose. To dispense the best of myself to serve humanity. My wish for the world is that everyone should find their cause and do what is necessary for it," Arius said.

The flow of the Don lingered in their silence.

Tao got up first. The sun wasn't yet high in the sky, and a small breeze along the water sent a chill through Arius, who rubbed his arms to warm them. Arius stood up a moment later to face Tao.

Tao extended his hand, and the offered shake became a hug. He took off the checkered hoodie he wore and gave it to Arius for warmth.

"Arius. The next time I see you, you won't see me," said Tao. Then he turned to leave.

"Tao," Arius said with finality. Tao turned his head halfway. "Thank you."

Chapter 31

Senna was buzzed in to the glass-lined lobby of the downtown condominium building. Three cream-colored spherical light fixtures glowed overhead, barely noticeable in the bright sunlight. She carried her hopes past the security desk to the tightly packed leather sofa, where she waited and watched the mid-morning activities of regular people.

Elevator doors opened on the far side of the lobby, and out came a pristinely manicured golden retriever, walking a man in his twenties decked out in fully licensed basketball attire. The faux pro baller talked into the air, either for his own benefit or for the benefit of whoever was on the other end of the tiny white sticks protruding from his ears.

A loud thump disrupted the serenity of the lobby as a teenager, holding up their cell while speaking on a video call, walked face first into the squeaky-clean entry door while trying to enter the building and ended up disoriented on the floor. The entry door opened and the golden walked its human over the teen into the urban jungle that lay beyond.

"Senna!"

Her host called to her after another elevator door opened, and she hurried over. The waves of her brunette hair swung over her black, button-up, short-sleeved shirt, and her leather cross-body bag bounced against her back.

"Been a long time since we crossed paths, Senna," her associate said. The elevator doors closed and they ascended to the thirtieth floor. "Must be important if you're willing to come to see where the magic happens."

Senna's associate was known as "the Archivist" for his next-level ability to dig out data from any digital source. Once they were in his condo he double-locked the door and enabled his security system. Senna followed behind as the Archivist blazed a trail to his bedroom through a maze of pizza boxes and pop cans.

"Last time we worked together, you sniffed out my violator's online footprint so I could track her in the real world. I still need that level of discretion, of course, but the chase is a bit different this time," said Senna.

"If it's been typed, scanned, searched, recorded, or stored anywhere on the planet and accessible by the internet, I can get it for you. Public, private, legal, or otherwise," the Archivist said as he pulled up a chair for her in his bedroom.

"Are firewalls a problem?" asked Senna.

The Archivist chuckled. "You're funny," he said, with a blank expression.

Beside the neatly kept single bed was his computer desk, where the Archivist took a seat behind a forty-nine-inch curved monitor. Above that, mounted on the wall, were two twenty-seven-inch monitors.

The Archivist rubbed his chin as Senna debriefed him on the process used to retain Tao. She told him how the young woman client she'd spoken to had contacted Tao through coded email from a particular website.

"If we want to get ahead of him, we'll have to go through the dark web," said the Archivist.

It was from the website Senna provided on the "clear web," the relatively small visible part of the internet, that the Archivist would dive into the rabbit hole. He went into the "deep web," the majority of the internet that was hidden behind paywalls, passcodes, and security access. Then he made a foray into the "dark web," a subset of the deep web that was specifically hidden and ever-changing and required hacker-like precision, experience, and patience to navigate.

The screen in front of the Archivist was flashing from one site to another like a sprinter, while the two above were slowly chugging along on various searches. Senna just watched as the Archivist occasionally shifted his gaze between his main screen and the two above it. About an hour had passed when all the screens became still.

The Archivist let out a breath and turned to nod to Senna. Her attention was directed to the top right-hand screen, where the Archivist had managed to dig into the messages from Tao's clear website. It was a record of who had reached out to him to request his services, and it included correspondence from her informant, the young woman who had hired him to take out the cigar man, Smoke.

She scanned the correspondence history, and something jumped out at her.

"Are those in chronological order?" she asked.

The Archivist nodded.

A shiver went up Senna's spine as the Archivist confirmed that in fact a query from Cole had come in just after the fire on the settlement. The record on the screen didn't stipulate who the mark was, but Senna knew it was no coincidence.

"You know who the mark is?" he asked.

"Cole spotted the file for the man aspiring to be River Enforcement's 'Most Wanted.' He does underground work for her," she replied anxiously.

"Sooo . . . if he's gone, then he's off your list. Good news, no?" the Archivist asked genuinely.

Senna's eyes blinked rapidly, then stopped.

"Unless her plan is to frame me for the hit. Regardless, the mark is my cousin. If anything happens to him, it won't be by her hand," Senna said decisively.

Senna told the Archivist there was a confirmation process that Tao used to let his clients know they'd been accepted. The Archivist nodded again and turned back. Senna watched as his screens came back to life, but she didn't have to wait long this time before he pointed out the confirmation on the top left screen.

"Sorry, Senna," the Archivist said. "It's on."

She called out the cell numbers for Arius and Tao from memory. "Triangulate the location of those two numbers," she said.

Two minutes later, the top screens each showed a flashing dot. The Archivist said the top left screen was Tao and the top right screen was Arius. Tao, if his phone was with him, was moving southbound along the Don Valley Parkway. Arius's phone was beside the Don River, stationary.

Senna's heart stopped. She'd left her phone in her car out of fear that Tao might track her. She asked the Archivist to make an encrypted call to Arius's cell. Straight to voice mail.

"Track it," said Senna. The Archivist unlocked his security system as Senna got up and walked briskly towards the door. "I know exactly where Arius is. I can get there fast. But if his phone starts moving, call me the second it does."

Minutes later, Senna's car was screaming across Lake Shore Boulevard as she prepared to veer onto the Gardiner Expressway. She put the Archivist on speakerphone when his call came in.

"Signal is moving west, away from the river. I pinged it and it shows it's still off, though, so you can't reach him," said the Archivist.

Her speedometer dropped substantially as she breathed a sigh of relief.

"Something else you might want to know," said the Archivist.

"Go ahead," said Senna. A tremendous weight had been lifted from her shoulders, and even though the weight was now like a yoke attached to her neck, it still felt like an easier burden to bear.

"Tao's vehicle exited on Richmond. I have your signal as well, and . . ."

"Yes, I'm moving to intercept," said Senna, cutting him off.

The Archivist guided her to an intercept route with Tao. When they were about a third of a mile apart, Senna hung up on the Archivist and thumbed through her contacts. It rang as Tao's vehicle moved into view coming the other way.

"Detective Mira," came the pleasant greeting.

Senna was seething. Her brain function had collapsed and she was about to go primal.

"How could you?" she said, as if forcing out her last words.

The silence came as the revelation set in, exactly at the same moment the two cars approached one another. Their eyes met for an eternal moment.

Chapter 32

In the eternity that Senna and Tao gazed at one another, they had an entire conversation.

"Is this how you're repaying a lifetime of friendship?"

"It's more complicated than you'll ever know."

"Never, not with him. There is no complicated. Just him. And you. And me."

"Sometimes there are bigger things at play in the world."

All of it, the entire dialogue, happened in their eyes within that instant, as the cars passed.

And in the instant that followed, Senna felt another eternity go by as she decided whether to pursue Tao or proceed to secure Arius. She hit the brake to spin the car around.

Tao accelerated to put distance between them, but Senna caught traction quickly and locked her eyes on him as her car lurched forward.

He raced across Richmond Street in the one-way traffic and made a hard right at Jarvis to go north. His eyes caught Senna in the rearview again. He pushed his luxury ride to outpace her car's electric lightning punch.

Senna clenched her teeth when she saw Tao toss his phone out the window.

"Where are you going now, then?" Senna asked out loud.

She mapped his route options in her head. If he veered left, he'd end up going towards Dundas Square, deeper into the downtown core and busier pedestrian roads. Too much congestion.

Going right would send him into Regent Park and Cabbagetown. Residential. Too slow, too many turns.

He was going straight.

"He's heading for Mount Pleasant. If he makes it, he'll have a straight run," Senna said. Mount Pleasant Road was like a secret back door into the city core that drove like a short freeway during off-peak hours.

Senna knew she could not catch him. She feigned the chase by keeping her car behind him, and she engaged her speakerphone to call the Archivist.

The Archivist sent her Arius's current position.

She gulped hard before hanging up to make the next call.

Two rings felt like twenty, and it was shocking to hear the line pick up after the third ring. She readied herself to speak as quickly as humanly possible.

"Merchant," said the voice on the other end.

"Merch, this isn't about me! Tao's after my cousin. Please, help me extract him," Senna pleaded, as efficiently as possible. When she was met with silence, she lobbed in a final plea. "He's in imminent danger."

Tao reached the ramp to get onto Mount Pleasant Road, and Senna broke off to let him go. She pulled over to the curb and listened to nothing but background noise from the police station on the other end.

She grabbed her phone from the dashboard and yelled out the coordinates the Archivist had messaged her. The line went dead.

Senna huffed. She plugged the coordinates into the car's navigation system. And hoped.

"He's a ghost. Again."

She continued towards the Bloor Street viaduct, wishing she could take her impulsiveness back. She should have left well enough alone. Then Tao wouldn't have ditched his phone, the Archivist would have continued tracking him, and he'd have been none the wiser.

"Come on," she said out loud, banging the steering wheel and refocusing on the navigation system. She took a deep, slow breath.

Senna hammered the accelerator as she exited off Bloor Street onto the Bayview Avenue bypass and pulled off into the Evergreen Brickworks site, restored industrial land that now provided space for a farmers' market, gardens, and environmental education. This was where much of the extracted clay had been made into bricks for Toronto's first impressive buildings. Senna couldn't help but think that not even twenty-four hours ago she'd seen where pieces of those historic downtown buildings had ended up, in Guild Park.

Senna breathed a sigh of relief as she parked beside the three police cars clustered in the parking lot. She got out to seek out the officers, and she thought about how Arius must have walked along the nearby Don River and ventured towards the Brickworks. It was something the three of them had done in the past.

She walked onto the Brickworks grounds and through the covered pavilions to emerge in the open air on the other side, facing onto the former gravel pit, now the site of a large pond. She continued onto the boardwalk, which crisscrossed the pond, and looked out for Arius or the officers. All she saw, though, were distant slopes overgrown with vegetation.

With two directions to choose from, she opted to go left towards a gravel trail, but as she left the boardwalk and moved up a set of metal stairs, two officers appeared in front of her out of thin air. They grabbed her by the shoulders before she could comprehend what was happening. Her arms were behind her back and in handcuffs a moment later.

She held her breath as the officers walked her back across the boardwalk to a trail on the other side of the pond.

"Officer, I'm the one that asked Sergeant, uh, Captain Merchant to send you here. Why am I in handcuffs, and where are you—?"

"Just a moment, ma'am," one of the officers interjected.

They walked up a hill to find two pairs of officers walking towards them. Another person was being escorted in the middle, in handcuffs as well. The captor's head was bowed solemnly.

Senna recognized Tao's checkered hoodie immediately.

"What?!" Senna gasped.

Arius looked up at her. His eyes gleamed quizzically.

In the blur of the moments that followed, she heard something about conspiracy relating to three murders.

Chapter 33

"I thought the settlement was priority one, Cole," said Steele as they walked into the opulence of the River Enforcement offices.

"It is. That's why we're taking advantage of Senna's hospitality. Let's flex our newfound power as lead agency for the wigrants' well-being," she said.

River Enforcement's Toronto headquarters had been built as an extension on one of the city's main water-treatment facilities, the R.C. Harris Water Treatment Plant. On the way in, they passed a small crowd milling around outside the marble entryway, snapping photos of the distinguished old building. Steele overheard someone saying it was named for one of the great city builders in Toronto. Steele had never imagined that this art deco fortress might be working hard to provide half the city's water. The backdrop of glimmering Lake Ontario was in competition with the glamorous façade of the "Palace of Purification."

"What are you going to do?" asked Steele.

"Turn the odds in our favor," replied Cole. The guide assigned to them by Senna was trying not to be obvious about his eavesdropping.

They approached what looked like an industrial computer lab. The control room had only a few people in white lab coats, but Steele sensed the sensitivity of their operation. The monitors wallpapering the room showed pressure and operational readouts from the various pieces of equipment in the facility. The guide was just about to take them inside when he received a call.

"I'm sorry to interrupt," he said to Cole, "but I'm told there is a video call for you. I can set up a teleconference in that boardroom over there."

Cole pursed her lips and nodded her agreement.

The guide tried to corral the River Enforcement staff inside to abandon the boardroom. They froze when Cole walked in, then sprang to their feet and hurried to the door. Steele smiled as he leaned against the smoked glass partition wall inside the boardroom that separated it from the hallway.

Their guide apologized for the mess in the boardroom. Maps were strewn alongside photos and dossiers. While their guide was distracted, setting up the teleconference, Cole sat at the table and discreetly inspected the documents. She quickly discerned they were related to the players in water-conflict zones around the world. On the bottom of the pile, an illustration stuck out from beneath the rest. Cole craned her neck for a closer look and recognized it as a graphic of the townships around Sydney, Australia, where colossal conservation efforts by the municipalities had successfully preserved the water supply. The situation in Australia was a standout example of averting disaster. Bravery and necessity had spurred bold water-reuse measures, including the processing of wastewater into drinkable water. It was like an alternate ending to what had gone wrong in Las Vegas.

A deep chime filled the room as the teleconference came to life. A plastic face with blond hair appeared on the screen.

"It's not the best time, Jone. How can I help you?" said Cole, somewhat impatiently, as the guide left the room.

"Cole. Things must have changed drastically since I was last in contact with the mayor. On behalf of the board, let me tell you, directly and clearly, that this whole situation makes us very uncomfortable," the face on the screen said.

"If you're as plugged in as you suggest, then you know that Axiom Water is now lead agency responsible for the wigrants. I'm here to order the pumping station to increase pressure to the settlement," said Cole.

"And what are the risks in doing so?" asked Jone.

Cole paused. "It means another part of the city could be compromised."

"Could?"

Cole paused again. "Do you know the exact situation on the ground in the settlement, Jone?" she asked.

"Cole, your involvement with Axiom Water may have helped build this business, but you're mistaken if you think you answer to no one. The board, your board, is responsible for this business. We're not a humanitarian agency," Jone insisted, managing to contort her bland face into something resembling an expression of displeasure.

"What you call 'involvement' I call 'leadership,'" Cole replied coolly. "I answer to the world's under-served masses. And you must have glossed over something in your corporate orientation or you'd know that, fundamentally, the business of Axiom Water is humanitarian. One People. One Water."

"The settlement was in better hands with Senna. I've heard

good things about her. And what I'm hearing about you these days is . . . not as good," said Jone.

Cole tensed as she watched the screen expectantly, waiting for the other shoe to drop.

"I'm hearing we may have another very serious problem," Jone continued.

Cole took an exasperated breath. It took all her willpower to keep her eyes from rolling.

"I'll be direct and clear with you, now, Jone," Cole said with a crocodile smile. "I'm impressed by your alpha tactics. You're the newest member of the board, and they all look up to you. But I don't have time for you now."

"Actually, you will. Tomorrow. When all five board members come to discuss this mess with you. Face to face," said Jone, smugly.

A deep chime filled the room again, marking the end of the call. The boardroom was silent and still. Cole looked to Steele and put one finger to her lips. She got up and led them out of the boardroom towards the control room.

"In your world, does that ultimatum mean what it does in mine?" asked Steele.

"It means whatever we're doing here had better work. Updating my résumé will be the least of my problems if it doesn't."

Chapter 34

Cole enjoyed a rare moment of peace as Steele navigated the twenty-minute drive from River Enforcement's HQ to the settlement. She slumped in the back seat and watched the world go by through the car window before closing her eyes.

As Cole snoozed, Steele adjusted his rearview mirror just a pinch. While splitting his attention, safely, between the road and Cole, he thought he caught a hint of a smile.

What felt like only seconds later, Cole felt the car slowing down as Steele drove into the settlement. That utopian moment came crashing in on itself as they arrived at the former Olympic village.

"Let's go remind ourselves what I just inherited," Cole said, as she leaned into the gap between the front seats.

The front gate opened for her and the wardens stood at the ready. Cole walked in a few feet and stopped to take in the vista.

There was a new stench on the site that was unbearable. Steele shot a scowl at the bravery of her breathing. "What I wouldn't give to get that sweet hog farm scent back. You're going to tell me we have to find where the smell is coming from, aren't you?" he asked, as he pulled a towel from his go-bag and tied it as a scarf over his mouth and nose.

Cole held her hand up, telling him to wait as she left to check in on the medical tent. All of the hundred temporary beds were now occupied. Steele watched as Cole spoke to several of the medical attendants. On several occasions during the conversations, a medic would point into the settlement.

On her way out, Cole stopped by one of the beds to comfort one of the patients. She held the limp grip of the woman with strawberry-blond hair, who was lying on her side. Her daughter, with filthy clothes and matted hair, sat beside her. Cole put her hand on the girl's shoulder but couldn't bring herself to meet the child's vacant stare. She returned to Steele with a despondent look. She closed her eyes and took another stifled, slow, deep breath.

"Right, then. As your British friends would say, 'In for a penny, in for a pound,' yeah?" Cole said through a forced smile. "I'm told it's this way."

Having passed the area that had been burned, they approached the nearest group of occupied tents. Cole paused at the first tent with an open front flap to politely peer in.

"Can we help you?" came a voice from inside.

It didn't take a moment for Cole to absorb the scene in the cubicle-sized tent. The woman who'd asked was sitting up on one of two small air mattresses set up on the ground inside. Her partner coughed gently as he rested on the other air mattress, along with a toddler. Between them was a small stack of tinned food and a large bottle of water. Cole presumed it was a welcome kit provided to the family when they arrived.

"Wondering if I can help *you*?" replied Cole.

"Oh, no. Thank you. We're okay. For sure we're much better off here," said the woman.

The only other objects in the tent were two silver aluminum

suitcases. She recognized the brand and tagged the price in her head at almost two thousand dollars each.

Noticing her gaze, the woman explained, "My partner and I were both IT execs in Silicon Valley. Vegas hit Day Zero but the drought shut us down long before. Our company had to stop manufacturing abruptly. We'd walked away and downsized to Vegas. I think people don't realize how much water is needed for a lot of different industrial processes, you know?"

"And your home. . . ?" Cole asked.

"What good is a mansion you can't live in, and that no one can buy? I count my blessings that we were among the fortunate few who could afford to leave," the woman replied. "We started from nothing, but I grew up with one basic principle, and it's this: If you have sustenance, security, and shelter, you have everything you need to own your destiny. We have everything we need now, for us and our daughter, and we'll begin again here."

As they walked on, Cole told Steele, "Ignore the high rises, and this is like the settlements outside of Cape Town. The big difference is that the people in the Cape Town settlements might never have known any other kind of life. But the people here, like that Silicon Valley couple, they came from something really different, something they figured they'd always have. They know what they left behind to come here."

Steele was walking ahead of Cole when they found the source of the smell pervading the settlement. They held their breath as they walked into one of the central rest areas, where a series of portable toilets sat. Even holding her breath, Cole struggled not to gag at the smell.

"This is the worst high school prank I've ever seen," Steele said, through the scarf held tight to his face. "What happened?" It looked and smelled as if a feces bomb had exploded.

They saw Gus approaching the scene, no doubt tipped off by the warden at the gate that they had arrived.

"Is it dysentery?" Cole asked.

"It's a waterborne bacterial infection. From the emergency water shipment that got mixed in with the clean supply. It got distributed and people drank it before they got the news. Some are still drinking it, hoping theirs won't turn out to be a bad bottle. As sick as the people in the medical tent are, this is what happened to the others," said Gus.

"People couldn't, wait . . . ?" asked Steele.

Gus shook his head. "The smell alone was making people vomit. If they didn't end up in the medical tent, they went back to their own places."

"Well, I want you to direct all available wardens to converge here and clean this up. I don't care what their regular duty is. Inside the hour, I want this area looking and smelling like a spring meadow," instructed Cole.

Gus jolted back and shrugged off the request with a sneer, but Cole stood firm. They both knew that Senna had handed responsibility for the settlement to Cole. Steele watched the two bulls standoff.

Obviously, nothing about this decision of Senna's sat well with Gus.

Nothing about dealing with Gus sat well with Cole.

A light breeze wafted the noxious odor directly into their brains.

Cole gagged slightly, and with a shake of her head she yelled her demands again.

Gus turned to walk away with a scowl on his face as he got on his radio to pass along the instruction.

Chapter 35

Senna and Arius were separated as the police brought them into the station. Senna was escorted through the bullpen, past the pile of broken glass that had been swept into a corner, and into Merchant's office. The constable escorting her removed her cuffs.

"This is really starting to feel like home to me," Senna said as she rubbed her sore wrists. "So . . . . I'm not under arrest?" She eyed the chair in front of Merchant for a moment but resisted the urge to sit down.

Merchant focused on the machine in front of him and slowly tapped at the keyboard with the middle finger of each hand.

Senna tried to keep her wits about her. "I want you to let Arius go," she said. "I'll make sure he stays out of trouble. He can be my problem." She knew Arius was innocent.

Still, Merchant tapped away. Every minute or so, he would stop, say "Yup," under his breath, and hit enter. Was he going to let her take Arius?

"Merch, if you're typing out your memoirs, I can free myself up in about fifty years when you're done the first page," said Senna.

Still nothing from Merchant, not even eye contact.

"You might find it's easier to use your pointer fingers to type, Merch," she told him.

Merchant held up his two middle typing fingers to Senna. Then he called the constable into his office and asked for Arius to be released.

The constable flinched and asked Merchant to repeat himself.

"You heard what I said. And when you do, maybe bring the new captain here an espresso and show her to a nice cozy corner office. Sound about right, Captain Senna? You're making the big decisions, you must be captain now. Right?"

Senna fell into the chair and stumbled over her words as she attempted to explain the mistake that had been made. She felt like she'd fallen through ice and was looking up to the frozen surface from under water. Arius wasn't the suspect they were looking for, despite matching the description the police had been given.

Merchant squinted at her.

The constable slowly backpedaled and sidestepped out of the office as Senna repeated that Arius was the target, not the killer.

"You know what, Senna? My wife says that each of us is the average of the five people we spend the most time with. Here I have a person with an assassin in her inner circle. Now I find out that your cousin-bestie, allegedly marked by your assassin-bestie, happens to be your 'Most Wanted,'" Merchant said, with his fingers interlaced and resting on his desk.

Senna's eyes grew wide. Her fingernail tapped the armrest as she shifted awkwardly in her chair.

"It's called police work. We do it sometimes. My point, Senna, is this. I can't imagine who the hell the other three people are who are bringing up the average in your circle," said Merchant.

She noticed him look beyond her into the bullpen.

"Five minutes with him. Please. And then I'm gone," Senna pleaded, with her hands pressed together.

He caught someone's attention and she heard footsteps enter the office behind her. Merchant held her gaze for one last, brief moment.

"Two minutes," he said. And with a wave of Merchant's hand, Senna was dismissed.

They made their way through the corridors of the police station towards the holding cells. The constable handed her a chair and gave her privacy as she neared Arius in his cell.

"Feels so twenty years ago," Arius said from a bench at the back of his cell.

"Hmph. Bit different this time," said Senna. She had her chair leaning back on two legs against the wall across from his cell. Her arms were crossed over her chest.

"Sure. Twenty years ago, we both had the energy to stand. Must say, though, I'm super impressed that you got the police to do your dirty work," said Arius.

Senna's hands fell from her chest to rest on her knees as her expression softened.

Arius's head turned sideways when he saw her reaction. He got up and walked towards the front of the cell to look at her. Senna looked down to her lap. She breathed slowly and steadily without saying a word.

The constable who had escorted Senna popped his head in for a second to see that everything was alright.

"Yeah. Bit different this time," said Arius. He returned to the back of his cell and sat.

Senna stood and walked up to the cell bars.

"I have nothing to do with it," she said.

The constable looked at his watch and popped his head in one more time to holler that time was almost up.

Arius nodded slowly. "Do me a favor. If you see him again, remind him of this for me."

Now the constable was announcing that time was up. He informed Senna that they'd be processing Arius, after which he'd be relocated to another facility while the wheels of justice cranked along on his process.

"I'll see you around, Senna," said Arius, as she turned the corner.

Senna recovered her car and was soon en route back to River Enforcement's HQ.

She entered the R.C. Harris Water Treatment Plant and made her way to her office. The majesty of Lake Ontario greeted her through her office window as she walked towards her desk.

Before she could sit, a plastic face with blond hair knocked at her office door.

"We need to talk, Senna. Cole is going off the deep end," she said.

"That's perfect, Jone. She's right where we need her," replied Senna.

20 YEARS EARLIER

Queen's Park, Toronto

I

Arius prepared himself as a crowd rallied on the large front lawn of Queen's Park, the site of the provincial legislature, where parliament was currently in session. On the lawn, in front of the sweeping steps of the legislature, an artist had crafted a scaled-down version of the legislature building made entirely out of empty water bottles, and he was placing the last few bottles to complete his work. It was unique not only in its structure, but also in the function planned for the end of the protest. The artist had rigged it so that it would implode as a symbolic gesture of the government's failure.

Arius had organized this event, and he was getting ready to speak to the excited crowd. Seven-year-old River was with him, excited to be part of the protest, and Arius took a moment to remind her that the purpose was to call out the lack of government action to control bulk water shipments. He told her they were allowing fresh water from Lake Ontario to be sold to private interests overseas.

"I'm all in favor of sharing our precious resource, Riv. But it's wrong when people sell the water to make a huge profit," Arius said, with his hand on her shoulder.

"My sister says that money makes the world go round, Uncle Ari. Oh, oh! Is that why she tells you to 'get real' all the time?" asked River, excitedly employing air quotes for the first time ever.

Arius chuckled. Nothing better than a seven-year-old's truth bombs!

"It's one of the many reasons, I'm sure," he said. "But money isn't the root of all problems, Riv. Love of money is. We can't escape the fact that once water becomes something we just buy and sell, then people will do everything for profit and forget about the social good."

"Everyone is a customer," River declared, with a swoop of her hand.

Looking at his little cousin, Arius noted that her dark hair made her look like her older sister, Senna, but otherwise she had the same family looks that Arius had inherited. Her olive skin radiated warmth, as did the vibrancy of her green eyes.

"The problem is, water is life," Arius said, "and not everyone can afford to pay."

"*R* stands for 'Revolt,' Uncle Ari," River cried. "Go get 'em!"

Arius remembered himself at her age. As a child, he'd had an irrational anxiety about homeless people, and there were many homeless in the nearby metropolitan Toronto. It was based on nothing more than childhood paranoia. Perhaps too much TV news with too little explanation. An imbalance of seeing problems every night at 6:00 p.m., with no solutions.

It was daunting when his parents corralled the family to help serve at the homeless shelter soup kitchen. Arius would recoil from the clients arriving for a hot meal, and his father would tell him to "Move in the direction of your fear."

His problem was solved one day when he looked across a tray of peas and rice to see a child his own age. People are the same, he realized. Everyone needs help. Some people just need different kinds of help.

At the Queen's Park protest, things started to go wrong before Arius even took the stage. The farmers were arriving. A slow-moving caravan of tractors had been making its way from the city's rural outskirts to support the protest, and these farmers had bottlenecked traffic by double-parking their tractors on the surrounding downtown roadways.

By now, thousands of people were chanting, "Make it right! Water is a right!"

The farmers had been asked to move their parked tractors, and they'd refused.

River was confused. "Why do you care anyway, Uncle Ari? Doesn't this just get more people's attention? Isn't that what you're trying to do anyway?" she asked.

"See the police, River?" Arius asked.

She looked around, then nodded.

"Well, the police are here to help us, because this is a legal protest, and we have a right to be here. But we have to hold up our side of the bargain and keep everything under control. As long as we do, then people can have more legal protests, a legal way to express themselves. But when you do things that disrupt other people's lives, like blocking traffic and making it hard for them to get to work or go home, then it's hard to get the police support."

"Don't you always say people are too busy with their own lives to care, Uncle Ari? Maybe they *need* something to shake them up."

Arius smiled. "So today, *R* stands for . . . ?"

"Rise," River replied, without missing a beat.

Before going onstage Arius handed his phone to River. Then he joined in with the chant as he made his way up to the microphone.

"Water is a right?" he shouted.

"Yes!" came the response from the crowd.

"Water is our right?"

"Yes!" the crowd yelled back.

"We're here to tell our government that we're not happy," declared Arius.

"That's right. Go on."

"Selling our water is not right."

"Yeah!"

He noticed three cars in the distance approaching the police cars. They looked like police cars, with sirens on top, but they were a different color. And right behind those three cars were three police vans.

He watched as Senna emerged from the lead vehicle. She engaged with the police officer coordinating the detail for the protest. From a distance, the interaction looked confrontational, but the dialogue ended almost as soon as it started. Senna took her phone out as she got back into her vehicle.

Out of the corner of his eye, he saw River, offstage, answer his phone.

"Our message to the members of Ontario's government . . ." he began, but he was interrupted by River, who had come onstage and was tugging at his sleeve.

He knelt down quickly, and she whispered in his ear. He gently took the phone and glanced to a friend offstage, who returned a knowing nod.

"River. Today, *R* stands for 'Retreat.' Do you understand?" Arius asked with firm resolve.

She nodded disappointedly, and his colleague came onstage, took her hand, and swept her away.

In his head, he heard Senna voice the words that River had relayed in a whisper. "Tell Arius to turn himself in to me, or the riot police will take action."

"The great poet W.H. Auden wrote, 'Thousands have lived without love, not one without water,'" Arius called out to the protesters.

He watched his friend skirt the periphery of the crowd as he whisked River towards Senna's car. The thousands of people gathered for the cause listened intently to his speech. At the same time, the riot police climbed out of the police vans and began to form a semicircle behind the crowd.

"This cause unites us all. The most dangerous thing we can do today is hand over our future to corporate barons. Our future is not for sale."

The crowd was focused on the stage and cheering, but no one was ignoring the fact that, behind them, shields were being raised. Arius slowly brought his phone out of his pocket as he looked out at the children in the audience. He made it look as though he was pausing to check his notes as he tapped out a short text.

Arius sent the one-word message to Senna. "Kids."

A voice came over the loudspeaker announcing that the police had been authorized to disperse the crowd. The word "authorized" lingered in Arius's mind as he looked over to the news trucks recording the entire event.

"Let's remember, we're here in this legal, nonviolent protest to champion our right to have a say in what happens to our waters, which are a public trust."

A two-word text came back to his phone. "Your call."

"This is a public trust! And I trust the public, not private profiteers. Give us back our future!" Arius's voice boomed.

Suddenly there was an uproar as tear gas cylinders landed at the back of the crowd. The riot police opened their line to make way for the crowd to exit. But Arius saw it go wrong from his elevated position on the stage.

◊ ♦ ◊

River was safely behind the riot police, but when the crowd broke through the gap, Senna thought her sister was going to get caught in it. River broke free from Arius's colleague and dashed towards her. Senna saw it happen, and ran to intercept her before she was consumed by the throng. Just as the two were closing in on one another, River tripped.

Arius couldn't see Senna throw herself on top of River as the crowd trampled through. He couldn't see the right side of Senna's face grind into the pavement as legs stomped over her.

When the crowd dispersed, Senna stood up, her face badly bloodied. And River got up, miraculously unscathed. She wrapped both arms around her sister and held her tight for a long moment. With the riot police now standing casually on the perimeter, Senna hobbled towards Arius with two men in River Enforcement uniforms. She shot lasers at him with her eyes for what had almost happened to River. Why had he brought her here in the first place?

The photo that appeared in two of the local papers the next day was taken from the back of the stage and showed Arius's back in the foreground, Senna and the two uniformed men in the center, and the riot police and lingering tear gas smoke in the background.

One paper captioned it "… Public Trust?" The other went with, "Water. Crime."

Senna called to Arius, "Under the authority granted to me by the City, you are under arrest for water crime. You are to come with these two wardens for detainment until your trial for inciting the misuse of water."

||

"You fired tear gas on children," screamed Arius from inside his holding cell.

Senna paused before lashing out.

"After I warned you, Arius. You see what almost happened to River because of you? And, by the way, it was minimal use at the back of the crowd. The kids were mostly in the middle," said Senna dismissively. The cadence of her speech was slower than normal due to the bandages on her face. The effect made her words drip with dramatic effect.

Arius leaned casually against the front of the cell, shaking his head. His arm hung out over the crossbar. Senna stood just as casually, propped up against the wall across from him.

"You've lost your mind, Drama Queen. Arresting someone for what? 'Inciting the misuse of water'? I mean, at first you were just fining people, and that probably sent the right message to the public to think twice. But this? This is going too far," said Arius.

"Abolishing slavery was a fringe idea when it first arrived. So was abolishing apartheid. The most powerful social movements started from the outside before they became normalized. Slavery and segregation may still happen, unfortunately, but at least they can no longer be considered the norm or acceptable," she said.

"Not the same, fool. Mandela fought against a system of oppression. You're *creating* a system of oppression in your effort to outlaw misuse and waste of water," said Arius.

"We're on the same side, you know," she said.

Just then, two hefty wardens came in with a chair each. Arius stood at attention immediately, his eyes bulging out of their sockets.

"Please don't leave me," Arius begged.

"Oh no. I am getting the Hell. Out. Of. Here."

"How strong are these bars?" Arius asked as she walked away.

Footsteps approached as Senna hollered her final instruction to the warden who'd stayed.

"Put those chairs as close to the cell as you can," she said, as she turned the corner out of sight.

He did, and in doing so looked to Arius with a shake of his head and fear in his eyes. The warden moved to the back wall as Arius sat on the bench at the back of his cell, hands clasped and head bowed.

River walked in first, her head down, with Ma right behind her. They both pulled out their chairs and sat quietly.

Ma tapped her finger on her knee for five minutes. The sound and silence were excruciating.

Finally, the bomb went off.

"Boy! You're out of your damn mind bringing this child here for your nonsense!"

With the first word from Ma's mouth, the warden jumped up and scurried away like a surprised cat. With any luck, Arius hoped, he'd gone to get him protection from the police. Arius knew when Ma's Caribbean accent came full tilt, there was no hope for civility.

"I come home and find a blasted note on my table, you're bringing this child. Do I look like a fool to you? Look at me, boy! Look at me when I'm talking to you!" she yelled, banging the cell bars.

"You some star boy now, eh? Aha. Some star boy out to change the world, eh? What change did you make back there? Can't even change your damn briefs in there, you're so stupid."

Ma sucked her teeth. She got up and started to walk away. Then she turned to come back, picked up the chair with one hand, and flung it against the far wall, where it smashed.

She turned to walk out again, flailing her arms and yelling out loud to the air, to herself, to no one and everyone at the same time.

"I guess Ma raised a fool. Aha. That's right. Ma raised some star boy FOOL!"

She turned back to River at the door, with an expectant look.

"Yeah, Uncle Ari! You show the Man what time it is! We won't stand for it!" yelled River as she stood up, banging the bars as hard as Ma.

Arius bowed his head again to hide his smile. If he hadn't, he figured Ma would have broken the cell down with her bare hands just to beat him!

III

"Your trial is in two days. How do you plan to defend your innocent plea? I've shown you the rules. You can see you have no chance," Senna explained to Arius, as he rolled his eyes.

Senna was persistent in her campaign of annoyance to offset Arius's campaign of ignorance. She told him there would be no gray area on the matter in court. The rules she worked from had been publicly sanctioned by the police commissioner and the mayor.

Their debate continued in the temporary holding cells that Toronto Police had lent to River Enforcement as Senna was getting started up. Police headquarters, where the temporary space was housed, was such a short distance to Queen's Park that they could have walked Arius from the arrest to his cell.

"First trials set precedent. I'm entirely ready to argue my case and put your rules to the test. And when I do, it will undermine everything you're doing," said Arius.

"Come on, Arius. Want me to get Ma back?" she asked gleefully.

"Whatever," was the only retort Arius could offer to stave off the embarrassment of the show Ma had put on.

"Where has Ma been staying, anyway?" Senna asked.

"With me at first, with River. Everything was going fine."

And then Senna had landed him in jail. When Ma had eventually cooled down, she'd decided that she and River would head back to her rural home in Georgetown to get some things and spend a couple of days there.

Later that afternoon, Senna told Arius that his trial would be further delayed. He berated her all over again for holding him on a ridiculous charge. The discussion degenerated into an epic shouting match that ended with Senna storming off and Arius trying to storm into the corner of his cell.

What happened the next day was unexpected.

Arius was sitting at the back of the cell when two wardens approached. They opened his cell door and Senna walked in.

Senna grabbed Arius by the hand and tried to pull him out of the cell.

"A police escort will ride alongside. And I have a driver ready for us," she said.

Arius was still sitting. "What are you talking about?" he asked.

Senna's eyes were full of tears. "There's been a water contamination issue in Georgetown. The hospital is slammed, so people are getting taken to the next town and even farther. There have been reports of a fatality from drinking the water," she said.

They ran out of Senna's station and through Toronto Police headquarters to the parking lot, where their convoy was fueled and ready. Arius and Senna jumped in the back seat of the assigned car and the outriders immediately turned on their sirens.

Senna got on the phone, trying to piece together what had happened. She got on the line with municipal officials, emergency workers, operations staff from the water utility, and hospital administration.

The outrider sirens blared as Arius looked through the window while their car blazed past one vehicle after another on the Gardiner Expressway. It was normally a forty-five-minute drive to Georgetown. The convoy continued off the Gardiner to another highway, then to yet another. The buildings flashed by in a blink, as though they were moving at warp speed on the ground. As the minutes passed, the scene outside the car window shifted from urban to industrial buildings.

The only thing that took up enough space to last longer than a blink was the airport. The clearest view was to Toronto Pearson's main terminal, which was like an island of transparency. Even from afar, it was evident how much natural light poured into the exposed steel structure.

Once they passed the airport, the world outside the car began to fade to nature. A few final billboards lingered, giving way to some sparsely placed warehouses, and then there wasn't much more than grass to be seen as they transitioned into rural surroundings and local roads.

With every minute that passed Senna looked more anxious. Arius looked to her with a curious upward nod, asking her what was going on. She could barely speak, but she solemnly explained what had happened.

It turned out that the water-taking from the neighboring town had a faulty intake. Those intake pipes were meant to work one way, suction only, with safeguards in place to protect against backflow. The fault meant that, rather than simply taking water, the operation had actually leaked flow back into the groundwater. Along with that leakage would come residue from old lead pipes. But something far worse had happened.

Senna closed her eyes and sighed gently.

It seemed the additional water-taking activity, combined with the backflow, had disturbed the soil that protected the groundwater source. The voids caused by that disturbance allowed other sources of runoff to enter into the community's drinking water. Those other sources . . . runoff from nearby farms that had picked up toxic bacteria from animal waste.

Senna looked as though she might be sick.

Just over twenty-five minutes after leaving police headquarters, they arrived in town. Senna had been trying Ma's line between calls along the way but there was no answer, so she asked the warden to go straight to the hospital.

The outriders pulled in to the ambulance loading bay, where Arius and Senna disembarked. The officers came in with them and, looking around, one of them voiced the question that was at the top of everyone's mind.

"What exactly happened here?"

"I've heard the expression 'as if a tornado passed through.' This is nothing like that," said Senna. "Looks like war descended here."

People of all ages were lying in beds in the hallway and on chairs in the waiting room. Buckets filled with vomit were all over the place, and people had to share since there weren't enough for everyone, which was causing even more sickness.

"This could have been avoided," Senna said stoically.

The officers followed them to an administration desk, where Senna gave Ma's name. She figured wherever she was, River would be there looking after her. The nurses behind the desk gave one another a brief, awkward glance before pointing them down the hall to another nurses' station.

There, they were given a room number a few paces down the hall. The officers hung back for their privacy.

Bolting into the room, they were relieved to find her. Ma was hooked up to an IV, weak but conscious. She was staring distantly out the window while the nurse attended to her.

Ma and the nurse turned to Senna when she stopped by her bed.

It was clear from the heartbroken looks in their eyes.

River had died.

Chapter 36

Toronto, 1 Day to Day Zero

Senna looked out onto the lake from her office, legs kicked up and crossed on her worn wooden desk, as she dialed the Archivist. As the speakerphone rang, she turned to fixate on the one framed photograph resting on the polished surface of the desk. River's cherubic face smiled back at her as the Archivist picked up.

"Yes, Senna," he said, as Senna reached out to pick up the photo.

"Hello?" he said again a moment later.

Senna shook herself into the moment and asked him if there had been any other activity on the site they'd turned up. He said no, and she filled him in on her car chase with Tao.

"With Tao's phone gone, I need certainty that a message will get to him. We know he monitors his site. You think you can get his attention if I feed you a message?"

The Archivist guaranteed it. Senna texted him coordinates for a meet and dictated a message.

"You said I'd never catch you. So meet me. Now. There's a way to save him," said Senna as she swung her feet off the desk.

"Are you sure about your choice of location, Senna?" the Archivist asked.

"I am. And I'm taking off now. If you guarantee he's getting that message, then I guarantee he'll be there before me."

As Senna prepared to leave, she walked up to a frame hanging on the wall that contained two art pieces. On the bottom was the original design for the River Enforcement logo, the blue *R* encircled by an olive branch. Prominently centered on the top was the logo's inspiration, a cutout from one of River's shirts containing a blue *R* inscribed within a circle.

She touched the shirt through the glass and wiped tears from her face. "I won't let what happened to you happen to another innocent," Senna declared as she grabbed her cross-body bag and departed.

The Gardiner Expressway was a freeway running into the city's downtown core, a notable portion of which was elevated. It was an object of both love and hate, appreciated for its ability to funnel vehicles in and out of the urban core and scorned for the fact that it separated the city from its waterfront. Underneath the elevated portion of the expressway could be found linear urban parks and paths constructed by the city, making productive use of the otherwise unused space. But in another portion of the lengthy underpass, in a prominent position near one of the expressway off-ramps, you could find a tent city occupied by the homeless, a community that existed in defiance of the city's opposition.

Senna walked through the encampment. She saw one of the residents graciously accept a tray of croissants from a car that had stopped at the intersection and bring it back to share with everyone as the car drove off on the green light.

Towards the end of the tent city, she saw Tao. Senna approached and sat down beside him.

"You've tucked Arius away, have you?" Tao asked.

"I know there's no safety for him anywhere from you. That's why I want you to get him out," said Senna.

Tao recoiled at the suggestion, then stood up to leave. "I don't want to get in the middle of your ridiculous turf war between Toronto Police and River Enforcement, Senna."

Senna reached out to grab his arm. "That's not what this is," she insisted. "It's not a grudge thing. I don't want that kind of heat on me. But we'll have to keep him covered once he's out."

Tao shook off her arm, but sat back down.

"You want me to protect him . . . when you know I accepted a contract on him? And if, somehow, you could get me or my client to cancel the contract, why wouldn't you just want him released? If he's not in danger from me, who is he in danger from?"

Senna bit her lip. "So. About that. The police think he's responsible for three murders," she said.

Senna explained the backstory with Merchant.

"So, you see, as difficult as it might be for you, it makes more sense to have him escape."

"Difficult for me? Who said—" Tao started.

"Alright, calm down, calm down," Senna interrupted. "I just mean to say, if Arius is released, then Cole might get suspicious. Maybe she thinks someone interfered with the contract. I don't know what she knows. But if he's broken out, she won't know how or who did it."

"What does this have to do with Cole?" asked Tao.

"Everything, Tao. Listen. Cole's efforts to save the settlement are futile. She's grasping at straws. I'm making a play to take over

Axiom Water. Imminently. And when I do, I'll control supply and demand of water. With that kind of power, I can look at the settlement and see what can be done to help them."

Tao stretched out his legs and leaned back on his hands. He bobbed his head as he thought through everything Senna had just put on the table. Cars whizzed by and honked intermittently.

Tao looked Senna in the eyes. "Is Arius still the wild card between Axiom Water and River Enforcement?"

"Just get him out, Tao. I have his knowledge to leverage, but he'll be safe with us. Once I have control of Axiom Water, I drop his 'Most Wanted' status. I'll shred that two-inch-thick file myself. He doesn't need to sacrifice himself to save the world for Cole's futile efforts," Senna promised.

"Is he in on this?" asked Tao.

"He has no idea. When I saw him, though, he did have a message for you," said Senna.

Tao asked with a chin nod.

"'Every man dies. Not every man truly lives.'"

Tao audibly breathed out, and he moved his hand to the back of his neck.

"Let him live. To help," Senna said with finality.

"I'll think on how to get it done," Tao replied.

Senna uncrossed her legs and got up.

"Take all the time you need. As long as he's out tonight," she said, brushing the back of her pants as she walked away.

Chapter 37

Back at the settlement, Senna tidied the small office in the supply warehouse. She'd drawn a curtain over the small double window, and the room had the feeling of a bunker. The low buzz of the fluorescent bulbs was the only sound that accompanied her as she swept some debris on the floor into a corner with her foot. She set a single chair in the correct position across from the desk.

She double-checked that the door leading outside was secure, then leaned back on the inner door that led into the warehouse. She crossed her arms and mentally checked the small room, shaking her head slightly.

Gus had made this his primary working space. A tall, brown, steel filing cabinet was against the wall on one side of the brown, steel desk. On the other side was a low table with a printer, and a small refrigerator. The desk itself had some neatly organized documents, with the file on Arius on top, but no personal effects. The single decorative feature in the office was a large photographic art piece that Gus had hung on the concrete wall across from his desk.

Senna plopped herself down in the desk chair facing the piece. The subject was two monks, wrapped in flowing red robes. One sat comfortably with his legs crossed on a large, flat rock poised in a crystal blue stream. The other stood on another rock, into which was carved sacred writing. Rolling hills of lush greenery framed the lazy stream in the background.

She reached down to her bag and then opened one of the desk drawers to make some final adjustments.

Senna rested her face in her palms with her elbows propped on the desk, peering intently at the monks. She longed to someday have the peace they exuded in the stillness of their meditation.

But today was not that day.

With an abrupt movement, she jerked herself out of contemplation and walked over to the monks. She lifted them gently off the wall, leaving only the exposed concrete, and set them down on the floor facing the wall underneath the covered window. Brushing her hands together to remove the dust, she nodded to herself and exited the office to look for Gus.

In the main area of the warehouse, Gus was working with the only staff member remaining on shift. It was the supply warden, and he was taking direction from Gus as he expertly maneuvered a small forklift. Gus acknowledged Senna's nod, and she went back to the office. She retrieved a bottle of water from the small office fridge, twisted the cap open, and sat behind the desk.

That was the scene the supply warden found when he walked in.

She closed the door behind him and motioned to the guest chair as she handed him the bottle of water.

The supply warden nervously accepted the bottle and, with a look of hesitation, took a swig from it at Senna's prompting. He twisted the cap back and asked how he could be of service.

Senna sat down across from him. "That's what I'd like to speak to you about," she said, as she rested her clasped hands on the desk. He gulped in response.

Senna asked if he knew what had happened in the settlement due to the confusion with the tainted water.

"Yes, ma'am. A lot of people got very, very sick. And I know it's because I got the bottles of bad water mixed up with the clean water. But I can explain . . ."

Senna smiled and patted the air with her right hand. The supply warden sat back, still uneasy but slightly comforted. She clasped her hands again.

"In a way, you did me a big favor without even realizing it."

The supply warden shot her a quizzical look.

"No, really," she went on. "Things have gotten considerably worse over the last couple of days. It's a perfectly miserable situation for Cole to inherit. The thing that's troubling, though, is that the problems started on River Enforcement's watch," she said sternly.

His quizzical expression gave way to grave concern.

"I built this. River Enforcement. And do you know what it is?" Senna asked.

The supply warden's head was bowed down. But he slowly nodded.

"You do know. Reputation. That's what I built. It's why the mayor of my city relies on me. He knows what I've done around the world. He knows I can keep our city safe. Our people," she said.

Then Senna leaned forward, supporting her weight on her arms as if her body were hovering over top of the desk. She asked the supply warden one question.

"Who are we protecting?"

"Our city," he replied.

She got up from the desk and walked over to him where he cowered in his chair. He shivered when she hovered tightly behind him and put her hand on his shoulder.

"That's right. Our city. Our people. Not these people," she said softly. "You did good. But very bad at the same time. The reputation of River Enforcement is paramount. Protecting Toronto is our duty here. For what you've done to jeopardize that, you're fired."

With that, she walked back around the desk and sat down. He slunk low in his chair as the news sank in. Senna watched him as she extracted something from the open desk drawer.

He looked up and saw the gun, he would barely have had a moment to register what was happening. Blood splattered onto the concrete wall where the monks had hung five minutes earlier.

"That type of mistake cannot be tolerated," Senna said convincingly to herself, as she unscrewed the smoking silencer. A single tear fell as she slid the silencer into her bag and returned the weapon to Gus's desk drawer. She dabbed her eyes dry, then, with a nod, she grabbed her bag and scanned the room briefly before leaving the office with the door open behind her.

Senna approached Gus in the empty warehouse.

"Look after the body and make sure the family is taken care of. It's a dangerous job at times, unfortunately. We can't always disclose the details," she said. "I'll be out for the night."

Gus nodded as he walked into the office, and nodded again with a deep sigh as he walked slowly around the supply warden's slumped body. He looked at the blood-splattered wall, then looked around the office until he found his own place of peace. He bent down to pick up the photograph of the monks.

He lifted it in the air to look at it, using it to block his view of the bloody scene in the office. He studied the monks. He eyed their peaceful poise, the serene calm of their surroundings, then focused on the crystal blue stream.

"Where will we get water?" he asked himself quietly.

3 MONTHS EARLIER

Las Vegas, Nevada

I

"Where will we get water?" the casino owner asked plainly, in an elegant Italian accent.

Colors looked up from his phone as the question echoed heavily around the executive boardroom, located high up in the posh Vegas casino resort. Desert sunshine poured through the room, but the looming query cast a dark shadow over the intimate gathering of the casino's senior leaders.

Another message notification vibrated in his hand as he felt an increasing number of eyes turn towards him for answers. His breathing quickened as he studied the last message on his device. He quickly tapped back a short response.

The casino owner spoke from the head of the table again, repeating his question. This time he was looking expectantly at the chief of operations he had come to rely on so heavily over their many years together. The playfully stylish individual set himself apart in the room full of suits. More than that, his insight was well respected.

Colors cleared his throat. He thought over all the things within his control, and what could possibly be done to contend with this problem.

But no words followed.

The other executives shifted awkwardly in their seats as Colors nervously tapped his phone on the table. He set it down to hide the tension that was uncommon to him. He wanted time to think, so he lobbed a question back.

"Remind us exactly what we're contending with here?" he asked, before he focused his mind on the colossal problem.

The tension in the room abated slightly with his engagement, and the casino owner explained the situation to the intimate team of finely dressed executives. He reminded them that over a billion dollars had been spent on providing water in the state of Nevada. The owner spoke about Lake Mead, the largest reservoir in America built by human hands, which provided water for drinking, power, and irrigation. It had been below full capacity for decades due to drought and increased water demand, but it had finally dropped below a critical threshold for power generation.

"And no one saw this coming?" chimed in the chief of security.

Colors cleared his throat again, unable to answer. He and the owner exchanged glances.

The owner told them that the state government had been voicing concerns for years and had ratcheted up alarm about a looming crisis.

Finally, with a begrudging nod, Colors dove into the fray.

"In other words, everyone knew it was coming. The watchers warned, the listeners ignored," he said flatly before bowing his head.

There was no longer any tension. Only silence.

Colors sat up, the sunshine reflecting off his shiny silver butterfly-collar shirt so brightly that the executive across the table from him squinted. Colors picked up his phone again and read out the message he'd received.

"The state has brought on River Enforcement to handle the situation, 'at this perilous juncture.' Senna herself has sent a note to the business community, citing all casinos in particular, insisting that any business that does not have a secondary power supply must wind up operations immediately."

It was as if a cartoon question mark hovered over each executive's head.

"We have backup power, don't we?" inquired the chief of security.

Colors explained that indeed they had backup power, but only for short-term situations. Their casino could not operate off the power grid indefinitely, and every other casino in Las Vegas was in the same boat.

"As chief of operations, I am responsible for this situation," Colors admitted.

"Years of drought isn't your fault," came an encouraging vote of support from the chief of personnel.

The owner lifted a hand as the chief of personnel was about to pipe in again. He reaffirmed that all the casino owners had banded together to refute Senna's absurd edict. The casino owners had collectively concluded that the shortage was fake news, and that business would continue. None of their casinos had moved a single step forward to act on the mandate for closure. Furthermore, he was going to the governor's office with the other casino owners to demand that Senna be kicked out immediately.

The chief of personnel sat back with a slight sneer, content that her question had been answered, but less than satisfied with the response. She stirred in her chair with unease, but her sneer ebbed as she wrapped her head around the situation they all faced. Around the table, the silence and slumped bodies echoed her feelings.

Colors had stopped mentally taking stock of the things in his control. He'd concluded that nothing he could do—in fact, nothing that anyone could do—would solve their problem. But as he took note of his dispirited colleagues, he had to wonder: was their silence acceptance? It couldn't be, if they truly understood what was happening.

"Hypothetically, though," Colors began carefully, "what would it mean if this were *not* fake news?"

The casino owner gulped audibly.

"Vegas would be unemployed," replied the chief of personnel.

"And . . . ?" Colors probed.

The chief of personnel squinted and leaned in slightly. The pause lingered into nothingness. No one was willing to wager against the unthinkable.

Colors couldn't sit anymore. He rose and crossed to the large glass wall that made their boardroom feel like a fishbowl and pressed his palm against it. He turned to face them; his silver shirt blended almost unbearably with the desert sunshine behind him.

"You hear the words 'Day Zero,' and you think of some far-off future in a distant land. Maybe a parched landscape in the far reaches of Asia. Your mind conjures an image of thirsty kids with distended stomachs in a Third World country. Never would you think that America's playground, home to over half a million people, would dry up so that none of the casinos could operate. Instant and almost complete unemployment in an entire city, overnight."

"For argument's sake, let's assume everyone gets very neighborly and helps one another out. They barter, share, and cooperate. But, after the power goes, is there enough water to even grow food? And before long, is there water to drink? In the not-too-distant future, if we all stay . . . we all die."

Later that afternoon, all of them in that room, along with everyone employed by the casino, received a message from the casino owner with the subject line "Day Zero."

"With great regret, I must notify you that, effective immediately, our operation is permanently closed. I pray that you and your families find safe haven."

II

Sweat was pouring down Colors' face as he walked through the front door. Without the air conditioning running, his modest suburban dwelling offered little reprieve from the sweltering heat of the Mojave Desert. He tugged at the purple cotton polo shirt that was sticking to his back as he rounded the corner to see his wife and young daughter trying to sleep on the couch in front of a small portable fan.

Ten weeks earlier the casinos had all closed, and he had not had a paycheck since then.

He nudged his wife gently. She opened sleepy eyes and smiled as she saw him standing over them. Colors held up the bunch of spinach that their neighbor had generously given them in exchange for a few hours of babysitting. He motioned to the kitchen as he held up the prized possession, and she carefully squeezed herself out from beside their daughter. She shook out her brunette locks as she got up to join him.

They held hands as they walked together through the spacious dining room, where their daughter's summer break activities and puzzles were strewn over the table. The next room was an expansive kitchen leading to the backyard. Four red-cushioned barstools were parked at a long granite island, and beyond that was a hefty stainless-steel range, a broad preparation counter with an oversized sink, and a restaurant-grade refrigerator. An open photo album lay slightly askew on the island.

As they entered the kitchen, his wife unlocked and opened the back doors wide, now that he was home, to let any breeze in. Lately, many of their neighbors had just packed up and left. Home looting was a real concern as people ran out of options.

Colors opened the fridge door and peered inside. Once abundantly stocked with organic meat, vegetables, and fruit, the fridge now contained three items: a small stick of butter, a few garlic cloves, and milk. Colors put half the spinach in and took out the butter and a clove of garlic. As he closed the door, pictures of his family stared back at him. He caught a glimpse of one taken only six months earlier, and he barely recognized himself with his then-robust physique.

His wife put a pan on the range, set out a couple of small plates, and spray washed the other half of the spinach before settling onto one of the barstools. Colors turned on the gas range and, as the pan heated up, quickly patted the spinach dry in a clean dish towel. The butter melted in the pan and he sautéed the garlic before adding the spinach for a few minutes. His wife watched him cook for a while, then bowed her head and massaged the back of her neck with both hands.

As only children with no surviving parents, they were each other's family. Their closest friends had lived in Vegas, but they had all walked away from their homes and belongings to return to their original hometowns across the country. And yesterday, he and his wife had reached the same decision.

Colors had explained to his wife that when Senna could not solve the Vegas "Day Zero" the state had brought in Axiom Water as a last-ditch effort. He'd attended a virtual town hall where Cole had explained the last alternative for those who had no options.

"There's a settlement, in Canada," he'd told his wife.

"Canada? But it's always freezing there, right? And there are polar bears?"

"Not all the time. And Toronto is a big city. No polar bears for miles!" he'd explained with a smile. "What Canada does have is about two million lakes."

Colors put the two plates down with a couple of bamboo forks and sat beside his wife. On the long granite island, their table setting looked like two small life rafts in an ocean. She offered him a forced smile as she lifted her head, then picked up the fork to start the only meal they would have for the day.

Colors pushed his plate aside slightly and pulled in the open photo album that had been lying there. It was one that he'd compiled and printed from a vast array of their digital photos as a gift for her birthday. He grinned from ear to ear as the memories washed over him.

The album was open to a photograph of their wedding day: a beautiful garden setting, his wife's even more brilliant glow, and the beaming faces of their parents. He gently touched his mother's face in the photograph.

The next group of photos started with a bare plot of land and documented the construction of their home. First the excavation, then the foundation, walls, and roof. The windows and doors were added as the custom-designed interior went from rough work to elegant finish. He wrinkled his nose at the cheesy photo that capped off the series, showing the two of them in mid-jump in front of their front door.

On the next page, their newborn daughter was in his wife's arms in the hospital. It had been a bittersweet celebration following the deaths, one after another, of their elderly parents. There she was on the baby scale, being measured and weighed. There she was swaddled in baby blankets. He flipped the pages slowly and watched her grow before his eyes. First, she was small enough to fit in a baby carrier as they strolled around. Then, a photo of his wife chasing her at the park. A few pages later was a photo of her first day at school.

Looking over his shoulder, she rubbed a tear from her eye, as Colors rubbed a tear running down her other cheek. He closed the album and turned to her. She closed her eyes and slowly nodded once.

"Fit whatever we can into two suitcases. We'll leave tomorrow," said Colors, with sad resignation, as he watched his wife weep. He put his hand on hers and they cried together.

"As long as we're together . . ." she finally offered.

Chapter 38

Toronto, 1 Day to Day Zero

The breeze from the lake had blown the undeniable stench throughout the settlement. Despite the ongoing cleanup efforts, the fumes continued downwind as if being blown right into the tent occupied by the woman from Silicon Valley. She brought her family out to stretch their legs in hopes that the open air would be kinder.

The toddler walking between her and her partner plugged his nose with his left hand without a word. Silicon Valley's partner did the same, but he smiled as he watched the toddler.

"I don't think he knows it's not supposed to smell like this," he said.

They walked counter-clockwise around their group of tents to see if there was respite anywhere. As they neared the northern perimeter fence they heard and saw construction equipment just beyond it. They approached a man in mustard-colored pants who was watching the activity with his little one.

Silicon Valley struck up a conversation. Colors told her that his wife was resting in the medical tent, so he'd brought his child to watch the big machines. He explained that his family was in cramped quarters in one of the high-rises, and Silicon Valley told him about their tent, and the reason for their walk.

"We're finding the water rationing is pretty brutal" her partner said. "How are you managing?"

"We're lucky, we actually have running water, but the other day, when we were out on a walk, my wife drank from one of the water bottles that just came in. That's when she took ill. If we'd just stuck with the water in our unit . . ." Colors wiped his eyes, then gathered himself. "You know, you wouldn't believe it, but I was once a powerful man. Water is going to strip everything from me."

One of the construction workers, who'd overheard a part of their conversation, came over to talk to them.

"Don't worry. Your problem should be fixed soon. When we finish our work later today you'll have water in the tent area," the worker said. "I don't think you can see it from where you're standing, but there's an old iron watermain down there in that trench where the excavator is. We're tapping into it. City says there's enough pressure for you now, so we're going to pull some lines off it to give you water."

"How can you do that if the water is still running into the buildings on the settlement?" Colors asked. The worker explained that they could "live tap" it while the water was flowing.

"So you can relax a little. With us on the job, you won't have to worry that the bottled water will run out tomorrow," said the worker, tapping his yellow hard hat and walking back to join the crew in the trench.

As he left, the drills and machinery ramped up again, so he couldn't hear them calling after him. They watched him disappear down a ladder.

◊ ◆ ◊

About twenty feet away, farther down the fence line, the site foreman was yelling over the noise, through the fence, to keep Cole up to date on his crew's progress. Steele watched them talk, entranced by Cole's face. He watched her put her hand to her heart, to thank the foreman for coming and working so quickly under emergency conditions. The foreman doffed his white hard hat and went back to work.

Gus was there too, but he had turned away to take a call. As he put his phone in his pocket and walked back towards the tents, Cole followed behind with Steele, who was moving at a surprisingly snail-like pace.

"Want to speed it up a bit, Grandma?" said Cole.

Steele smiled as he eyed the gap between them and Gus.

"Never told you how I lost my father," said Steele, just loud enough for her to hear.

Cole's expression became stony, but Steele persisted.

"He got very sick, very suddenly. I was overseas when I got the word. Didn't have enough time to get home to see him."

Cole stared straight ahead and said nothing.

"I've seen death in many forms. And from it all I've come to realize this: death is hardest on the living. Missing his last days stands out, head and shoulders, above all my other regrets," said Steele.

They walked past the cleanup operation in the rest area and then beyond it, as the construction noise faded off in the distance. A long moment passed before Cole acknowledged his unasked-for history.

"From your tone, I'm guessing you have warm memories to comfort you. No?" she asked, looking him straight in the eye.

"It helps. Despite the regret, what comforts me is how we lived," Steele said.

"Sorry about your dad," Cole calmly offered. "Was he a cold-blooded criminal?"

Now Steele stared blankly forward.

"Then mind your damn business and shut your mouth," Cole said sharply.

She hadn't noticed that Gus had stopped abruptly and turned to face her, and she nearly bumped into him.

"This may not be news to you, but I wanted to let you know, to be sure," Gus said to Cole. "Arius has been arrested."

Steele caught what Gus missed: her micro-expression, the smallest flash of a smirk.

"River Enforcement brought him in?" asked Cole.

"The police have arrested him," replied Gus.

"For what?!" Her genuine surprise at this detail was obvious.

"I'm told he's been brought in for murder. Three counts, including the two linked to the settlement."

"That can't be right!" Cole yelled.

Gus raised both his hands in the air. "Hey! Don't shoot the messenger."

Steele took a half-step back and longed for the comfort of enemy fire in hostile territory. It would be better than this bloody awkward situation, he thought.

"Look, I understand that you're concerned. But far as I can tell, he was a loose cannon. River Enforcement would've had him before too long anyway. And that brings me to something I want to talk to you about. Privately?" Gus politely suggested.

Cole politely declined with her eyes.

At that moment, an ear-popping boom cracked through the settlement.

Chapter 39

"Everyone settled in?" Jone asked.

"My guy Gus has them all settled and snug," Senna replied. "Only one piece of the puzzle is missing. Soon we'll be celebrating the marriage of Axiom Water and River Enforcement, thanks to you."

"Thanks to *you*," said Jone, nodding to Senna.

The two walked together north along the winding path known as Philosopher's Walk towards Bloor Street. The path had for generations been a favorite of students at the nearby University of Toronto, since it offered a bit of green and serenity for contemplation in the middle of the urban jungle.

"I thought this was a great spot when we used to study here. It's nice to come back now that we're all grown up," Jone said pensively.

"All grown up?" Senna said, with one eyebrow raised. "I don't know about *that*."

The path led them to the Royal Conservatory of Music, with its chic glass extension wrapping around the original, historic Victorian building.

"I don't need to know what exactly is about to happen," said

Jone. "Better for me not to know, actually. But do you think Tao can pull it off?"

"If anyone can, it's him. He told me he considered six possible options. Six. The one he chose is the one he thinks is the most fitting," she explained.

Senna wouldn't have shared the details even if Jone had asked her to. How could she possibly explain that Tao had told her that his options had originally been designed for terminating Arius? Three were scenarios to terminate him inside the Toronto Police headquarters jail cell. Two would have done the job as Arius was being transferred to prison in Kingston, and the last would have taken care of it right inside Kingston's high-security penitentiary.

They had now passed through a gate, designated by two stone pillars topped with wrought-iron lamps, and emerged onto bustling Bloor Street.

"Where's your guy meeting me?" Senna asked.

"Right here, at the Crystal," replied Jone. To their right was the Royal Ontario Museum, with its imposing modern crystal façade that jutted out to dominate the streetscape.

As if on cue, a white van slowly passed in front of them and came to a stop.

"You're in good hands," Jone told Senna, and she gave her a pat on the back as Senna climbed into the vehicle.

The driver was a strapping, clean-cut man. He was in his early thirties, Senna guessed, as they made small talk en route to their destination. A few minutes later they were passing Toronto Police headquarters, going eastbound. The driver made a short stop on a side street to allow Senna to pull on overalls and a hat in the back of the van.

As he turned the van around to go westbound, he reminded Senna where the cameras were located. They passed the police headquarters again, and the driver rounded a corner and found the underground entrance to the residential building beside it. He parked in a spot designated for maintenance vehicles and propped the appropriate sign up on the dashboard.

"Showtime," said the driver, as they got out of the vehicle and grabbed two bags of equipment from the back.

The driver buzzed them through the card-access-only areas and they got onto the elevator. It ascended to the lobby, where two people got on. Senna managed a quick glance at her partner as the couple argued about where to go for dinner.

When they got to their own floor, Senna and the driver got off the elevator and carried their bags down the hallway. The old maintenance room Tao had flagged was so unused that they passed the door twice before they even noticed it.

The driver picked the lock, and once they were in, Senna oriented herself quickly and found the designated spot. She looked at her watch: they had less than two hours to get the job done.

An hour and a half later, all the necessary bricks had been removed, leaving only the panes of glass from a bricked-up window. Senna and her associate dusted themselves off and made sure the room was ready. He handed her the key card and stowed his overalls into one of the bags. She thanked him before he made his way out.

He got on the elevator where the same couple was on their way back down. Engrossed in their ongoing debate about what to get for dinner they barely noticed him get on. He let them off and followed them out on the ground floor, waving to the building security on his way out.

Back in the old maintenance room, Senna was sitting, staring at her phone. She looked around the room at the defunct equipment that had been left to gather dust. She shook her phone nervously and at last gave in to her anxiety. She dialed his number.

"A bit busy now," said Tao as he shuffled on his end of the call.

"You're sure about this?" Senna asked.

"Exciting times, girl! Not every day you get to take on an entire protective police detail. Relax. I've been in the building before," Tao replied coolly.

"Great. That helps a lot," Senna said sarcastically. She shook her hands vigorously to help calm her nerves. "How long ago, anyway?"

"Ten years. An inter-agency training assignment with their tactical unit. They're top-tier, and I'd rather not deal with fully geared tactical officers, so can we chitchat later?"

Senna stopped shaking her hands and closed her eyes.

"Alright. Alright." She took a deep breath. "I'm secure and waiting here. Waiting for your ready," Senna said, and she looked at her watch before hanging up.

Chapter 40

The glass-block and pink granite cubes of the Toronto Police headquarters stepped back as the twelve-story structure rose from College Street. Sandwiched in the heart of the city, its multiple tiered roofs were lower than many of its surrounding buildings. It was one of the features Tao liked most about it: he knew there would be no snipers there.

The schematics Tao had pillaged showed no internal connection from the police headquarters to its neighboring buildings. It was, however, connected to several buildings by external walls. One of those was the residential tower where Senna waited, which met the police building at the highest roof level.

Inside headquarters, at the top of the elevator shaft where the pulleys were, Tao typed diligently on one of the two laptops he carried with him. One laptop was showing live closed-circuit camera footage inside the elevators, and the other intruded on the police communications and electronics. Tao wore a visor that could toggle between night vision and infrared, but for the moment it was just perched on top of his head.

He synchronized the communicator in his and Senna's ears to eavesdrop on the comm frequency the police were using. He switched channels for a moment to let Senna know he'd located Merchant, waiting by the armored vehicle with the tactical officers. He switched back to hear that two officers had now gone to retrieve Arius from his cell on the lower floor.

"Prisoner on the move," came the first message from the lower level.

"Awaiting your arrival in the secure parking garage," said Merchant.

"Copy that. Stand by," was the response. Tao captured that response with his digital recorder and prepared it for replay.

His monitor showed Arius entering one of the three elevators with two officers. The doors closed, and Tao turned on the radio jammer in the elevator. Then he released a flash grenade hidden in the elevator ceiling, along with a small canister filled with knockout gas.

"Contact!" yelled the officer in the elevator, signaling a problem, but the message went unheard. A few seconds later, all three men in the elevator were unconscious. The knockout gas would last only ten or fifteen minutes, and Tao hoped to be long gone by then. He sent the elevator to the very top, just below where he was nested, while maintaining all the elevator indicators in the building as if it hadn't moved.

The elevator arrived, but he wanted to wait for . . .

"Getting old here, officers," came the message from Merchant.

Tao hit the playback. "Copy that. Stand by," said the recorded message.

Tao's body, tethered to the elevator pulleys, launched out over the elevator as he left his nest. He opened the elevator's top hatch and let himself down slowly. Once he reached Arius, he wrapped his arms around him. With a tug on the retractor, the cable pulled them both back up and out, and he closed the hatch behind him. He lifted Arius off the top of the elevator into his nest, climbed up, and released the tether. He sent the elevator back down to where it had started.

Now Merchant's voice came over the comm again.

"Situation report?" Merchant asked.

Tao quickly closed down the laptops and packed up. He rolled Arius in a black blanket and put a black mask over his head. Then he threw his gear over his body and picked Arius up in a fireman's carry.

"Officer Garcia. What's your wife's name again?" Merchant asked, seeking an authentic response.

Merchant knew something had gone awry. The police comm channel exploded with activity as he called for updates and for backup to be sent to confirm where the officers were with their charge. Tao listened as he moved from the main elevator shaft to get to the freight elevator shaft, which went to the highest part of the roof. He'd locked the indicator on the freight elevator before shutting down his laptop, but he had to physically cross through a door from the maintenance area into a hallway to get there.

He popped down his visor and turned on the infrared setting. The clock was ticking, and it wouldn't be long before they locked the whole building down. Two officers were standing in the hall talking. Waiting was burning at Tao, and the dead weight slung over his shoulder was wearing him down.

Damn you and your fried food, Arius. Ever do any cardio? Tao thought.

As the comm channel activity increased, the two officers in the hall checked their radios and moved away from Tao's location. He waited anxiously as they rounded the far corner down the hall.

Lifting the visor, he quickly went through the maintenance door and hit the button for the freight elevator. The doors opened and he backed in.

He switched his comm to speak directly to Senna again before hitting the button to go up.

"Coming up. Confirm infrared signatures on the roof?"

She used her visor to look through the dusty old window panes.

"Negative," came her reply a moment later.

Tao hit the button and came out on the roof. "Make ready for breach," he said.

Senna readied for impact on one side as Tao approached with Arius.

All the windows at the part of the residential building where it met the police roof were false on the outside. But Tao had found one that had been bricked up inside, in the old maintenance room.

"Breach," said Tao.

The sharpened object she used was similar to that used by firefighters when breaking a car window. It was quiet but effective in shattering glass. She did this quickly for four panes and Tao squeezed through with Arius.

Less than five minutes later, Arius started shuffling in the back of the white van as they drove down Bay Street. He stretched and scratched his head as he pulled the mask off.

"Anything happen while I was asleep?" he said with an irritable yawn.

Senna patted his back. "We've got work to do, sleepyhead."

Chapter 41

Cole ran back in the direction of the explosion. She saw a geyser of water appear, then abate, as she got closer to the construction site. A crowd of wigrants gathered inside the fence watched as yellow hard hats scrambled to get out of the open trench.

She waved furiously to get someone's attention. A soaked construction worker came over quickly to tell her that the old iron watermain had ruptured. He told her it had corroded so badly that it burst when they tried to tap into it. The water to the settlement was now turned off completely.

"No, no," Cole said quietly to herself as the construction worker looked back to the trench.

Gasps ran through the crowd as a limp body was pulled from the trench. A harness had been secured to the worker and his colleagues played tug-of-war against the weight of their fallen brother until he was safely on the ground. One of them checked his pulse and nodded his head vigorously with hope.

The worker told Cole, "There's still one more down there! We didn't get a harness on him, and the trench is filling with water," and he hurried back to help the recovery effort.

Staff from the medical tent came running to attend to the unconscious man, as the workers peered anxiously into the trench.

Steele climbed the eight-foot chain-link fence, maneuvered himself nimbly over the top, and jumped down. He pushed his way through and found the foreman, and almost immediately after, Steele was making his way down the ladder into the trench. Some of the construction crew yelled at him to stop while others told him where to search. The foreman yelled something to one of his guys on the other side and pushed the rest of his crew back so he could watch Steele.

Minutes went by, and then Cole breathed a sigh of relief as she saw Steele come slowly back up the ladder with the unconscious construction worker in a fireman's carry. The construction crew cheered him on, and then they helped lift their colleague off his shoulder.

On the other side of the fence, Silicon Valley and Colors had navigated a path through the wigrants, kids in tow, to reach Cole and Gus.

"Does this mean there won't be water for the tents?" they shouted. People near them heard and started calling out their own questions. Silicon Valley tried to silence the crowd so she could hear an answer.

Gus intervened by imposing his towering stature. "Give us a minute, please, ma'am," he said, simply and firmly.

Silicon Valley watched the backs of Gus and Cole as they walked away from her.

Now Gus took the pawn from his pocket and forced it into Cole's hand.

"Look. Things are going downhill fast. We need to talk about this before it's too late. Tell me, how did this end up in Arius's possession?"

Cole pressed her lips together, looked briefly at the familiar object in her hand, turned, and threw it over the fence.

Gus watched the marble pawn sail in the wind, as if by watching it closely he could safely catch it.

"Why do you even care?" shouted Cole.

"I care because I care. What kind of question is that?!" shouted Gus. He peered back to the crowd and calmed his voice. "You're tied to an alleged arsonist with no concern for human life. If I know the truth, I can get you clear of him."

"Oh. So, you're looking out for me? How sweet of you. After spending all these years in the good graces of the one woman hell bent on bringing me down," cried Cole.

"I'm just trying to do right by you," Gus said in exasperation.

"Huh." Cole looked him in the eyes. "Do right by me. Look out for me. Who are *you* to do anything for *me* after you threw me away?!" Cole said defiantly.

Gus's entire body contorted, as if Cole had landed a series of knockout punches.

"Threw you away? How could you say—"

"Kicked me out. Bags packed at the door and sent off without even a goodbye. Not even an explanation!"

"Don't you understand it was for your protection? I couldn't be in touch with you because—"

"Because if the family of the man you murdered found me, I'd be in danger. Yes. I found out, eventually."

Furious, Cole crossed her arms and turned away from him. Her anger was like a bubbling cauldron, and she knew she was dangerously close to falling slave to her emotions.

"If you had let me choose," she went on, "I'd have stood by you, no matter the danger, whatever the outcome. Never, in any circumstance, would I have chosen to leave."

"I could never have allowed that," said Gus quietly.

Cole snapped back to face him. "Just get out of here!"

Gus stared at her, in shock.

"You don't get it, do you," she said. "You let it happen, the day I joined your crew."

Gus's eyes filled with tears. And in that moment, to Cole, the towering figure of authority seemed like just a frail, scared boy, yearning for what he loved, afraid he would never be loved in return.

"I don't care if I ever see you again," she said, dismissing him with a wave of her hand. She turned her back again and wiped her face.

Gus tried to appeal to her head, if not her heart. "You can't do this without me."

Without looking back, Cole just said, "Goodbye, Gus." Gus stood still, waiting, but when she didn't relent, he pushed back through the crowd.

Silicon Valley grabbed his arm and asked her question again. "Will there be water for the tents?"

Gus simply pointed to Cole. "That's the woman in charge of everything now. Talk to her."

Two wardens ran up to Cole, anxious to speak with her.

"We were cleaning the rest area when the water stopped," said the first.

"The bottled water is finished, and it's grim at the medical tent. And there's no water into the buildings," said the second. "What happened?"

"They have to fix the watermain," said Cole. "The water has been turned off."

Steele, still drenched from head to toe, walked up to Cole at the fence.

"Are you okay?" Cole was reluctant to admit, even to herself, how worried she'd been when Steele had disappeared into the trench.

"I'll be fine," he said. "What's going on?"

She looked back at him blankly.

"It's here," Cole solemnly replied. "Day Zero."

Part Three

The River

DAY ZERO

Toronto

Chapter 42

The ocean of billowy clouds was slowly being painted orange by the sunrise. Sounds of drilling and sawing emanated from the construction site as the crew labored on into the morning. They'd had to wait while industrial pumps worked strenuously to get enough water out of the trench, and since then they'd been working through the night. Now the foreman wiped sweat from his brow as he turned off the floodlights that were no longer necessary.

"Red sky in the morning, sailors take warning," said Steele. He and Cole were watching the construction through the fence. Cole took a call, and then hollered to the foreman to keep going as quickly as they could.

"There's a problem on the west side of the settlement," she told Steele, with a tone of weary resignation. "Here we go."

They found themselves in the middle of a standoff between Silicon Valley and a man in mustard-colored pants, whose small child stood lethargically beside him.

The warden who had called Cole stood watching Colors, and Silicon Valley's family watched Colors too, anxiously, from behind their tent flap. Colors held an unopened water bottle gingerly in his hands. The warden gestured to Silicon Valley to tell her story again.

"Like I told the warden, I went for a morning walk with my family, and on our way back, I caught him stealing our water."

The warden apologized for bothering Cole but told her he couldn't reach Gus.

"I'm sorry, but we drank all of ours. I'd buy more if we could," said Colors, clinging tightly to the bottle.

"We all had to pay for our first set of supplies," Silicon Valley reminded him. "After that, you get what you're assigned and that's it. They told us anyone caught stealing would be incarcerated."

"She's right," said Cole. And she said to the warden, "You really have no choice."

Colors handed the bottle back to Silicon Valley, and the warden took his arm to escort him to the security compound at the south end of the settlement, by the lake. But Colors's child stood idly by, her face drawn and her eyes lifeless.

"My wife is sick. Please, try to understand," Colors pleaded. "What will happen to my child?"

The warden looked towards the child, and then to Cole.

"I'm sorry, sir. You understood the consequences," said Cole tentatively.

From behind Cole came the odd sound of footsteps on grass and gravel. She turned to see Senna walking towards them. Her sleek black electric car was parked on the grass behind her, the early-morning sun reflecting dazzlingly off the hood. The car's silent electric propulsion had allowed it to creep up stealthily through the settlement as the scene unfolded.

"Take the kid with him," Senna hollered to Colors's escort.

The warden looked over to Cole, who closed her eyes and nodded reluctantly. Colors's facial expression warmed as he reached out and called to the child. The little girl toddled over, and the warden took them both away.

"This was supposed to be a safe haven, Senna, a refuge . . . not some shantytown resort," said Cole scornfully.

"You're in it now, sweetheart," said Senna. "You threw a Hail Mary pass in Vegas and I caught it for you. Toronto has bought in to our partnership . . . the partnership you agreed to when you took custody of the settlement."

People were now emerging from their tents and listening to the exchange.

"I didn't buy in to a hustle," replied Cole.

"What hustle? You squeezed 250,000 people into a spot for 20,000. Overnight. Wigrant or not, life comes at a cost. Water is the critical path, the most expensive and challenging resource, so River Enforcement stepped up," said Senna.

"Stepped up?" asked Cole quieting her voice. All those eyes looking on made the hairs on the back of her neck stand up. She put her hand on Senna's chest and walked into her, pushing her back so they were several feet farther away from curious ears. "Your Hail Mary catch will let the water-poor die while the water-rich outside that fence survive."

"Get real, Cole. Life costs money. You think anyone can afford this? You know better than anyone else, that bottle of water she's holding over there would cost more than my car in some countries," said Senna.

They turned to brave the blinding glare off her hood. The glimmering sun soaked into the illegal tint on the windscreen that blocked any view inside the vehicle.

"Fine. Maybe not *my* car, but *a* car," said Senna.

"Get off my site," said Cole, pushing past her. She and Steele walked away towards the medical tent.

When Cole and Steele were nearly at Senna's car, the front passenger door opened.

Arius stepped out of the vehicle. He closed the door behind him, took a deep breath, and walked over to stand alongside Senna.

"I think I'll stay," said Senna.

Chapter 43

"**Y**our Robin Hood is here to save the day," said Senna. Arius fidgeted uncomfortably beside her, as if looking for something in his pocket.

Cole turned back to face Senna.

"Come. I want to show you something," Senna told her. She locked arms with Cole. "Arius, you'll keep an eye on Cole's guard dog, won't you?" she asked.

"Sit boy. Stay. Staaay," Senna said, pointing a finger at Steele.

They walked through the tents while Senna explained how she'd been counting down the moments till today.

"It's our big day, sweetheart!" Senna said. "Today, you have a big decision to make."

Cole remained silent.

"Pat yourself on the back," Senna went on. "You tried. Really! Sending people across the country with hope. Squeezing families into decrepit conditions. Fire, water bombers, water smugglers. What a ride! Look, you gave them the gift of time. A few more days with their families." Her voice dropped to a whisper. "But it's time to let them go. The reality is, there's always a price to be paid. For the world to survive, the price is steep."

They passed the warehouse that was functioning as a hostel. Two wardens had another middle-aged man in handcuffs there, as Colors looked on with his daughter.

"Do you think Gus would like to join us?" Senna taunted.

At that, Cole struggled out of her awkward arm lock.

"Gus is good at what he does, you know. Even if you don't agree with him," offered Senna, as Cole looked away. "And for the miracle you're about to fail at, I thought you'd want all the help you could get. Let me show you what you're up against."

"I'm not up against anything but you," retorted Cole.

"Think again," said Senna.

They neared the security compound where Colors and his daughter had just been taken. Senna explained that the security compound had been tiny when the settlement was established. But within days they'd realized they would need all the space they could afford. There was an outdoor area where the families of those incarcerated could visit them under supervision. The prisoners themselves were confined to tents and guarded by armed wardens.

In the visiting area, a man was speaking to his wife, and clinging to her in an embrace. Their two children were with them, and the older child, probably seven or eight years old, wept softly and gently wiped tears from his face.

"Bet you thought all the applicants were screened," Senna said to Cole.

"For what, an inability to express emotion?" Cole shot back, her sense of frustration mounting.

Senna rolled her eyes and asked the warden for background on the people they were watching.

"Evidently they have family money," the warden explained. "The husband's family manufactures automotive parts, but the husband himself is not involved. I don't think these two actually do much of anything themselves. No pressure in life, no backbone. Coming up with money to get here was easy, but apparently they don't have access to it here, and they didn't come prepared. Living in such a trying situation is a drastic change. And the husband is taking it very hard."

"So they're idiots," said Senna.

Cole couldn't hide her disdain for Senna's remark. "They've hit a hard time for the first time in their adult lives. And they're having difficulty making the adjustment," said Cole.

The husband embraced his wife again, and they separated. The wife was escorted back to the security tent. The husband, carrying their younger boy and holding the hand of the older son, walked away from the visiting area. When he saw Senna, he approached and began to plead with her to release his wife for stealing someone else's water ration. He put his young child down and dropped to his knees, begging for her help.

"Please, Senna. My children need their mother. I'm helpless without her." He grabbed at Senna's leg, and the nearby wardens on duty intervened. Three large men were on him almost instantly.

"Don't touch her," said one of the wardens, as he picked the man up and threw him aside like a rag doll. Then they held him down like a violent criminal.

Others in the visiting area saw the abusive treatment and started shouting their objections.

"Stand down," Senna calmly directed the wardens.

Two of the wardens got off him immediately, and the third slowly released his grip on the man.

"Let him be, let him be," Senna continued. She met Cole's

gaze and the two of them turned to continue their walk through the settlement.

Cole turned to back to see the children clinging to the man and tending to him as onlookers consoled him. Cole thought it must have been a meteoric fall for that family, and possibly for everyone in this settlement who'd gone from riches to rags. She sympathized with the poor soul.

"This is why the world needs us. People are weak and can't be trusted to look after themselves," Senna stated bluntly.

Chapter 44

"What's his name, anyway, your security guy?" Senna asked as they made their way back to her car.

"Steele," replied Cole.

Senna offered a blank stare.

"Stop," said Cole.

Senna shrugged, with just a hint of a smile.

"What do you want from me?" Cole asked.

"Everything," replied Senna.

"My company," said Cole.

Senna nodded slyly. "With your cooperation."

Cole looked at Senna with an icy gaze.

They were passing the tent that belonged to Silicon Valley. She was standing outside to watch the power play that was unfolding, her family was tucked securely behind the tent flap.

Cole called out to her. "What was your entry fee?"

Silicon Valley replied with the upfront figure her family had paid to cover the first three months.

Cole ran the numbers in her head. "Hmph. Sounds like a lot more expensive cars in your future, Senna. And what if I don't cooperate?" Senna smiled. "You think you can just walk in off the street and take over my company?"

They had reached Arius and Steele. Senna put her arm on Arius's shoulder. He shuddered slightly but stood his ground.

"Get arrested much? Not quite Robin Hood anymore, eh, Arius?" asked Cole.

Arius felt sick to his stomach looking back at Cole.

"I guess no one should get upset if they're framed for murder then, yeah?" he said.

"And I guess trusting you was a better choice? Because that seems to have worked out *so well* for me," replied Cole, archly.

"Steele, what do you think about this predicament that Senna's cooked up for me?" Cole asked. "Do I bow to her ultimatum?"

Steele thought for a moment. "If you cooperate, and she takes over Axiom Water, you lose any chance you had of saving the settlement. But then, if you don't, she just leverages the information she gets from her confidant here and she throws you in jail. Does that sound about right?"

"Which one takes longer?" Cole asked him.

He nodded his answer, and she smiled in agreement.

Cole turned back to Senna. "Yeah. I'll stick with 'get off my site' for today, Senna," she said, with a beaming smile.

Senna just waved off the drama and walked back to her car, stopping only to admire it for a moment.

"Whatever. Arius, let's go," she yelled back. She gave a two-finger wave from the forehead as she got in the driver's side. "I'll be in touch real soon, Cole."

Arius made his way to the car, and collapsed into the passenger seat.

◊ ◆ ◊

As Senna drove off, she put her company phone on speaker and called her personal cell, which she'd lent to Tao.

Arius listened as she told Tao, with a light and airy tone, how the situation had played out.

"It went even better than I'd hoped," she said.

"Good to know," Tao replied. "I did my part and delivered that dossier I put together to Merchant."

"Okay. Sit tight. I'm bringing Arius. That dossier is sufficient to clear his name based on his whereabouts and activities?" she asked.

"Exactly what was needed. I'm monitoring the police response to the information. And don't worry. I'll harbor the fugitive. Bring him to me and we'll go underground."

Senna hung up and reassured Arius that he'd soon be exonerated.

Back at the settlement, in the medical tent, Colors's wife was having a violent seizure. Cole froze when she saw the medical staff race into action. Then everything fell quiet.

For a moment, everyone stopped breathing. But the woman in the makeshift hospital bed had stopped breathing forever.

One of the medics approached Cole. "There was nothing more we could do. After the poisoning and the dehydration, she was just too weak to make it."

Not another moment passed before the technicians started preparing her body to move.

"So quickly?" asked Cole, as the bed was being wiped down and medical supplies were refreshed.

"We lost fifteen overnight. Mostly seniors. This was the youngest. There's a huge backlog so we turn the beds over immediately," offered one of the technicians matter-of-factly.

"Usually Gus notifies the next of kin."

"Her husband is incarcerated in the holding tents," one of the wardens explained. "And the daughter of the deceased needs the bed right now!" he demanded frantically.

Cole's eyes grew wide as another warden ran in carrying Colors's unconscious daughter in his arms. The little girl's skin was pasty and gray. They explained that she'd passed out just after she and her father were confined to the security tents.

The child was given the bed, and a medical attendant checked her vitals, hovering over her with her instruments and listening intently with a stethoscope.

"She's very weak. I don't think she'll survive the night," said the medic.

Cole shouted an instruction, and one of the wardens ran over to the security tents to get Colors.

At police headquarters. Merchant was in his office reviewing a dossier seemingly provided by an inside source at River Enforcement. One of his uniformed constables was hovering at the door, and Merchant beckoned for him to enter.

Merchant handed him the file.

The constable expertly flipped through the dossier, his eyebrows rising higher as he scanned each passage and page. He stopped and studied the last page of the dossier intently.

"Senna?" the constable inquired.

Merchant nodded slowly.

"Do you want me to dig into this further?"

Merchant took the dossier back and thought for a long moment.

"No. I'd want more than this to move on."

Chapter 45

Cole sat across from the faces of her five board members on the video screen at River Enforcement's office in the R.C. Harris Water Treatment Plant. Steele paced along the boardroom's smoked-glass partition wall. Curious River Enforcement staff trying to look in were sent scurrying away by Steele.

"We're seeing you face to face this afternoon. Why did you need us all so urgently?" asked Jone.

"Because I need to buy some time," replied Cole. She subtly bit the inside of her bottom lip as the board members sat silent. "I'm asking you to approve an expenditure that goes beyond my authority. And I need it now."

Their mouths dropped open when she disclosed the dollar amount and described what it was for.

A board member named Allan spoke up next. "To be clear, you've opted to involve us in a humanitarian mission. You know where we stand on such matters, and I don't know how this expenditure helps in the long term."

"You've been very clear in the past that we're running a business, Allan. I'm asking you to park your concerns and trust me on this one," Cole replied.

Allan asked Cole to hold, and her screen went dark while the board talked privately. Cole was sitting with her hands clasped on the desk when the screen came alive again a couple of minutes later.

"We've discussed it, and we're worried that parking our concerns now means parking them forever," Jone began, in a disgruntled tone. "But the situation in Las Vegas was regrettable. If Axiom Water can make things better here, it would be excellent publicity that could lead to a break for us into the Canadian market."

Just then Senna burst into the boardroom. Cole's eyes met Steele's for just a moment. He gave the slightest shake of his head. Cole relaxed in her seat.

"Hello," said Jone, in an upbeat tone.

Cole and Steele exchanged glances again.

"Good day. Nice to see you all again," said Senna, "and I hope Axiom Water will stay awhile. I'm sure our work together can set a template for future partnership."

Cole barely held back a scornful sneer.

"We've heard what's happening from Cole. Is there anything further you'd like to share with us?" Jone asked.

"Oh. Cole's the expert here. I've handed over operational control to her, so I know we're in good hands. Today will be very telling, I'm sure," said Senna, with a twinkle in her eye.

◊ ◆ ◊

On behalf of Axiom Water's board, Cole ordered lunch. For a quarter million people.

Food trucks peppered the settlement, and there were lineups everywhere that took on serpentine shapes. Cole and Steele were on site supervising the food service. Everyone seemed to be getting what they needed in an orderly manner, until an argument started brewing between two men at the front of the gourmet taco truck line.

Steele approached them. "Problem here, gentlemen?"

One of the men was still in line, but the other was hoisting three bags of food and six bottles of water. The men stopped and sized Steele up. He had no uniform other than his air of authority.

The man in the lineup voiced his complaint. "This guy is being greedy. Is there going to be enough water or food left for everybody here? Look at this line! What kind of pig is this?"

"I don't owe him an explanation," said the other man. "I've got three families in my small unit and no running water. They sent me down for all of us." He organized himself and turned to walk away.

"It's getting tense with all these people crammed in here," Steele said to Cole. "But it was a nice end run around River Enforcement's water restriction. For one meal, anyway."

Behind them, the sound of clapping and cheering was building.

"Think that's for you?" Steele quipped.

Cole looked down at her phone and saw the message she wasn't hoping for. She knew who the applause was for.

"It is, actually. Let's go," she said, leading him towards the growing applause. They started pushing through as the crowd grew denser but rather than go into the heart of it, she led them around the periphery to get behind it.

"Did you find it strange that Jone was so warm with Senna?" asked Cole.

"Is that her usual style?" Steele asked.

"You saw her before. She's an icy lady whenever I deal with her."

They found two vehicles parked where a couple of people lingered. As they approached, one of the people looked down to his tablet and acknowledged her.

"You can wait inside the vehicle, Cole. He won't be long," came the instruction.

Steele waited while she got in the car. The mayor returned from his impromptu appearance and slumped in.

"Cole. The calls started coming in almost immediately after you turned down the water in the Liberty Village neighborhood. I certainly hope this is a short-term measure," he said.

"If short-term means years, then yes, Mr. Mayor. For us to service ten times more people than the city thought would be here, we have to appropriate resources from somewhere," said Cole.

"You know, Senna's approach was working just fine from where I sat," said the mayor.

In her head, Cole saw the bodies piling up and regretted her feeling of gratitude that nothing had hit the headlines or made it back to the mayor's office.

"Uh-huh," said Cole.

"You know, I'm the mayor for *every* resident of this city, including the people in Liberty Village. Everyone told me the settlement made sense for these wigrants. Win-win, they said. We're saving the rich people of Las Vegas," said the mayor.

"You mean the good people," interrupted Cole.

"Rich people *are* good people. They spend their money here and keep my economy going. I'm not winning when you're creating the same problem for my city that you're trying to prevent for these wigrants. Rich or not, fix my problem, now. Wait, what are you doing?" asked the mayor as Cole reached across his body.

She slid the window down so he could hear the throng.

"I've fixed your problem," said Cole. She opened the door on her side and got out.

Chapter 46

Cole stormed away from the mayor's car to meet Steele. They were walking back towards the throng of people when a horn honked behind her. She turned to see the mayor's car had pulled up, and his window was down.

"Fixed it, have you, Cole? Just down the road from here, you'll find a hoard of homeless people," said the mayor, combing his hair over with one hand.

"That's my problem because . . . ?" asked Cole.

"Because someone just bought free food for 250,000 people. Think that will attract any attention? When word gets out, you'll find a lot of people knocking on your door. Still want to ask me whose problem it is?" the mayor asked.

Cole turned and walked briskly away. Steele, hesitating, held the mayor's glance for another moment, then turned to follow her.

"That's right, son," the mayor called out to him. "Talk to your boss and tell her to sort out the mess she made." The car drove away.

Steele did a short jog to catch Cole.

". . . the mayor putting this mess on me?" he heard her say. Apparently, she'd started a conversation without him. "And Senna sitting high and mighty."

She slowed her pace, calmed her breathing, and eventually stopped. Her reprieve from the misery of days gone by was proving to be short-lived. Wardens handling crowd control were getting yelled at by the wigrants in the long lines. People were trying to hoard water bottles to bring back to their dwellings, and skirmishes were breaking out all around.

"Senna was right about one thing. We can't manage this on our own," Cole said, without looking at him.

"I'll find him," Steele said confidently. His reassurance was a surprise moment of reprieve for her.

Steele approached a warden who was getting yelled at and put a hand in the wigrant's face. Steele identified Cole and asked the appreciative warden if he could track down Gus. The warden happily called in the inquiry and waited a minute for a response. He asked again. A moment later a response came back.

"Apparently he's looking after some guests?" the warden told Steele.

"Thanks." Steele began to walk away, but then he put his hand on Cole's shoulder. "Wait," he said.

He casually walked back to the warden. "I hate it when my boss does that to me," he said.

"What's that?" replied the warden.

"Leaves me all the heavy lifting while he goes gallivanting somewhere. Nice gig," said Steele, as if wearing a River Enforcement uniform himself.

"Tell me about it. Wish *I* could take the priority guests to their fancy hotel," the warden said in a friendly tone.

"Yeah. Good luck, brother," Steele said, offering the warden a fist bump.

Steele shared the story with Cole as they made their way to the eastern perimeter.

"Priority guests?" Cole asked. "News to me."

They avoided the rest area, where the smell still lingered. Unused janitorial supplies lay around the perimeter, waiting for water to return, and, with no other choice, people bravely lined up to continue using the facilities.

As they neared the security compound, Cole prompted Steele to reprise his role as the authority figure.

"It's going to be a two-person act this time," Steele said.

He instructed her to pull out her phone and stare at it. As she did, he surveyed the wardens manning the security compound and selected his victim. Then he directed her to look flustered.

"Exactly how, now?" asked Cole.

"Just look at your phone and think about your father," directed Steele, getting into character. He dispatched himself to speak to his new warden friend, whose name he picked up from his badge as he approached.

"Warden Flores. Forgive me. I'm escorting Cole from Axiom Water over there to an important meeting. She's in an awkward spot because she just realized she's lost her list of priority guests. Help me spare her the embarrassment, will you?" asked Steele.

The warden looked him up and down, then looked over at Cole. One hand was on her head, which she was shaking, and the other was thumbing madly through her phone. He looked back at Steele, who flashed a pair of authoritative puppy dog eyes.

"Look, uh, Mr. . . ." began the warden.

"Steele," he replied.

"I can't give you anything. But I can show it to you. Short list, anyway. Here, take a look," said the warden, displaying a list on his phone.

The fourteen names didn't mean anything to Steele but were easy enough to memorize, especially since they belonged to three families.

"I owe you, brother. Thanks so much," said Steele as he started to walk away. And with one brick removed from the fortress of trust, it was easy to eke out one additional piece of information.

He turned back quickly, as if having forgotten. "Shucks. Are they staying at the Royal York or the Plaza?" asked Steele.

"Royal York. I wish, eh?" said the warden with a chin nod.

"Tell me about it," replied Steele.

He returned to Cole and told her to look relieved. She mouthed "Thank you" to their warden friend, who smiled back sheepishly. They walked away quickly and Steele told her the hotel where they'd find Gus. He'd guessed it would be one of the two "fancy" hotels nearby. It was when he shared the names of the guests that Cole stopped in her tracks. Their full names.

"Do you know who they are?" asked Cole.

"A quarter million people, and three families are treated like royalty. Politicians?" asked Steele.

"Let me tell you the names of my five board members," said Cole.

At the first two names, Steele was silent. After the third name, he took notice. At the fourth name, he went pale. At the fifth name, he was breathless.

"River Enforcement is harboring the families of three of your board members," said Steele.

"Senna has my board in her pocket. She's been baiting a trap for me," said Cole.

Chapter 47

Senna had just received a distressing phone call in her office at R.C. Harris when Gus busted through her door. On his way to speak to her, he'd received a disturbing message from a warden at the settlement that suggested he review the names of Axiom Water's board members.

"You played us both!" Gus shouted.

"Not now," Senna said, as she got up to gather what she needed before leaving.

"Yes. Now!" demanded Gus.

Senna stopped and turned to face him. "Thirty seconds," she said, tapping a foot impatiently.

"We'll take as long as we need to establish how you were playing both me and my daughter. Look, you wanted me on board to encourage my daughter to partner with you. But having me give the luxury treatment to her board members' families just so you can oust her from her company? That's cold and—"

"Stay. Leave. I don't care," yelled Senna. "But nothing's happening till I get back!"

◊ ◆ ◊

Moments later, Senna was safe in her car, and the acceleration of the sleek electric vehicle pushed her back in the driver seat as she rocketed off onto Queen Street, headed westbound. Her phone rang and she put it on speaker to get a status report.

When the call finished, Senna took three deep breaths. She slid her window down and then reached into the glove compartment and took out a blue police-style light. She almost never used it, but when magnetically mounted to the roof of her car it enabled her to travel through traffic seamlessly, like an emergency vehicle. She reached outside to pop the blue light on top of her car and voice-dialed a call. Senna cut off Cole's voice when she picked up.

"I'm sending you an address. Meet me there. Now!" said Senna before hanging up. She called out the instructions for the text message.

On the west side of the downtown core, in Liberty Village, firefighters were desperately battling an apartment fire.

Ten minutes later, Senna and Cole were standing together watching the firefighters make a valiant effort to save an eight-story glass building overlooking a rail line. The street was closed for blocks. The fire was on the sixth floor. Smoke billowed out of the windows and the media trucks were reporting live from the scene.

Liberty Village was named for Liberty Street, the first street convicts would take once freed from Toronto Central Prison. The prison had closed in the early twentieth century, and the area had since become developed and gentrified. Retaining some of its industrial feel, the new glass-skinned towers had sprouted to impose their will on the landscape.

"Did you call me because you think I'm a firefighter?" asked Cole.

"Toronto Fire called *me* because of an unusual problem. The water pressure is drastically low, and they wondered if I knew why it might be happening. And if I could do anything about it," said Senna.

Cole looked at the burning building. "Can't the pumper trucks increase the pressure?"

"Not enough for a fire on the sixth story with the low pressure they have," said Senna.

Senna already knew that, as soon as she'd got operational control, Cole had increased the water pressure so the wigrant settlement could be properly served. That meant the pressure had to decrease elsewhere, and there was a drastic drop in Liberty Village. Senna wanted Cole to admit it, and to see firsthand what she'd done.

"Even if we decided to change it now . . ." said Cole.

"It's already too late," finished Senna.

"You called me here to answer for this," said Cole.

"I called you here to see this. The consequence of your decision," said Senna.

"And what would you have done instead, Senna? You'd have just left the wigrants without water. The same people who've lost everything they own. The people who left their homes and businesses with almost nothing but the clothes on their backs. You'd have just left them to die in a settlement while the city around them thrived?" said Cole.

Senna looked over at the flames. They looked to be diminishing. She took her phone out and pressed some numbers on the keypad.

"That's the number Toronto Fire called me from. You tell them whatever you want to tell them," she said to Cole.

Cole took the phone from Senna as one of the firefighters approached them.

"Senna? Thank you for coming. I'm sorry to bring you out here for nothing. I guess there's nothing we could do," he said.

Senna waited for Cole to jump in with something, anything, but the firefighter just continued in his husky, smoke-ravaged voice.

"We weren't able to do much with the pressure, like we told you, but we got in and doused it from inside with chemicals. The building's fire suppression helped isolate it, and we finished the job. What you're seeing now is just some residual smoke," he continued.

"Thank you very much," Cole finally offered.

The firefighter's expression changed then, and Cole felt a chill of apprehension.

"The suppression system isolated it, but we couldn't knock it down quickly enough with the low pressure. We weren't able to help the occupants. A single mother and her son both died due to smoke inhalation," he said. With his report complete, he looked down, patted his gloves together, and turned to walk back to the truck.

It was the first time either woman noticed the ambulance among the fire trucks. They stood quietly together, staring at it. Senna finally broke the silence.

"There are three million people in Toronto. Are you going to put them all at risk to save 250,000 wigrants?" she asked, not even trying to mask the anger in her voice.

Cole touched Senna's shoulder and looked her in the eyes.

"Arius told me what happened to your sister, Senna. I'm sorry. But this is different. I won't abandon these *refugees*," Cole said emphatically. "I won't let them die because the world turned their back on them. For something entirely out of their control."

"Different?! It's exactly the same, Cole. Sharing water killed my sister. Now, Toronto is on my watch. It's my responsibility to make sure that theft doesn't harm another resident of my city. The blood of those two people you just killed is on my hands too."

Chapter 48

Senna had tried to calm herself with a late lunch at her favorite downtown spot. She exited the market restaurant, walked past the extended indoor patio area by the entrance, and perched herself on a platform that had once been a central fountain of the atrium. Bankers hurried by at their unnecessarily frenzied pace.

She was waiting for Gus.

Light poured down through the glass ceiling held high above by intertwining steel arches. She watched for him to come down the indoor avenue known as "the crystal cathedral of commerce," which connected office towers on either side. The parabolic ceiling arched over a corridor that created the illusion of a tree-lined country road. She was enjoying the closest thing she'd felt to a serene moment when she saw Gus approach, dwarfed by the six stories of open air above him.

"What kind of monkey is this?" said Gus, looking up at a bronze art installation on the fountain.

Senna turned halfway to glance at it, scrunching her nose. "I've always assumed it's a dog," she said.

Gus sat. "I want out," he told her.

"Not so fast there, champ," replied Senna.

"Champ? Am I a six-year-old boy bouncing on your knee now? What happened to, 'Stay. Leave. I don't care'?"

"That's behind us now. I just had the benefit of spending some time with your daughter, and it was a good reminder," said Senna.

Gus looked around uncomfortably at the passing pedestrians. Being belittled was one thing, he thought, but it was another thing to be belittled in public. He consoled himself by considering the imaginary bubble everyone around him was in. Everyone eating at the indoor patio fifty feet from where they sat, everyone walking by—they were in their own world. And he was sitting, invisibly, in this atrium with Senna.

"A reminder of what, exactly?" Gus asked hesitantly.

"Of why I hired you. I wanted your daughter to join forces with me," Senna began.

"You want to destroy her and take control of her company. That's abundantly clear. And I'm supposed to stand by now and help you," interjected Gus.

Senna nodded in agreement. "Be that as it may, you and I were right to team up. You had no hope of getting to your daughter, right? No good is served by you leaving."

Gus felt the blood rush to his face. He let his thoughts go with the passersby, and the rush relented, his breathing became more even.

He was considering what Senna was driving at when something caught his eye. A group of four diners, sitting apart from everyone on the patio, had been having an intense discussion. He could see their faces clearly, but they were too far for Gus to hear their words. What he'd noticed was a change in the expression of the speaker, for just an instant, that showed a shift in the power dynamic of the conversation.

He turned back to Senna. "What good is a deadbeat dad as bait to you? I can take my chances on making amends on my own."

Senna rolled her eyes. "Hmph. Can you now? Okay, here's my apology for what I said earlier. Does your daughter know what happened before you pulled the trigger on that water deal?" she asked.

A diner from the group on the patio stole a glance at this man whose face had just gone pale. A man whose power had just been stripped from him.

"Coming onboard with us was a Hail Mary pass. If you try to leave River Enforcement, or help your daughter in any way, I'll be glad to share the details of your life before she left you," said Senna.

Gus's head was spinning wildly.

"Ha. Did you think I wouldn't have the resources to piece together the history you hid from her? Come now. I would never have brought you on without my own insurance policy. In truth, I'm amazed you were able to hide the rest from her. Maybe I should worry that you're too slick," continued Senna.

Gus steadied himself. With the scrutiny River Enforcement had put him under, in addition to their routine internal monitoring protocols, he felt like a lab rat.

"So, you keep me on the hook. But what am I really doing for you by staying?" asked Gus.

"Give yourself some credit. You've handled the settlement very well," said Senna.

"It's a glorified administrative position. But I do the best I can with what I have," said Gus, playing his cards carefully. He knew Cole wanted nothing to do with him, but he had to figure out a way to get a message to his daughter.

Senna leaned back, her arms propping her up, and looked up to the glass ceiling. She took in a deep breath.

"Nevertheless, what do you want?" she asked, and then let out a long exhalation.

"I understand you're pitching to Axiom Water's board," Gus said.

Senna flinched ever so slightly. "And?" she said.

"And I want to be in the room. If you really respect my handling of the settlement, then bring me into the room, in case any questions arise," offered Gus.

Senna closed her eyes, her head still tilted upward to the ceiling. "Despite the fact that she kicked you off the settlement . . . You're really that desperate just to see your daughter?" she said.

She opened her eyes and leaned forward, then got up abruptly.

"I'll text you the location for dinner. Meet me there, and when we're inside, answer only when I speak to you," said Senna. "Not a word without my permission," she insisted.

And she disappeared into the crystal cathedral of commerce.

Chapter 49

Cole left the sidewalk to cross Yorkville Avenue, walking between a Lamborghini Huracán and what must have been James Bond's Ferrari. She noticed a passerby sneering at the Huracán, likely unimpressed by the cheap quarter-million-dollar hunk of metal polluting the road space in his neighborhood. A Mercedes rolling by barely missed her as she stepped into the street.

"Car should come with a driver's license for all that money," she whispered to herself.

"Didn't know I'd need to help you cross the road," Steele said to Cole as she joined him on the other side. "Anything special I should know about the place we're going?"

"Save me from what's about to come. I despise having to be told by my board to invite Senna."

Steele wished he could. Save her. Care for her.

"Anyway, the place we're going is run by an old friend of mine," continued Cole. "Control the controllables."

"You mean, like, spike someone's drink," Steele offered.

Cole remained stoic, ignoring the comment.

They walked in silence through the intimate urban upscale surroundings. The sign in the window of a women's clothing retailer read "By Appointment Only." The suit displayed in the window of the men's apparel store next door probably cost three months' salary. Steele skirted his eyes past a window displaying fine lingerie, lest his mind wander. And wonder.

On mission, he told himself. *Focus.*

When they entered the Italian trattoria, the host escorted them upstairs. Cole took the lead up the steep staircase as Steele trailed a step behind, making a concerted, gentlemanly effort to lower his gaze from her curvaceous figure.

Client, client, he reminded himself, nearly stumbling forward in disorientation.

They passed another small dining room and a crowded, perched patio that overlooked the casual scramble of Yorkville Avenue. As the door opened to a private room boasting exposed brick walls and rustic chandeliers, the scent of fresh bread wafted towards them from the appetizers set out on the table.

Gus stood behind Senna's chair, as if guarding her. The small room could seat twenty people but, aside from Gus, only six sat at the table set in the middle. Her five board members sat around the table along with Senna. Two servers stood nearby at the ready.

Cole took the empty chair at the head of the table and Steele took up his position standing behind her. While everyone exchanged greetings, Gus passed a small note to Steele during their handshake, and very subtly nodded towards Cole as he did so.

Steele took out his phone, as if to check a message, but used it instead to cover his unfolding of the note. The message was nothing but a single word, and it meant nothing to him. As returned his phone to his pocket he side-eyed Gus, who paid him no mind. He kept the folded note in his hand.

"Shall we get down to business, then?" asked Allan.

"Dinner first," replied Cole. She gave a royal wave to the staff, who got right to work, and moments later, seven fragrant bowls of minestrone soup were served.

When they got to the main course, Allan navigated some of the less daunting items on the agenda to break the silence, which, to that point, had been punctuated only by the clink of utensils on plates.

As the dessert orders were going in, Cole leaned back at Steele's prompt. He discreetly presented Gus's note to her. Cole looked down at the note, squinted slightly, then turned back to the table.

The note said "Nimzowitsch."

Cole knew exactly what that meant. The word denoted her father's favorite chess opening.

Amidst the looming threat to Axiom Water and any chance of saving the wigrants, one word cut through the anxiety and tumult of that moment. Gus was calling to her. He wanted to help.

Cole was transported to that small kitchen table in Bo-Kaap, her father squeezed sideways in the tight space, watching over the game. Watching over her. Fond memories of the Saturday morning chess games rushed back, but her head would not allow the stranger she called her father to find his way back to her heart. She refused to be won over.

The door to the private room opened and the desserts were brought in.

Allan cleared his throat.

"Cole. You may be wondering why we've asked Senna to join us," he began.

Cole dabbed the corners of her mouth with her napkin and sat back quietly, ready for the pending coup.

"I think you've heard our dissatisfaction with your recent moves. Now, we sit at the helm of a humanitarian crisis, our good reputation about to be stained despite our trust in your best efforts. We've been presented with a bold and exciting opportunity by Senna," said Allan, as he looked over to Jone.

Taking her cue, Jone tabled the proposal.

Chapter 50

"It is clear you have failed, Cole. Senna has offered to run Axiom Water to help get us past this dilemma. She has a more aggressive plan to curb water use in the settlement that we feel we can stand behind. She has a long history of experience on the ground here in Toronto, too, and we believe that is a tremendous asset," said Jone.

Cole let Jone's words hang in the air. The decision had been made. But . . . she had to fight.

She questioned the board's concerns. They pointed to the poisoned water supply as being squarely Cole's fault. They talked about the necessity for medical tents aligning with Cole's adoption of the settlement. They even took a page from Senna's book and cast suspicion on her about the fire at the settlement.

The nerve of them, she thought. *Facts be damned.*

She waited for Senna's killing stroke: someone would bring up Day Zero. The final thread that would unravel all of her work.

Through it all, Senna quietly picked at her tiramisu. She savored the treat as much as the barrage taking place before her eyes. She watched the volleys back and forth between the board and Cole like a spectator at a tennis match. Cole alleged that she had no choice but to look for a water source due to limited supply at the settlement. She declared that the poisoned water could not have been anticipated. The board shot back that she was hiding behind excuses. Senna watched and waited. Waited and readied to pull that last thread.

Cole was holding back everything she knew about Jone's family living it up for free while others struggled through life in the settlement. She understood Allan to be a principled man, and she wondered how much he knew.

Finally, having waged a good fight, she relented.

"You're in good hands, then," Cole told them.

Senna choked on her tiramisu, coughed, and tried to regain her composure.

"I will bow to the wisdom of the board on this matter . . . on one condition," said Cole.

The comment floated in the room like a bubble to be popped.

"What's the condition?" Jone finally asked.

"No final vote on the matter till tomorrow," Cole said.

The board members exchanged glances. Senna sat dumbfounded with her fork in midair.

"We accept," Jone said begrudgingly.

Cole got up and left the room without another word. Steele trailed behind her, his eyes lingering regretfully on the untouched plate of mini-zeppole, powdered with cocoa dust, left at her spot. He closed the door behind them and followed her down the stairs into the main dining area. Cole walked towards the open kitchen and stood, as if waiting for something. Steele inserted himself between her and the kitchen.

"What just happened?" he asked, over the clanging of pots in the busy kitchen behind him. He thought she looked oddly composed, given that she'd practically just signed away her company.

She stepped nearer to him. He fidgeted uncomfortably over the sound of his own heartbeat and was about to ask what she was doing.

Cole whispered into his ear. "Steele. I can't trust myself for the next move," she said.

"Move?" he asked uncomfortably. Steele was hopeful but uncertain of what was happening. He knew the bonds of friendship could be forged through stressful experience. Until now, though, there had been no signs that he could see.

As the kitchen noise quieted for a moment, she stepped back slightly.

"The Nimzowitsch defense is a flank opening my father often used to lure me in with when we played chess together. He would let me think my pawns controlled the crucial middle board while he waited, concealed and ready to attack," said Cole.

Steele's eyes widened with a slow nod, despite his sinking heart.

"He's baited Senna?" he asked. He watched Cole's thoughtful nod back. "And you trust that?"

For a long while, all that could be heard was the bustle of the kitchen and the table chatter in the dining room. He watched her.

Something was different.

The cauldron of anger had cooled.

Cole breathed in, for what felt like the first time.

"He had no place in that room. Senna thinks she's playing him, but he's got the upper hand on her," replied Cole. "She's watching him closely. Whatever he does, he's at risk of being caught, and if Senna finds out about his treachery, it will be personal."

For a moment again, Cole was a teenager in the sunlit kitchen at the chessboard with her father.

"Everything he's doing, it's for me," she added.

Steele knew he should be happy. It was what he'd wanted for her all along. But now, in this moment, in this situation, he seriously questioned whether this was in her best interests.

He reached out to touch her arm. But Cole's attention had been caught by a figure emerging from the kitchen. The head chef smiled at her old friend from Paris and inserted herself between the two of them as Steele quickly pulled his arm back. Chef kissed Cole once on each cheek.

"Wonderful to see you here, darling. Everything good?" Chef asked Cole.

"Almost perfect, Chef. There's just one last thing that I need," said Cole, in a hushed tone.

"Whatever you need," said Chef.

Cole pulled a scrap of paper from her bag and grabbed a pen from Chef's apron. She wrote the name "Ruy Lopez" and handed the note to her.

"My father is in that room. No mistaking who he is—just picture my face on a man. It is of the utmost importance that he receives this note without anyone knowing," said Cole.

"Count on me," said Chef.

They hugged, and Cole walked out with Steele on her heels.

Chapter 51

"What's wrong?" Steele asked.

Cole was in the back seat of the car with her head in her hands as they entered the settlement.

"If I don't get this right, that little girl will die tonight," said Cole. In her mind's eye, she saw the pallid face of Colors's daughter, lying amidst a small sea of beds. It was as if she were right in front of Cole's face. She rubbed her face briskly again, trying to shake it off. "Lot on the line with this move."

The noise of the settlement jarred her back to reality as they got out of the car.

"Why are we here again?" asked Steele, trying to relax his shoulders and stay aware.

"Ruy Lopez," said Cole.

"Some Spanish dude you need to see?" asked Steele.

"Not quite. He's a Spanish priest from the sixteenth century. The sequence of moves named for him is a long-game attack on the center pawn. It was the opening I used the first time I beat my father," said Cole.

Steele came to a sudden halt, and Cole stopped too.

"I'm the one who's been trying to convince you to make

amends with your father, I know," he said. "But . . . I don't know if this is right."

She hesitated. Then, "I have to trust my instinct, Steele," she said with finality.

She started walking again and led them into the central part of the settlement.

Gus came into view around a corner, walking ahead of a group.

"This is them?" Cole asked Gus.

Gus nodded and looked behind him at the fourteen people, new arrivals being escorted to the small confines of their tents. In their coded chess exchange, Cole had instructed Gus to turn the advantage in their favor.

They were conspicuously well dressed, in contrast to the haggard wigrants. Some people peeked out of their tents to see their new neighbors. Others closed their tent flaps as they walked by. The faces of the adults were sullen, defeated.

One man in particular was not taking it well. He was the father of the family coming in towards the back of the group. One of the wardens had him by the arm and was forcibly guiding him to his tent as his family followed. Steele recognized the warden named Flores, the same man who'd unwittingly helped him secure the list of "priority guests."

The man being escorted was repeatedly trying to shake off the warden. He kept yelling that this was outrageous, and saying he'd call his sister. Steele shifted his attention from Flores to the captive man. It seemed only minutes ago he'd been looking at a more female version of this face.

"You're dumping these families here? Now?" Steele said quietly to Cole.

She nodded nonchalantly.

"That's why you asked for the time? You wanted to make sure your leverage was out of play." Steele, smiling, was equal parts impressed and disgusted by her maneuvering.

Cole looked to her father.

"The police have been uneasy about Senna ever since she was spotted with a person of interest in the Union Station killing. Seems one person was tied to that death, as well as the two wigrant terminations. A dossier has landed with the police, under the guise of an inside source from River Enforcement. Senna thinks this is information simply exonerating Arius. Indeed, it suggests Senna instructed her wardens to complete the two wigrant terminations."

Gus's eyes widened at the notion.

"Did our guests here try to reach Senna?" Cole asked Gus.

"I was their primary contact so they had no direct line to her. Of course, they reached their sponsors on your board. We couldn't stop that," said Gus.

Cole knew then that Senna would know. Gus was exposed.

Cole picked up on an increase in the chatter coming over the wardens' radios, but the noise wasn't coherent. Warden Flores reached back with one hand to respond, with the other hand remaining on his captive.

Gus's phone began to ring.

"Something's up," said Steele, picking up on the same vibe.

Gus answered. Cole and Steele waited.

Gus listened to the voice on the other end without saying a word.

Warden Flores looked to his fellow wardens, who were also listening in to the dialogue over the radio. He stopped in his tracks and asked for confirmation of the orders coming through. The displeasure of the man he was escorting turned to despondent inquisitiveness. He asked what was happening.

Voices began to rise in the background. Steele stepped towards Cole, stood immediately beside her, and put a hand on her shoulder.

Warden Flores released his hold on the man and huddled together with the other wardens.

Gus ended his call. "Senna has instructed the wardens to return the families to their hotel . . ." he began. Cole had a bad feeling about what might be coming next. "She has convinced your board to hand her the reins. And . . . something else is happening, but I don't know what," said Gus.

Steele broke into a sweat, worried that Cole's plan had backfired.

Gus's breathing became labored as he dropped the last bomb.

"I'm sorry, I didn't know. I was focused on getting the families here," he said.

As the wardens looked over at Gus, Cole, and Steele she could just make out what they said: "Breakout."

A group of women rushed up from behind the wardens yelling loudly about the fact that they had no water. Cole recognized the face of Silicon Valley, standing hand in hand with the woman she'd seen in the security compound. Silicon Valley had led a revolt.

The wardens began to run towards Cole as Silicon Valley jumped on Flores. Two other women joined in and started punching and kicking him.

Steele tightened his grip on Cole's shoulder. She turned to him as he looked back in the direction of their car, then at her.

"Go!" he said.

Chapter 52

C ole burst into a full sprint, followed by Steele. Gus trailed behind them, doing his best to keep up. But when Cole heard him groan, she turned to find him collapsed on the ground.

"Dad!"

"Go, go!" yelled Gus, as he struggled to get back up.

Steele stopped and turned to look too, just as Cole darted back towards her father. He called out to her and ran in her direction, towards looming danger.

Behind Gus, the wardens were trying with little success to help their comrades who had been overwhelmed by the attack from the crowd. Flores was on the ground, and the other wardens were trying to pull his outraged attackers off him. People were coming out of their tents to see what was happening and to cheer on the other wigrants.

Cole pulled Gus to his feet and, with Steele's help, the three of them turned abruptly and fled once again.

Two of the wardens broke away from the mass then and, seeing the three fugitives, one of them quickly drew his weapon, took aim, and pulled the trigger, just as the other warden knocked his hand upward.

"She wants her alive," he explained.

When Steele heard the gunshot and the crowd screaming he quickly used one arm to pull both Cole and Gus to the ground. He felt bad to have to strong-arm the older man. *Better than having him take a bullet,* he thought.

Cole shot Steele a brisk, heartfelt thank-you glance. The look ignited a warmth inside him. *No time,* he remembered.

Steele looked back to assess the danger and saw that the warden had holstered his weapon. The gunshot had also disoriented the mob, and that gave the wardens a chance to rescue Flores and pull him away.

"Where we going?" Gus asked gruffly as Cole helped him up.

"Just keep running," Cole told him.

The wardens were chasing them, but tracking them and navigating through the maze of tents was slowing them down.

Steele charged ahead as Cole ran with Gus. A warden came around a corner, not expecting to see them running his way, and Steele launched him backward through a tent opening with a brutal body check. The surprised hollers from inside the tent were muffled as the warden landed on someone inside.

Steele was running full out to try to catch up again when he saw another warden round a corner in front of Cole. This one was not surprised to see them, but he really wasn't prepared for what happened next. Cole took a move from Steele's playbook and body checked him to precision. She sent the warden reeling back with the upward contact of her shoulder to his chest.

They wove around the tents, desperately hoping to evade the wardens behind them. Steele took a risk and told them to take the straightest line possible. All the weaving was slowing them down. It might be only a few moments before the wardens caught up. There was no doubt where they were headed.

When they got to the western edge of the settlement they saw their car . . . and three wardens standing around it, waiting. Steele grabbed Cole by the arm and hauled her and Gus back into the settlement behind a tent. Their car, their freedom, was only twenty feet away.

Steele was surveying their surroundings, trying to formulate a new plan, when he felt something solid tap him on the shoulder.

"I grabbed it from his belt when I body checked him," said Cole. She was holding the warden's radio.

Steele gave her a smirk and grabbed it. He covered his mouth slightly to mask the volume and took his best shot.

"Subjects spotted along the west edge moving towards the northwest entry point," he reported.

Two of the wardens headed out, but one stayed behind.

Cole and Steele looked at one another. She twirled her index finger in the air, signaling him to call on the radio again.

Steele pushed the radio button, about to make another attempt, then saw Gus holding his hand up.

"May not be the fastest sprinter anymore, but I still got a trick or two left in me," Gus said.

Steele shook his head. Cole grabbed Gus by the arm with a look of concern, but Gus shook it off with a smile. He walked away from the tents towards the car.

"Warden," said Gus.

As the warden got a closer look at his former superior, he pulled his baton nervously and directed Gus to get on the ground. They heard Gus tell him to calm down, that he was ready to turn himself in. Gus slowly turned to be cuffed. Then there was the faint sound of a car window sliding down.

There was so much happening that no one had paid attention to the outlandish vehicle that had sauntered in. The large car that looked like a children's toy was idling perpendicular to the parked vehicles.

Then there was another very distinct sound.

A pop. Gunshot.

When Steele looked, he saw the body lying on the ground.

Chapter 53

S teele and Cole both saw Gus standing over the warden's body, and a familiar face approaching Gus from the idling car. It was the big brute Steele had laid out in the swanky hotel lobby two nights earlier.

Gus took a swing as the brute holstered his weapon, but the behemoth ducked and punched him in the stomach. He threw Gus over his shoulder and tossed him into the back seat of the car before driving away.

Cole and Steele ran to their car. Steele reversed in a flash, then threw the car into drive and slammed the accelerator as the two wardens he had fooled appeared in his rearview mirror. He caught a glimpse of them getting on their radio before he sped off.

They raced the toy car westward across Lakeshore Boulevard. Cole gritted her teeth, grappling with the decision before her.

Settlement. Wigrants. Death.

Gus. Father. Death.

Save a quarter million people.

Or try to save one.

Steele could see the water broker's car getting away. If he lost sight of them, which way should he go? There was a flurry of activity on the stolen radio, and they heard the make, model, and license plate of their car being identified.

"What direction are they headed?" they heard Senna ask. A clear, accurate response came back, to Cole's dismay.

Cole pulled out her phone to make a call.

Tao picked up immediately.

"Police have what they need?" she asked, then listened for the response. "They're not moving on it! We're out of time!"

"Eyes on Senna, fifty feet," said Steele, looking into his rearview mirror.

"West across Lakeshore, then straight up University," Cole yelled to Steele, the phone still in her hand. She turned back to see the dark-tinted windshield of Senna's sleek electric car mercilessly in pursuit, a silent, blue rotating light on the roof of the driver's side.

Black Lightning.

She called new instructions into the phone before hanging up. She looked ahead at the broker's toy car with despair as they broke off pursuit.

Steele raced way beyond the speed limit to keep their distance from Black Lightning as they barreled up University Avenue.

"Stop the car!" Cole told him. At the intersection of University Avenue and King Street they got out of the vehicle. Steele left the keys in the running car as they ducked down the stairs that led into the subway station.

They heard Senna slamming her door and cursing Cole for making her leave her car in the street. They made their way onto the northbound subway platform, moving as far forward as possible as the familiar three-ding chime of the subway rang. Senna appeared on the platform just as the doors closed behind Cole.

Senna and Cole locked eyes through the window as the subway pulled away. A muffled voice announced the next stop over the PA system.

"What did he say?" he asked. Cole put her hand in his face.

Four stops later, the platform was decorated with replicas of antique columns in honor of the Royal Ontario Museum, which the stop was named for. The Mexican Toltec warrior greeted Cole and Steele as they disembarked. They stood beside the train as the passengers left it, staring each other down. As the chimes rang, Cole and Steele dashed for the stairs that would take them to street level.

Cole looked up to the light at the top of the stairs, wondering nervously what awaited them. The setting sun blinded them for a moment as they emerged onto University Avenue near the side entrance to the museum. They turned to see Black Lightning idling at the curb, the blue light quietly turning.

Steele wondered what the hell was happening as Cole hustled him toward the back seat.

Arius put his arm around the front passenger seat and turned to smile at them. He accelerated the machine forward as he pulled the blue light off the roof and closed the window.

As Senna alighted at street level, Black Lightning breezed around the bend of University Avenue southward, out of view.

"Good thing you caught their license plate," said Arius. It was his first full sentence since they'd made their getaway from Senna.

Arius and Tao had been hovering in a car nearby when Cole reached them on the phone. Arius was dropped off to get Black Lightning and do the pick up outside the museum. They were on their way to rendezvous with Tao, who had tracked the car carrying Gus back to the broker's house where the assailants were now holed up.

"Tao told me after the break out that the hit on me was a ruse," said Arius. "But he never explained . . . why all the drama to break me out of the police station, then? If Senna was convinced it was real and talked Tao out of it, why wouldn't she just have me released from jail, knowing I was safe?" he asked from the driver's seat.

Cole explained how she needed Senna to think she'd sold Arius out. At the same time, when Senna was on Tao's trail, he'd planted breadcrumbs on the dark web to lure her in even further. Senna wanted Arius's intel badly, but once she "convinced" Tao to call off the hit, Cole was worried that Senna would clue in if he was so easily released from prison by the police.

Arius thought it over.

"But if I was broken out, Senna wouldn't be the wiser. Damn. So, Senna thought she had you over a barrel. Your dad and me in her pocket. Your heart and your secrets," said Arius, shaking his head.

Cole scrunched her nose at the descriptions, but let it be.

"Merchant needed time to get through the dossier Tao prepared, so I had to buy as much time as possible while keeping the wigrants alive. And I had to get my board to approve the merger when Senna was ripe for a takedown."

"Everything came to a head today when the board handed control to Senna. At the height of opportunity, that's when she was most exposed," said Cole. "The grounds for your arrest were shaky to begin with, and the plan was to exchange your freedom for the person who was really behind the recent deaths. Tao's real clients would remain anonymous, but . . ."

Cole slouched, a tear running down her face for what would not be.

Arius understood.

The moment was pivotal. To save the wigrants, Cole's plan had hinged on striking at the critical moment when Senna thought she was completely in control. Right now. But the trap hadn't sprung.

"The wigrants will die. Because I failed."

Chapter 54

They had left the shore to approach the broker's house by boat not long ago. Steele's energy was now intensely focused on navigating the Zodiac through the dark of night, using his night-vision visor to scope out the shore ahead where Tao was waiting for them.

They pulled ashore and brought the gear to where Tao was nestled in the foliage at a corner of the property near the lake. He told them he'd seen four people go into the broker's house with Gus. Steele huddled them together to ensure they each knew the part they would play. Arius would use his drone to survey the site with infrared cameras. Tao would take up a sniper position. Steele would enter the building with Cole behind him.

They popped communicators in their ears and synced them together. Arius unpacked and readied the drone for launch as Tao grabbed his gear. As Arius reviewed the infrared drone feedback, Steele reminded Cole to stay behind him and keep one hand glued to his shoulder at all times while they advanced.

"Tao's right. Five bodies on the premises. One by the side door, looks like two near the back on the lower level, and I presume Gus is sitting on the main floor, with the broker standing next to him," reported Arius.

"I'm set up on the east edge in the trees. I have sightlines to the main floor and to the target. Our guy by the side door is not carrying a radio. I'll keep eyes on him as you move to the back. The house cameras and door sensors will be disrupted in ten seconds, but if they're watching, they won't think it's a coincidence, so move fast," said Tao.

Steele looked back to Cole. She nodded and put her hand on his shoulder as directed, but just before he moved, she spoke to him.

"This is my father, Steele."

"I got you," he reassured her solemnly before returning the night-vision visor to his face. "Let's move."

"Green light, green light."

Steele and Cole ran to the darkest part of the backyard and made a beeline up the middle to the back door.

"No bodies by the door, but watch the corners upon entry. Breach," said Arius.

Steele quietly manipulated the door lock and they entered the lower level. Within five seconds, Steele had dispatched the first man with his silenced weapon. Cole stepped over the body as they moved through the cavernous basement where the second man was sitting watching television. Another silenced round was fired before they were clear to move upstairs, but their quiet advance was shattered by a shout from the broker on the main floor.

"Movement outside, stand by!" called Tao before Arius reported that the side door man was down. "The broker must have picked up on the cameras and alarm. Watch yourself, Steele. It's just you and him."

Steele and Cole were in the main floor kitchen outside the room where they'd first met the broker. He heard the broker calling his men.

"Broker's parked himself at the wall between the windows, Steele. I don't have a shot. Repeat, no shot," called Tao.

"Can you move to a better vantage point?" Steele asked quietly.

"The only sightline to him now is from the front lawn," Tao replied. A moment later he added, "I'm going."

Steele told Tao they'd distract the broker and instructed Arius to ready the drone to crash into the window beside Tao's sightline.

"You know how much this thing cost me?!" Arius complained.

"Arius!" Cole called out, hushing her instinct to yell. Everyone heard him huff over the comm. Steele looked back to Cole and nodded.

She walked into the room alone. Gus sat on the couch with his hands tied. The broker stood over him, holding a gun.

"Welcome back, my lady. You know, before you arrived, I was telling your dad about my own father. You didn't know him, did you, Cole? He's the man your dad blackmailed to get his water deal through," said the broker.

Cole shook her head, then looked at her father whose head was bowed.

"Unlike my uncle, my father was an honest man," the broker said, waving his gun around.

"He was a politician," Gus rebutted. "Sorry to break the news. If he'd been honest, I'd have had nothing to blackmail him with."

Arius and Tao signaled their readiness and Steele told them to wait for the sign.

"That's your apology?" said the broker.

Gus looked directly into Cole's disapproving eyes, and, with tears filling his, he sat up straight.

"That's the truth. I accept the consequences here today. For your part, you need to accept the facts of the past," said Gus.

The broker accepted the apology and raised his gun, aiming it at Gus. Cole yelled out loud and rushed forward to stop the broker. At that instant, the drone flew into the window. The crash disoriented the broker long enough for Steele to bust into the room through another door.

A single bullet entered the window and hit the broker in the back, just as Steele's silenced weapon shot him from the front. As the broker slumped to the floor, he squeezed his trigger reflexively and discharged a shot.

"Guys? Guys? I hope that was the sign, 'cause you just wrecked my favorite toy," said Arius.

Chapter 55

Gus winced in pain, but it was Cole who was in agony as Steele drove to the hospital.

The stray bullet from the broker's gun had lodged itself in the left side of Gus's abdomen.

They sat in the back seat of the vehicle they'd abandoned when they'd fled the broker's house in the Zodiac after their first visit. Gus was clutching his abdomen, where Steele had applied a makeshift pressure bandage to the wound. The vehicle darted eastbound on the Gardiner Expressway through the light late-night traffic.

Cole told her father how tonight's moment had been pivotal. She had needed Senna arrested tonight in order to take back control of the settlement and save the wigrants. But the ploy with the police had failed and there was no way she could coax Senna out without her knowing she was walking into a trap.

Despite the searing pain, Gus was insisting that he help resurrect Cole's mission. And she would have none of it.

"You shouldn't have come for me," Gus said to Cole wistfully.

Cole gently put her arm around him. "I wasn't going to leave you to die," she explained. "You're safe now. Safe from the broker. Safe from Senna."

"And all those people will die if you don't let me help," Gus replied.

Cole shook her head.

"Senna might be fooled if *you* try to bait her. But there's something she can't resist," Gus suggested as he looked into his daughter's eyes.

Cole refused to accept the suggestion. "No. She'll kill you. No. Hurry up, Steele. We have to get him to the hospital."

Gus appealed with all the might he had left in him. He went on about how hard he had struggled to keep the wigrants alive. How he'd worked and toiled to keep order for these poor refugees.

The words penetrated into Cole's soul.

She remembered the appeal of the strawberry-blond girl, when she'd first set foot on the settlement. She could vividly recall the helplessness in those young eyes. She tried to shake the image from her head.

The car was in the right-hand lane for an exit off the Gardiner that would take them to the hospital. If they wanted to engage Senna, though, Steele would have to veer left back onto the expressway. He looked back to check on Gus.

As if reading Steele's mind, Gus met his eyes and subtly nodded.

"You don't need to worry about me, young man. I've survived far worse," Gus said, to make a show of it.

"Almost at the hospital exit, Cole. We need to decide now," Steele said.

A stream of images flashed through Cole's mind.

Her dad sitting with the chessboard at the kitchen table.

The morning sunshine illuminating the side of her father's face.

Auntie lying dehydrated in her bed.

Her friends piling on a poor father as he stood in line to get water for his kids.

Steele saw nothing behind him in the rearview, but a large tractor trailer was approaching on their left as the median approached. He couldn't slow down, but in just a few seconds they'd be committed to the hospital.

The visions raced frantically now through Cole's head.

Her bags packed at the front door.

Gus walking out on her again in the Paris café.

The fire at the settlement.

The broker's gun going off.

And then . . .

The little girl lying alone, dehydrated, under the medical tent at the settlement.

"Cole?!"

"Left, left!" Cole shouted.

Steele veered hard to the left, just in front of the median crash barrier and in front of the tractor trailer, which was blaring its horn. He accelerated hard.

Everything in real life became a blur.

Cole got Tao on his phone. He and Arius had taken the Zodiac back across the lake to retrieve Senna's Black Lightning. She told him to let Senna know where Gus was. Senna still thought Tao and Arius were on her side.

Tao told her how to reach Merchant, and Cole made the call.

The car careened across Lakeshore Boulevard, then turned up Bathurst Street. A few moments later, a River Enforcement vehicle appeared behind them.

"Senna," said Steele.

Gus's curiosity got the better of his pain, and with his teeth clenched he turned back to see the River Enforcement vehicle for himself.

"Where is Senna's car?"

Cole and Steele both smiled.

The River Enforcement vehicle turned on its mounted lights. Steele was distracted and he missed the turn on to College Street that would have taken them towards the police station.

"Missed our turn, Cole."

"Up to Bloor Street, Steele. Let's draw enough attention to bring the police to us then."

Their car wove in and out of the local traffic on Bathurst as Senna's vehicle closed the gap. Steele made a hard right on Bloor Street to go eastbound on the portion of the street that had been narrowed for bike lanes.

The crystal façade of the Royal Ontario Museum, the "ROM," hung over the street in the distance.

Senna's car slowed to divert around the late-night pedestrians. As Cole's car advanced, she looked back to see the gap between their vehicles growing slightly. And as the onlookers watched the chase, some drunken students approached the intersection they were nearing. Steele snuck by but Senna's car was forced to stop as the young people scattered clumsily to the other side of the street.

"We need Senna closer, Steele!" And just then she saw a sea of lights approaching fast in the distance beyond Avenue Road. "Stop the car!"

Steele turned hard and nudged the car over the curb in front of the museum.

She reached over to Gus's door to open it and pushed him out. He grunted as he exited onto the sidewalk, and soon she and Steele were supporting his weight as they all walked towards the ROM.

Behind them, Senna's vehicle braked hard, and five other River Enforcement vehicles stopped in front.

Everything stopped.

Cole and Steele turned their backs to the ROM and put up their hands.

Chapter 56

The immense crystal façade of the ROM hung over them like an avalanche frozen in time. Senna smiled broadly as the River Enforcement vehicles circled the group of three, the wardens with their firearms drawn at her command.

Cole stood beside Steele, looking out at the array of authority vehicles spread out before them. They still had their hands in the air. Gus leaned on them both, finding it harder to stand with each moment that passed.

Senna studied the trio at the center of the scene. She studied Gus's stance, his tall frame wrapped strenuously over his partners. Something was clearly wrong with him, but not as wrong as she'd have it, given her own way. She cautiously approached them, the only figure moving in the frozen scene, as if trying not to tempt the avalanche above them. Cole moved slightly to her right, as if trying to block a path to Gus. Senna shot Gus a disapproving gaze, the only shot she could venture.

"Their blood will be on your hands," Cole said.

Senna raised an eyebrow. "They had a choice. And so did you," she told Cole calmly.

She walked right up to them, put her face beside Cole and her hand on Cole's shoulder. Then she spoke in a whisper.

"Unfortunately, the Axiom Water leadership wasn't up to looking after a losing cause. Their blood will be on your hands alone, Cole."

Senna patted Cole's shoulder and took a step back. Cole furled her brow.

"I was responsible for the settlement when the water was turned off . . ." Cole said, her voice trailing off.

"Don't forget the contaminated water shipment," Senna answered, not bothering to whisper now. "Oh yes. I believe you'd asked to be left in charge. Tsk, tsk. You'll get to know my friend Captain Merchant from Toronto Police. It's alright, sweetheart, I can give you some tips on how to handle rough people in jail. And fortunately, your board is very forward thinking. They've approved a merger and identified a new CEO. I'll be announced after all the people you let die are gone. What a mess—"

Senna's sentence was cut off by the approach of police vehicles from both sides. Her smugness gave way to anxious curiosity as ten police cruisers circled the scene from all directions and police officers emerged with weapons drawn. She decided the timing was opportune to arrest Cole—a very satisfying outcome.

The River Enforcement wardens nervously held their weapons. Several of them turned curiously towards the police presence behind them as the scent of exhaust fumes hung in the still night air.

"Did you forget to call the army?" asked Steele.

Senna ignored the comment. She looked back and saw a familiar face emerge from one of the police cars. He walked through the maze of vehicles with an officer accompanying him.

"Ugh, my arms are getting tired. Can we just get arrested?" Steele muttered to Cole from the side of his mouth.

From around the side of the ROM, another vehicle quietly approached. A slick, dark vehicle with a tinted black windshield. Merchant caught a glimpse of it and turned to the officer beside him, who then took out his handcuffs.

The scene seemed to fall silent as one sound caught everyone's attention. The dark vehicle's door opened. A figure in a waist-length peacoat emerged. Arius stood and gently rested his arms on top of the vehicle. He caught Senna's eye.

"Blood is thicker than water," Senna said with a playful smile.

"Very fitting expression. Do you know what it actually means?" Cole asked, with an equally playful smile. She looked at Merchant and lowered her hands.

Arius then fixed his gaze on Cole, who returned it expectantly. He signaled her with an index finger salute from the forehead.

The color drained from Senna's face.

"People have come to think, incorrectly, that it means that the bonds of family override all other relationships," Cole explained. "But its origin is 'The blood of the covenant is thicker than the water of the womb.' The opposite, you see? The bond between Arius and me, the covenant for water, surpasses your familial relation." And Cole gave Steele a small nod.

Senna stared quizzically as Steele cautiously lowered his hands as well.

As Merchant and his officer approached Cole, she motioned to Gus. Merchant left his officer a step behind and leaned in to hear what the injured man had to say.

"I've told my daughter the location of . . . he is . . . was . . . a River Enforcement warden. Shot dead. She knows the location of the weapon used, which your lab will confirm. On the weapon, you will find Senna's prints."

Merchant nodded to the dying man. He glanced back to his officer, then toward Senna.

"You are under arrest on three counts of conspiracy to commit murder, and suspicion of first degree murder."

Senna turned to Merchant. "What?!"

"Put your hands behind your back please, Senna," replied Merchant.

Senna stepped towards Cole, her face turning red. "You wanted the board to approve the merger!"

"Control supply and demand of water? Wish I'd thought of it myself, but I'm glad to take responsibility now that it has dropped in my lap. Everything had to be in place. Once that was done, I knew that putting the families of the board members in play would make you pull the trigger," said Cole.

"And I'm responsible for murder?!" declared Senna.

The wardens gawked curiously at one another.

Cole leaned in close to Senna's ear and put an arm over her shoulder.

"You might know some rough people. I happen to know an assassin with a conscience. You heard of him?" asked Cole.

Senna closed her eyes, thinking back to the dossier on Merchant's desk. The dossier from Tao that she had never looked at herself.

"Senna, your hands," Merchant demanded.

"I was just doing the right thing," Senna cried in exasperation as the cuffs went on.

"I'll look forward to those tips on how to handle rough people in jail, *sweetheart*," taunted Cole.

Cole couldn't help but smile. She heard Merchant's words fade out as they walked away. "It is my duty to inform you that you have the right to retain and instruct counsel without delay. You have the right to . . ."

"And to think I almost lost you," Cole said loudly as she turned thankfully to Gus. And in that same moment, Gus collapsed to his knees.

"For God's sake, someone get an ambulance!" Cole screamed.

Steele helped Gus lie back, making him as comfortable as possible. Cole heard an officer call an ambulance on his shoulder radio, but she still kept crying out in shock.

Steele reached up for her hand. She looked in his eyes. He shook his head.

It was time.

Cole breathed hard as the tears began streaming down her face. She looked back to Steele. The look told him what she needed at that moment. He got up and walked away, leaving her alone with her father.

She gathered herself and held her father's hand, for the first time in forever.

"Dad. I understand now."

Gus looked at his daughter's face, admiring it, learning it again.

"I understand why you sent me away," Cole told him. "It was the only thing you thought you could do to protect me. You sacrificed the thing you loved most, to save the thing you loved most."

Gus nodded with a beaming smile.

"Just as you had to do," he said. "You saved me. You'll save them all."

She bowed her head and wiped her eyes with one hand as she held his hand with the other.

His expression made his entire body glow, even as he closed his eyes for the last time.

Epilogue

Cole was holding a little girl's hand as the child looked up with wide, bright eyes and told her story after story. The little girl with strawberry-blond hair told Cole how she'd had a dream that a boat saved her life.

Cole pointed to a freighter in the harbor and told her to wave to the captain on the top deck. The morning sun gleaned off Neptune's trident, the mark of the ocean freighter that had docked the night before and started distributing freshwater into the settlement.

The docked freighter was so close to the settlement that it towered over the southern perimeter. But what might have been a looming, threatening presence had instead been welcomed like a beast of burden carrying precious gifts from afar: in this case, enough fresh water for the whole settlement. Even the shadow it cast was a welcome reprieve from the late-summer heat. And the watermain repair had been completed, so water had been restored to the high-rises, too.

In the settlement, a major cleanup effort was underway. Every tent was empty as all the refugees were collecting garbage and cleaning up the grounds. The wardens worked alongside them, equally engrossed in the task.

Cole was looking after the little girl, so Colors pulled on elbow-length rubber gloves and a mask and he made his way towards the rest area, where he grabbed a bucket and some cleaning supplies. As he did so, he passed a warden sharing a canister of fresh water with a woman he recognized. It was Silicon Valley.

Silicon Valley waved to Colors, and then, looking past him, she saw Cole.

"Everyone! She's here! She's here!" Silicon Valley shouted.

People looked over and noticed Cole as if for the first time. A single clap could be heard in the distance.

"You saved us!" came a voice.

The single clap was soon joined by another. Then another, and another. A cheer was added and the sounds soon grew into a symphony of praise.

Cole tried modestly to calm the crowd but it only encouraged them more. Resigned, she smiled to them and put her hand to her chest as an expression of her thanks. When they didn't stop cheering, she turned to the crowd to address them. One of the wardens handed her a megaphone so she'd have a chance of being heard. Arius and Tao came and joined her. And of course Steele was nearby, keeping an eye on things.

"Last night, River Enforcement and Axiom Water merged as one company," said Cole. "Within hours, the new company's CEO was arrested on criminal charges, and the board made me CEO of Axiom Water once again. My first act was to have this fresh water delivered to the settlement to avert the Day Zero crisis."

The cheers from the crowd were ear-piercing. It took ten minutes for her to calm them down.

"Which leads me to my second act. I have appointed Arius Roy, here, with the responsibilities that River Enforcement once had, but under Axiom Water's banner. In effect, Arius now watches over water demand, and I oversee water supply," said Cole, with a look towards Arius. He whispered to her that it might be nice to talk about some board restructuring.

Cole nodded knowingly.

"And Arius. It was either her, or everyone here," Cole said.

"Senna and I may have disagreed, but she's family. It's going to take some time," said Arius.

They smiled and nodded to one another. Arius and Tao then went off towards the docks, where more freighters were waiting to offload additional water shipments.

Steele waited patiently for the crowd to disband, but it was organizing itself into a receiving line instead. People were lining up to hug and speak with Cole. He stood by and watched for an hour as person after person expressed their thanks to her. Finally, after a long while, the rest of the crowd disbanded. Steele stopped Cole as she began to walk away. He put something into her hand.

"This was found during the cleanup."

Cole looked at the black marble pawn in her hand. She gave Steele one of her brightest smiles, and Steele felt as though time stood still.

Then, "I have some good news and some bad news," Cole said authoritatively.

"Bad news first. Always," said Steele.

"You're fired," she said.

"Wow. It might have helped my ego if you'd have let me quit first," he said, deflated.

"Maybe the good news will help your ego. Since there's no longer any threat to my safety, I really don't need you to be my bodyguard any longer."

"Still sounds like 'You're fired' to me," Steele replied.

Cole smiled, and blushed. She moved closer to Steele.

"How do I say this? Um. I like how you protected my body." She glanced up, shook her head with embarrassment and slapped her palm to her face. "I don't think that's how you say it."

A rush of heat flashed through Steele, and he cracked a real smile for the first time since he'd started working with Cole. He rubbed the back of his neck and cleared his throat.

Cole put her hand on the back of his head and kissed him fully on the lips. Steele was knocked backward.

"Uh . . . maybe since I'm out of a job . . . I could hang out here for a while?" he suggested.

They stared out at the lake together. The water glistened under the morning sun.

Afterword

In times of crisis, people pull together in unexpected ways. From late 2017 to early 2018, a severe scarcity really did force Cape Town's inhabitants to think strategically about their relationship with water. Following three years of unprecedented drought, dam levels were extremely low. With "Day Zero" looming, the city was facing the very real possibility that it might be the first metropolitan city on the planet that would no longer be able to provide running water to its residents, forcing them to go to distribution points.

The crisis catalyzed residents, business, and industry to action. With only three months of water left, the government throttled back allocation of water for agriculture. On the heels of that effort, water tariffs and fines were levied in addition to strict prohibitions for heavy users that included restrictions for swimming pools, lawns, and similar non-essential uses.

The net result of the communal restraint, bolstered by a return of average rainfall in June 2018, was that water reserves were buffered and dam levels rose, and Cape Town was able to call off Day Zero indefinitely. The crisis served as an example and a case study for cities around the world, not only with respect to the effectiveness of extreme water conservation measures, but also as a commentary on social inequality. In Cape Town, a problem that was constantly being managed by the poor had only just been realized by the rich.

Water is a precious gift, one that calls us to action to avert similar crises wherever we live. As recently as 2008, Barcelona struggled with water availability. São Paolo, the largest city in the western hemisphere, continues to face similar challenges. South Africa's climate is mimicked in California, southern Australia, southern Europe, and parts of South America. Despite this, Australia is a shining example of water reuse.

There is always work to be done, but humanity has made important advances. For example, more than 2.1 billion people finally got access to clean drinking water between 1990 and 2012.

Water flows around the planet, through our countries, into our cities, to our homes, and into us. Tracing its path can be very telling.

Water connects us all.

Acknowledgements

I 'm greatly appreciative to those individuals who gave of their precious time to provide meaningful feedback on various manuscript drafts. Kind thanks to: Michelle Berquist, Julius Lindsay, Greg Turfus, Victoria Kramkowski, Peter Morris, Saud Juman, Anisah Ahmad, Paul Villard and Irshaad Ahmad. Beta readers like you are an author's dream come true.

My very first draft was read by dear friend Allison Baker, who promptly encouraged me to publish immediately. A vote of confidence of such magnitude will always linger with me.

I appreciate the interview with Chris Clementoni along with referrals and insights offered by team members from Youth Without Shelter. Thank you Anastasia and Moe. Your work makes this world better. What you've shared with me fuels even further curiosity, a tremendous present for an author.

Thank you to the mentoring and guidance provided by Sam Hiyate. Your encyclopedic knowledge and sage wisdom were helpful at all the right times.

The insight and knowledge provided by my editor, Catherine Marjoribanks, made every page better. Heather Morin remained forever patient and professional with me during our cover art work. Kathryn Willms made it all possible with her gracious guidance through the self-publishing process. Thank you all very much.

I appreciate the patience my kids had with me through this journey, which actually spans much of their lives to the time of first publication. There may have been some bed times when my mind was, ironically, immersed in plotlines rather than story time. Despite this, Daniyal and Nyla, you encourage and teach me every day.

It is hard to put into words the appreciation one can have for a partner that supports and nurtures your crazy dreams in a way that helps you believe anything is possible. To the extent that two simple words can convey the depth of gratitude one can possibly feel for another human being, I say to you, thank you Anisah Ahmad, for the sacrifices along the way and for sharing in this labor of love with me.

Peace and Love.

About the Author

Muneef Ahmad is a public servant and civil engineer of over 25 years. He was born in Guyana, South America, and raised in Canada. Having always enjoyed edu-tainment, the climate-fiction genre became increasingly appealing. His purpose-driven mindset inspired *Day Zero*, Muneef's first novel, as a way to ask readers, what if? He lives with his wife and kids in the Greater Toronto Area in a house seemingly owned by their cat. You can visit him online at muneefahmad.com or on Instagram: @MuneefTheWriter.